It all happened ... one moment they were looking at an empty stairwell, the next they were under attack.

A man and a woman. He was in dark battledress, a Bethel warrior easily discernible even as he flew through the air. She was in a short battle tunic, camo style, with the colours of Kyas. Both of them had blasters.

There was confusion both amongst the front line warriors and back in the tech room. They had been dealing with a shapeless, invisible mass; now they had two flesh and blood warriors.

Even as they hit the ground – he smoothly, she stumbling slightly but still keeping her feet – they began firing.

An Abaddon Books™ Publication
www.abaddonbooks.com
abaddon@rebellion.co.uk

First published in 2006 by Abaddon Books™, Rebellion Intellectual
Property Limited, The Studio, Brewer Street, Oxford, OX1 1QN, UK.

Distributed in the US and Canada by SCB Distributors, 15608 South
Century New Drive, Gardena, CA 90248, USA.

10 9 8 7 6 5 4 3 2 1

Editor: Jonathan Oliver
Cover: Mark Harrison
Design: Simon Parr
Series Advisor: Andy Boot
Marketing and PR: Keith Richardson
Creative Director and CEO: Jason Kingsley
Chief Technical Officer: Chris Kingsley
Dreams Of Inan™ created by Andy Boot

ISBN 13: 978-1-905437-02-3
ISBN 10: 1-905437-02-1
A CIP record for this book is available from the British Library

Printed in the UK by Bookmarque, Surrey

# A KIND OF PEACE

## Andy Boot

Abaddon
Books

WWW.ABADDONBOOKS.COM

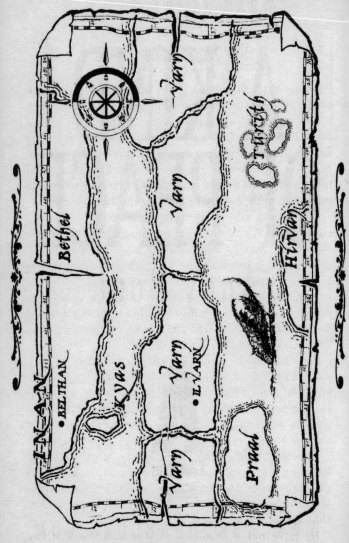

# CHAPTER ONE

## Year Zero - Period Three

Jenna watched Simeon prowl up and down the deck of the *Peta*. A straight line from one side to the other, a turn on his heel and back again. If there had been a floor covering he would have worn through it. If the floor had been real he would have ploughed a furrow. In truth, the constant pressure was making that point more and more fragile, and she was having to devote more and more energy to keeping th floor intact.

Which was why they were going more and more slowly. Which was making him more and more anxious. Which was making her more and more annoyed.

"Simeon," she muttered through teeth gritted as much with anger as concentration.

"Hmmm?" He paused mid-pace and turned his gaze on her. His eyes were burning with a light that seemed distant. Then he sniffed the air like a hunting dog. "We've slowed down, Jen..."

She breathed through flaring nostrils, almost snorting in frustrated anger. Dragged from her bed, fed some ridiculous story and now attempting to penetrate the airspace of another land in violation of the treaty. And he was complaining about the fact that they had slowed down!

"Simeon," she began, fighting the urge to shout, knowing the break in concentration could have dire consequences. "There are reasons. Good reasons. Why we have slowed. And you, are one of them. Scratch that. All of them."

He gave her a peculiar, unfathomable look. Okay,

she knew she had been speaking like a newscaster, but being so terse was the only way to say it without yelling.

For one moment she could forget he was a warrior, standing before her in combat garb with weapons secreted in every fissure of the black fighting suit. With that expression, he looked like her pet: a ridiculous, stupid creature with an unswerving sense of loyalty and no intelligence to back it up.

It was how she thought of anyone below her in rank. Nothing personal. Although he did seem to be an archetype at times.

But at least the mood was broken.

"Simeon, let me explain it as simply as possible. I cannot devote my full energy to maintaining direction and speed when I have to divert a considerable amount towards keeping the structure of the ship intact." She paused. He still looked like her pet, Fermy. Keen, but none-too-bright, struggling with the concept of not shitting indoors. Still, she'd trained the creature eventually. Lower ranks were just the same.

She continued: "You! It's you. A holoship is like any material construct. It's prone to the same stresses and tensions. And you're putting a lot on the one spot, which I'm having to try and keep from dissipating under that pressure..."

"...and that's why we've slowed down," he nodded as the idea sank in.

She wanted to call him a 'good boy' and ruffle his ears. Instead, she said: "If you want to occupy yourself, tell me again why I'm doing this and risking the termination penalty. I don't think I could have been fully awake when I agreed to it..."

Simeon grinned. This was something he could get his

teeth into. Maybe if he went through it again, he could work out were he'd soiled in his own keep.

And maybe he could work out how to put it right.

# Signing Day - Year Zero

It was to be a momentous day. For over five hundred anums the war had raged between the two great nation states of Inan. Those smaller lands that relied on the big two for their trade, and for support in times of trouble, had been forced to take sides, to support one or the other. Generations had been born, grown, and died knowing nothing other than a state of attrition between the two halves of the world. Millions of people who had no conception of anything other than an 'us-and-them' state of being.

It was no wonder that the peace had been a shock to the systems of individuals and nations alike. A complete turnaround in thinking was required. Those you had hated since the day you were born were now your allies. You were to embrace them, and their way of thinking. You were supposed to join as one and look to the future; a future where the wealth of Inan would no longer be squandered on war, but would be utilised to make a better life, a better standard of living, for all.

From the outside, a noble and utopian aim. But what if you were on the inside, and had been educated from birth by the State and your parents to think the opposite?

It was no wonder that everyone at the signing ceremony for the peace treaty seemed to be furtive, on edge, and distrustful. The delegations muttered in corners, casting suspicious glances at each other. It occurred to Simeon 7 – so named because he was the seventh son of a seventh son called Simeon – that in all probability the other delegates were probably moaning about the hardness of the castle beds, or the dreadful food. Certainly, that was all the delegation to which he was attached seemed to do... but that life-long distrust was a hard one to dismiss out of hand.

It was for this reason that the venue for the peace conference, and the subsequent treaty signing, had been so hard to determine. Certainly, the largest nation states – Varn and Bethel – could not allow themselves to cede to the enemy by meekly travelling to the lands of their former adversary. Other nation states, although smaller, were closely allied to one or the other.

It left one nation state: the continent of Praal. A barren, hard land with people of an equal disposition, they had somehow managed to keep themselves aloof for the best part of the five hundred anums, siding with one or the other at various time, depending on their own agenda.

In truth, they were a primitive people compared to those of Varn or Bethel. Technology had proceeded at a slower pace in this land, as the inward looking populous had developed their magical skills. Simeon had spent sleepless nights looking out of his window in the castle (those damned beds - and he a warrior used to discomfort) working out how many units of warriors, how many land tramplers, and how many blaster ships it would take to lay waste to the country around. Not many. In truth, the land already looked like the victim of a scorched earth policy.

But Praal had one thing that had enabled it to maintain independent status: magic. Whereas in other lands magic was an academic discipline confined for the most part to the academies, here it was a part of everyday life. Only the evening before, Simeon had witnessed a servant curse softly to himself after dropping a wine jug, and then mutter a few words, make a few gestures and somehow – in a manner that the eye could not quite catch – the jug had reformed.

If Simeon had managed that back home, he would have been boasting of it for days. More likely he would have just made a spatial hole where the wine had spilled on the floor. Everyone said they could make magic, but it was like playing sport, or playing an instrument. Everyone said that the game you didn't see, the performance you hadn't heard, was their best. Here, it was a matter of course.

So, as he had looked out that night over the sparse vegetation of the surrounding dry, hard lands and the winking lights of the distant town, with no building over ten storeys, he had realised why the people of Praal didn't care about technological advancement. Why they didn't care to ally themselves to one nation state, and why Praal was a perfect place to hold the peace talks.

He glanced back into the room, and at his bed. Ruefully, he mused that magic was all very well, but it wasn't helping him get a good night's sleep, and he needed such a thing if he was to competently peform his duty at the signing. The chances of trouble breaking out were slender, but they were still there. That was why warriors were necessary.

But a warrior who could not keep his eyes open, and whose stomach complained with indigestion at the appalling food, would be little use in a crisis.

Particularly a warrior with something to prove.

With a sigh he had retired to the hard wood base and lumpy, badly stuffed pallet that passed for a mattress.

He tried to shut out the discomfort by thinking about Jenna. That didn't help. At that time he thought he would never set eyes on her again.

With another sigh he consoled himself with the thought that if trouble were to erupt, the chances were that the other warriors present would feel as rough as he did right now.

The talks leading to this day had been interminable for a warrior. What could these people find to talk about for so long? It was a simple matter: you didn't want to fight anymore, so you signed a piece of paper saying it was over and that anyone who started aggression would find the others united in coming down on them. Simeon didn't understand economics, but even he could see that all against one would soon isolate and wither the aggressor. Even if that aggressor were Varn or Bethel themselves.

So what did they find to talk about for so long and at such length? So much hot air that, if it were harnessed, it could augment and surpass the clanking heating system that inadequately attempted to counter the freezing Praal nights.

Like all the warriors who were there – a maximum of ten from each nation state – he spent much of his time hanging around, talking of past battles with his compatriots and casting aspersions on the prowess of the delegation in this corner or that. Just as the other warrior delegations were doing about his people, he was sure. They roamed the grounds, making sure to avoid each other lest pride or some imagined slight should cause confrontation. They had been warned severely about the costs of any such fracas. They ate too much of the inedible food through boredom, and suffered the dyspeptic consequences. They took too little exercise. Training was banned for fear of being seen as incitement. They drank the terrible teas and infusions, wishing they were wines and ales. These, too, had been banned for the obvious reasons. Not that this ruling seemed to apply to the politicians and diplomats who drank freely with their meals. They were the ones drawing up the peace, and yet they could get drunk and argue if they wished.

Hypocrisy. Another reason why the warrior delegates were uneasy with their stand-down status in this place. Everyone knows that a diplomat, by his very contradictory nature, is the least diplomatic creature to crawl the lands on his scaly belly.

Yet, despite the distrust and disbelief that radiated from the warrior delegates, the treaty was actually being agreed and drawn at a surprisingly rapid rate. When Simeon had expressed his surprise at this to one of his brother warriors, the thick-set and scarred visage had creased into a grin.

"Why do you think they picked this shit hole? There's nothing else to do except come to an agreement with speed. Own up, Si, would you want to spend any longer than was necessary stuck here?"

The answer was a definite no. Praal was an inhospitable land. The people were okay. Those he had encountered in the castle – either amongst the staff or in the Praal delegation – were friendly enough, if a little distant. They would answer your questions or comply with your requests, but would not engage you in any kind of conversation. There was something about the way that they spoke to you, the way that they looked at you. It was kindly yet condescending, as though you could not possibly understand what was going on in their minds.

It should have made the warrior blood boil. It didn't. There was something about them, a sense of a greater knowledge that made you hold back. Fear wasn't really the word, but rather a kind of awed respect.

The environment didn't help. If the outside was forbidding then the castle itself was no better or more welcoming. Built in a spiralling circular design with interior walls and corridors that twisted on each other as they ascended to the top level, much of the castle was lit artificially with only the sleeping quarters and some lower corridor levels having windows that admitted the soft pink glow of the sun.

Within the walls of the castle even the artificial light and heating systems could add no warmth to the bare stone walls. To the touch the stone was numbing. Mined from the depths beneath the earth it was this stone, and the few other minerals which Praal held in its natural vaults, which formed the basis of their scant wealth.

The sooner these talks were concluded and the peace signed, the happier the warrior delegates would be, and the sooner they could go back to their lands and away from this weird place.

And now that day had come, Simeon watched as the politicians and diplomats were joined in the main hall by a group of shuffling, ancient men. Each was dressed like an academic, each in the fashion that reflected his homeland, and each sat at the right hand of his Chief Minister.

A murmur of confusion spread through the hall. It echoed off the cold stone. The warrior delegates exchanged puzzled glances, shrugs of bafflement. Many of the diplomats looked equally at a loss: this was evidently something that the Chief Ministers and their advisors had kept to themselves.

Simeon was not baffled. He already knew who these ancients were.

He didn't, however, know that it was the last time that he would feel in full possession of the facts, and in control of his fate, for some time to come.


A few days before, a rumour had spread through the warrior contingent from each nation state that a signing was nigh. In the meantime there was still daylight to be killed, although often the only way to know this would be to venture out into the scorching heat of day or freezing frosts of night.

It was during one of these dead times when Simeon stumbled on the real reason for the treaty. Although, like a true warrior caste, he didn't realise this at the time.

It was the seventeenth day of the last month in the old calendar. The day the peace was sealed was to be the first day of Year Zero. Many of the older warriors were making jokes about how it would make them seem younger to start counting their age again from zero. It was a feeble joke, and even though Simeon would be the last one to think of himself as a mental giant, still he was a little smarter than those who found the joke still funnier at the hundredth time of telling.

Daliel had tired of this too. The squat, heavy-set and scarred warrior was older than Simeon, but this did not make him keen to perpetuate the joke.

"Being older just means I've heard more of that stupid humour," he murmured to the younger man, "let's take a walk before I break all protocol and start a fight.

With my own men, at that." He chuckled, the sound reverberating in his barrel chest. "They can't demote me any lower, so I guess that'd be me out of a job. And how else am I going to support my wives and children..."

This joke did make Simeon smile. Daliel had seen action in every part of the planet, and had – so rumour had it – left a string of women holding babies and looking for recompense, all searching for a warrior with a different name.

Simeon welcomed the chance to escape the boredom, and also to spend time with the man he had first met as a fellow prisoner of war. Taken in different battles, both had ended up in the same encampment in the highlands of Kyas where they had served out their time farming crops for the nation state. Despite the island's proximity to Bethel they had been allied to Varn. Acting as a home for war prisoners had been a canny way of preventing decimation from the air, and had allowed them to continue the war with the much larger nation state. It also made repatriation easier when the hostilities ceased, pending the drawing up of the treaty.

For reasons that neither man understood they had been taken from the same encampment and briefed as members of the same warrior delegation as soon as they had been repatriated.

"I tell you this my friend, I preferred the farm and the lack of freedom to this place," Simeon whispered with an involuntary shiver as they climbed to the top level. In all the time they had been in the castle they had not observed the view from the rooftop observation post. It looked like this may be their last chance.

Daliel suppressed another chuckle. His girth, turning from muscle to fat with age and inactivity, wobbled beneath his black tunic. "I think that there was more than the love of the land to hold your interest at the camp."

Simeon was nonplussed. He thought that he and Jenna had been discrete; particularly in view of her position. He tried to frame an answer, but was saved by an unlikely intrusion.

A wizened old man, dressed like a Bethelian, shambled around the corner. The peevish expression on his face was reinforced by his tone of voice.

"I was wondering when I would find anybody in this open sewer. It's cold, it's boring, and now I've locked myself out of my room. So what are you going to do about it?"

The two warriors exchanged a glance. The old man did not take kindly to the pause.

"You two are men of Bethel are you not?" he snapped. Dumbly they assented. "Well then, while I have to be in this Gods-forsaken place then the least I can do is rely on you men to assist me. I do not wish to expend unnecessary energy on such a ridiculous matter as a locked door!"

Without waiting for an answer he turned and shuffled off down the corridor. The two warriors looked at each other, shrugged, and followed him around the twisting stone passage.

They were now in a part of the castle they had not seen before. It was almost at the highest level and in this section were bedchambers that were not, as far they were aware from their duties, occupied by any politicians, diplomats or warrior delegates. But certainly one, at least, was occupied by this old man of their nation, who now stood outside the door seething. Without preamble, he started as they approached.

"The audacity of these people. They invite us to their

land, then house us in this uncivilised pit of filth and to make it even worse, they have the temerity to cast a charm on these damn doors so that they are self-locking!"

"If you knew that then why did you leave?" Daliel asked in a reasonable tone.

"My dear man, if I couldn't break a simple charm then I would not be worth the honours bestowed on me," snapped the old man. His papery skin wrinkled into a frown.

"So why don't you break it then?" Simeon asked. It was, he felt, a reasonable point. The old man obviously did not feel the same way. He glared.

"You, sir. Who are you?" Simeon thought about lying, and then reasoned that it would probably backfire on him. When he had introduced himself, the old man sniffed. "Hmm... I shall, no doubt, have cause to rue that name. Now break down this damn door!"

The two warriors once again exchanged glances, eyebrows raised. Their material weapons were the equal of simple magical charms true, but the use of such would raise an alarm. As Daliel reached for his blaster, Simeon stayed him.

"Stay here with, er, with this worthy," he murmured. "I've got a better idea."

Setting off back down the corridor it took only a few moments to find a Praalian castle worker. He explained the situation, ignoring the seemingly sardonic stare of the man, and waited until a security warrior had been fetched. Whereupon he explained the situation again. Nodding a brief assent, the Praalian warrior strode ahead back to the spot where the peevish old man waited with a distinctly embarrassed Daliel. Simeon could hear the old man's voice as they approached, complaining at length about the men of Bethel.

The Praalian warrior unsealed the door with a brief pass, sparing the old man barely a glance. Before he went back into the bed chamber, the old man fixed Simeon with a steely glare.

"I could end your life with the raise of an eyebrow if I wished. Today you have been lucky, Simeon 7. Remember my name, for I am Ramus-Bey and I will not give you cause to disrespect me a second time!"

With which the old man swept imperiously into his chamber, the Praalian warrior closing the door and making a pass over the lock before giving them a look that held just the hint of a mocking smile.

When Simeon stood in the great hall as the treaty was signed with ceremony before the tables groaning with Praalian delicacies, he was the only one outside of the select coterie who understood the presence of the old men. Three days is a long time to ponder an old man who knows magic caught in a corridor. Long enough to figure that if an elderly guest who got curious occupied one bedchamber, then the others on that stretch of corridor could equally be occupied by those who did not have the same restlessness.

And long enough to figure out what his talk of magic had really meant.

# Year Zero - Period Three

"So you figured it out before anyone else. Well done. Just shows how smart you are. Was that why they picked you to guard Ramus-Bey?"

Simeon didn't answer at first. There was something in her tone that smacked of sarcasm. Not that he blamed her. If he was so damned smart, they wouldn't be here now.

"I tried to catch Daliel's eye. I figured he would have guessed too. But he was too busy watching the signing. Maybe he thought that was when any trouble would start, if it was going to. There had to be some reason they had us warriors there right?"

"Well there was, wasn't there?"

"Sure. But none of us knew that until later."

Simeon moved to the view-screen. He looked out over the seemingly endless sea. On the horizon the pink glow of early morning was beginning to break, the scant rays of light revealing water that was wine dark, with only white breakers flicking the surface.

"The thing you've got to remember is this," he continued. "At that moment we were all still thinking in terms of conventional warfare. We had no idea what was happening in the academies. Who had, outside a few people in government? You know what those people are like. Devoting themselves to magic, to the ways of the Gods, to knowledge, to pure abstract thought.

"Now we've got used to the idea that the academies hold the fate of Inan in their balance – strange how these things become so normal so quickly– but at that actual moment they were just a bunch of old men. Some of them looked a bit lost, a bit senile. And Ramus-Bey looked pissed off."

"He must be in paradise now then!"

Simeon breathed out heavily, suppressing the urge to curse her. For one, he found it hard to curse the most perfect woman he had ever met. And second, you never cursed the Ensign of a holoship when you were standing in it. Especially not when you were over the middle of an ocean. Instead, he contented himself with: "You don't have to help if you don't want to Jen."

She snorted. "Simeon, sometimes you can be a complete moron! I'm here, aren't I?"

# CHAPTER TWO

## Signing Day - Year Zero

The heads of conference waited until the swell of sound had swept around the room and subsided before electing to continue. From his position at the back of the hall, it seemed to Simeon that they were smug in their knowledge. He had a glimmering of a notion that he should never ever trust any of these men.

Finally the Chief Ministers of Varn and Bethel stood and faced the assembled throng. They were on a raised dais with their entourages seated to their rear. At their right and left hand, spread across the dais, sat the Chief Ministers of Turith and Kyas: as befitted smaller nation states, riding the coat-tails of the big two, they had much smaller delegations at their rear.

The Chief Minister of Praal sat to one side. He had no delegation to back him up. He sat with only a wizened old man for company. Why not? They were standing on his land, and his people had been aloof for most of the war's immense span. He had a slightly amused expression about the eyes as he surveyed the warrior delegates standing in groups across the floor of the great hall. The old man ignored them, concentrating his impassive gaze upon the dais, eyes seeming to search out the other old men. To study them like insects on the ground.

Simeon snapped back to attention, aware that the Chief Ministers had begun to speak, but that he had not registered a single word. He took a brief look around at the delegations and at those seated behind the Chief Ministers. All were at rapt attention as the two men took it in turn to speak.

"... and so it became necessary for us to end the ceaseless strife, to attempt to make a better world. That is why we speak to you today, via holovid, as a world. This is a most momentous day. Never in the history of comm-systems on Inan has a simultaneous broadcast has been made worldwide. Every comm-receiver on the planet can hear our words. But we want you to do more than hear. We want you to listen."

Bethel's Chief Minister stepped back a pace, allowing his Varnian counterpart to shuffle forward and take the lead. It became clear to Simeon that this was a carefully choreographed speech in which both men had been given equal time and prominence. It was perhaps an unworthy thought, but he wondered if half the interminable delay in this peace conference had been caused by the need to squabble over the order and form of the speeches, rather than their content.

No matter. The Chief Minister at centre stage had started to speak.

"People of Inan. As you hear our words, translated into every dialect and tongue across the globe, realise that the traditions in which you were raised have now become defunct. The hatreds that existed between our peoples no longer matter. They must cease to be. The other is not your enemy, he is your friend. For half a millennium we have battled against our brothers, even as the sun turns and the crops grow to harvest. We have developed tech that has enhanced our existence, but have turned our backs on the Gods."

Simeon's glance flickered to the Praalian Chief Minster. His expression hadn't changed. One thing he liked about the Praalians: a gambler's face. Never play against them.

"...and in so doing have confined ourselves to the

surface. We do not know what lies beyond, even though we now have the tech to explore. But there are those who have made it their life's work to explore the spiritual side of life. They have ignored the mere material motives of their governments. They were right. Instead of war, they have devoted their lives to the soul, to the spirit, to knowledge."

He stepped back. Simeon was glad. Maybe they'd get to the point now it was the man from Bethel who was to speak. That was the thing about the Varn: didn't know when to shut up.

The Chief Minister from Bethel stepped past his flamboyant counterpart with the briefest of glances. Simeon kept his smile inside. If looks counted for anything, they'd be back at war right now.

Composing himself without skipping a beat, the Minister stared out over the heads of the delegates and began to speak, addressing his words to the comm-pickups that were located through the hall.

Simeon couldn't spot them. The hall seemed to be bereft of anything remotely resembling tech. Even the light and heat was expertly concealed behind the seemingly simple facade. But he was missing the speech...

"While we mere men have been waging war, those who chose to devote their lives to learning have been cloistered in the academies, searching for a greater truth. There are some who have found this. You see them seated up here with the leaders of the nation states. Although they are not familiar to you, I – we – assure you that they have a far greater import than we could ever have."

Simeon suppressed a whistle. Figured that his guess was near the mark. It would have to be for a Chief Minister to downplay his own importance in the scheme of things.

"People of Inan. For many anums these men have been

exploring the breadth and depth of our world's knowledge. They have looked at the secrets of magic. While we have grown lazy, relying on tech to take the place of our own will, they have eschewed the use of such short cuts. Rather they have explored the true meaning of magic. They have become the greatest masters of substance over form. Indeed, such is their thirst for knowledge and their mastery of their arts that they have learned to prolong their lives in order to continue their studies. These men are older than we can imagine, and will in all likelihood outlive us all."

A rumble of disbelief spread around the hall. Simeon could imagine it being echoed in every home, workplace and public holovid across Inan. And, to be truthful, you could understand the doubt. Five old men, a couple of them looking a little confused at all the fuss. The old man from Praal looking like anything could be going on behind that face, as cold and impassive as the stone of the castle walls. Another of the ancients looked embarrassed, like he'd rather be anywhere else but here, and the old man from Bethel, who Simeon had met just a few days before, looking even more peevish. If the practice of magic brought you serenity, then this one had skipped some lessons.

Simeon scanned the immediate crowd, looking for Daliel. All the warrior delegates had clustered together according to race. Despite the fact that this was a peace, there was still a feeling of security in numbers, in the familiar. Daliel should be near. Even amongst other warriors a squat, heavily scarred man in a black tunic should be easy to spot.

The Bethel contingent were a dark blot on the floor of the hall. The warriors of other castes were wearing ceremonial dress, a riot of colours that clashed in reds, oranges, greens and yellows. Insignia blared garishly. The Varn believed in brightness, their sartorial sense having infected other nation states over the anums. Bethel, on the other hand, was defiantly drab. Black with just the one insignia to break the shadow on ceremonial garb.

Of course, this did have a tendency to make them blend into one. Simeon scanned the room for Daliel.

He wasn't there.

Before he had a chance to ponder why his comrade had vanished, the unrest was quelled by the unprecedented move of both the Bethel and Varn Chief Ministers stepping forward to the front of the stage. It was well rehearsed, and in some ways a very small gesture. Yet it held a gigantic significance. Neither yielded to the other. Both were equal.

Two momentous revelations in one day. Within moments. You could feel the shock wave across the globe. It was as though the world had stopped spinning. No wonder that they were to call this Year Zero. After this, things could never be the same again.

When the rumble had subsided, both men spoke together. It was a symbolic gesture of indescribable importance. Across Inan, every man and woman focused on them. In the hall Simeon forgot everything except each syllable that fell in unison from their lips.

"From these men we have learned the wisdom of the ages. We have learned that there is such a thing as absolute power, and that those who possess this have power over the dominions of land, sea and air. But we have also learned that if all share this power then every man and every woman is an equal.

"Our lives are about checks and balances. If one of us has this power and can wield it, then he can reign supreme by threat of absolute annihilation. Likewise, if all have this power, then dare one use it at the risk of retaliation?

"We say no. None shall be so blind as to take this route. Together we are strong. Apart, we risk the destruction of our very mother Inan.

"We cannot take this risk.

"And so we have decreed that from this day forward we shall no longer be at war with each other. Never again will one nation state raise arms against another. The peace that we shall sign today will lead to a new era of peace and prosperity for our planet. And it is thanks to these men. These men of peace, whose learning and great wisdom has shown us the way forward.

"Now let us show these great men to the world, so that the world may know those who have ultimately given us peace."

It was like some strange holovid show where people are paraded before a vidscreen for entertainment, showing off some obscure talent. During the long downtime between missions, and in the dreary times on the prison farm, Simeon had whiled away the time watching such shows, wondering at the willingness of people to make fools of themselves for the fun of others... including himself, it had to be said.

As the portent of the two Chef Ministers of Inan speaking as equals died away, it struck him that this presentation of the peace treaty to the planet resembled nothing more than a cheap holovid show. Their words had been carefully chosen to skirt around the truth, prodding at it from the corners and edges, lifting the covers a few degrees to allow the people a look inside while not actually spelling it out for them.

But Simeon didn't need it spelt out. Not because he was an intellectual, but because of something the tart and miserable Ramus-Bey had said to him: that he could wipe him out with a raise of the eyebrow.

Ultimate destruction. Magic may be about the spirit, about the manipulation of reality by the will and the unseen forces it can draw upon to create its desired aim, but all that sweetness and light has a flipside. Those forces could be used for destruction as much as creation. If these old men, in their respective academies, had attained such a level, then...

Could it really be possible that these collections of bones and wrinkles held the world in the palms of their shaking hands?

As the ancient Mages of Varn, Bethel, Kyas, Turith, and finally Praal were paraded before the world, he could see in each of these unspeakably old men the potential for Inan to be snuffed out as the result of an attack of bad temper. Certainly, he could see the irascible Ramus-Bey falling prey to such a rage.

Wegnak and Comul, the Mages of Kyas and Turith respectively, were tired old men who looked like they would rather be anywhere than here. Nervous out in the world after so long secluded, they seemed ill-at-ease. Not so Vixel, the Varnian Mage. Like many of his race, he had an easy confidence and flamboyance about him, almost playing to the unseen audience.

Ramus-Bey was short, barely acknowledging the hall, let alone the watching millions. Simeon had him sized-up; a spoilt academic used to having his own way, irritated at being dragged from his secluded studies and paraded like a piece of livestock because of the whims of politicians. To be truthful, Simeon could not blame him and yet, if this were to be allied to what seemed to be a natural talent for the polar opposite of amiable, then it could make him a dangerous man with a whim.

In truth, the only Mage to act with any dignity, and to inspire any trust, was the Praalian Mage. Despite his great age and seeming physical frailty, he had a bearing about him that at least gave the illusion of a straightness of back. He stood tall, with an air of authority that the others seemed to lack. He stood aloof, like many of his race, from the facile games of the Chief Ministers. Noticeably, he was the only Mage that either Minister declined to guide by touch. Where they had felt free to manhandle the other old men, they both demurred from laying hands on the Mage called Kathel.

As he stood before the hall, he seemed to search out the comm-pickups and direct an unblinking, unflinching gaze to the whole population of Inan.

He was inscrutable, yet the only one that Simeon felt any of them could trust with the planet. By their very nature, the people of Praal shared few of the conceits of the other nation states. And, by extension, a Mage who had focused his energies on studying the very nature of the universe and beyond had refined those nation state characteristics to their finest point.

Yes. Inan was safe with him. But the others?

Politicians were capricious. These old men shared some of those characteristics by the very fact of their places of birth.

Simeon wondered if he was alone in thinking that, behind the show, this peace would not be the easy ride that the Chief Ministers were so eager to present.

While this had been preying on his mind the Mages had been returned to their seats and the penultimate part of the treaty signing was taking place. Praalian servants brought an ornate table into the hall and onto the dais. While this took place, the Chief Ministers returned to talking in turn – the strain of speaking in unison obviously being too much for them to continue at length – and spelt out the terms of the peace. In essence, Bethel and Varn kept parity, while Turith and Kyas acceded territory and economic expediencies of war. It was clear that these two would return to their status as adjuncted nation states. Praal held aloof and self-sufficient as always.

All change was no change. The hierarchy of the planet remained as before. The only thing to alter was that the warrior forces stood down. Instead of combat, select cadre would be engaged in defensive duties within their own boundaries.

This last caveat did not go down well in the main body of the hall. Warriors without income were men with little prospect of other work. The war had raged for so long that there had been generations of men who knew nothing but how to be a warrior. Simeon was amongst them. He should have been thinking of how this would affect his future.

Instead, he was wondering why Daliel had only now entered the hall and why he was making for him through the massed black of the Bethel delegation.

"Where have you been?" Simeon asked as the squat warrior came within earshot. "You should have seen the performance. All show, no doubt, but..."

"Enough! We can talk of this later. First you must come with me." The warrior's heavily scarred visage carried a mien more grim than was usual.

Simeon did not have a chance to protest. Daliel took his arm in a firm grip and set off for the entrance to the hall. Despite their unusual behaviour, their fellow warriors had no cause to pass comment. Their attention was focused on the ceremony.

Two copies of a large, illuminated document were laid on the ornate table. The size and style of the document had been decided in conference to act as a signifier. It was bold and dramatic and was a gesture of intent to the waiting world. But it served its purpose: as the Chief Ministers of Bethel and Varn signed, side by side, swapping copies before each was signed in turn by the other Chief Ministers present, so the audience in the hall – and doubtless across the globe – were held in awe, their collective breath paused at the portent of such a moment.

Finally, the war was over.

Simeon did not witness the signing. By the time that the first two signatures had been scratched on paper, and the document swapped to be counter-signed, he was already outside the great hall.

"Daliel, it might be ridiculous but it's history," Simeon said, "so you'd better have a good reason for making me miss it."

"I have, son, I have. Tell me, is there something that's worrying you?"

Simeon frowned. "Not worry, but... it's those Mages. They're all old, probably older than we're supposed to be, and probably senile. Look at that old bastard from our land. You saw what he was like the other day..."

"Yes, I did. More importantly, so did you," Daliel said, cutting across him. "Did nothing strike you as strange about that little encounter?"

"Not as strange as your manner," Simeon returned sharply. "Tell me, why do I get the feeling that there is more going on here than I know about?"

"Because there is," Daliel said simply. "But not here. Come." With which he began to move in the direction of the chambers they had stumbled on a few days before, leaving Simeon in his wake. Frowning heavily, the confused warrior followed his compatriot.

"I'll tell you what's been bothering me about the other day," Simeon started as they ascended a spiralling stairwell, "for a start, how come one of the Mages was wandering about on his own? Where was the security for such a valuable diplomatic asset? And if they're so powerful, then how come he couldn't break a simple charm on a door?"

"Is that all?" Daliel asked.

"Isn't that enough to be going on with?" Simeon countered.

"Ah, true enough, son. But isn't there something specific that worries at you, about your encounter the other day?"

Simeon's face must have writ large his puzzlement for Daliel laughed when he looked at him. By this time they had ascended to the level of the chambers where they had encountered Ramus-Bey a few days before.

Then it dawned on him.

"Why are we here?"

"Philosophers have joined Mages in asking that question since the very beginnings of time," Daliel intoned with a hint of mockery. "Who are we to question..."

"That's not what I mean and you well know that!" Simeon snapped. "There should be no way that we could get near the Mages without being stopped by warrior security. They might be all-powerful, but they're also old men. Physically, they could easily be taken by surprise and overpowered before they had a chance to act, or raise alarm. We should have been stopped long before we got this far."

"Maybe the warrior security aren't that bothered?"

Simeon shook his head. "They're Praalians. They don't do anything in short measure. Unless..." He looked at Daliel, searching for clues in his face. It had to be...

"Unless they're requested to hold back."

Daliel grinned, his scarred face split by an almost beatific beam. "I knew you were the right man for the job."

Simeon wanted to ask what that job may be, but the older warrior continued, leaving him with little chance to interject.

"You're right about the Praal of course. They're as close to neutral as anyone gets on Inan, but they can see the sense in co-operation. Particularly given the circumstances." He put his arm around Simeon's shoulders, guiding him on their further ascent. Given that Simeon was head and shoulders above Daliel, and that the older man was squat where the younger warrior was lean and wiry, this was not as easily achieved as may be supposed.

"Look at this place," he continued. "You think that the lighting and heating are well-concealed pieces of tech? You think that their warrior security relies on hidden comm-transmitters to monitor any movement? No, son, they don't need all that. They use it on a low level, sure, but in secure places like this they use magic. All the light and heat in here comes from charms. Likewise, their warrior security for these places are highly trained, and can remote-view from anywhere in the building or surrounding area.

"They knew we were coming up here the other day. They knew, and we had their permission. Ramus is a tetchy old bastard and he's been driving them mad. Hey, their security chief even raised an eyebrow when he told me about it. You have to push one of them a long way for that. They've let him roam to a degree because he's not been in any danger. With all the Mages in one place, it might have been tempting for a warrior with ambition to try and tilt the odds for his nation state."

Simeon made a moue of distrust. "Is that what we were supposed to be doing when we came up here? Because if it was, then you should have told me, 'cause I had no idea. It never entered my head... and it certainly wasn't put there."

Daliel threw back his head and laughed. "See, that's one of the things I like about you son. Sense of humour. One of our concerns was that this could happen. That was one of the reasons the peace treaty was held on this continent, in this place. No one was going to get past the warrior security in this place. But once we get outside... This is how it works. These Mages are frail old men despite their power. They're going to need bodyguards for the rest of their lives. Knowing of Ramus's little habit of wandering it seemed like a good way to introduce Mage and guard."

Simeon stopped, disengaging Daliel's arm from his shoulders. His tone hardened. "Which is why he found it hard to keep that stone face. Still, at least someone knew what was going on. Well, two of you... Tell me, Daliel, just who are you?"

The older warrior faced Simeon, looked him square in the eye, and shrugged. "In many ways, I am who I say I am. My name is Daliel and I am a warrior. Have been all my life."

"But that's not all..." It was not a question.

Daliel shook his head. "No, son, not just that. I've worked in Intel for the last eight anums. I was recruited because of my record and worked in the field amongst our own people. My task was to sniff out spies, and also to look for new talent. Recruitment, if you like."

"What about the prison farm?"

Daliel shrugged. "Bad luck. I was captured in action. I had to keep quiet and hope that they didn't have Intel that would sign my death decree. I could say nothing about it to you when we were on the farm."

"But Jenna..."

"Would I consider you a security risk for that? A spy, perhaps? No, not you... whatever else, you don't have that in you. Which is why I made sure that we were co-opted to the warrior delegation for this conference. And why I arranged with the Praal warrior security to come up here and introduce you to Ramus-Bey."

Simeon's mind was racing. First, he had to assimilate the fact that everything he had thought about his friend was wrong. Second, the fact that he had put his life at risk with Ensign Jenna of the Kyas. Doubly so, considering what her own side would have done to him.

But at least the puzzle of why he and Daliel had been picked for this conference was solved. That was some scant consolation.

It was only when Daliel turned and carried on climbing, beckoning the younger warrior to follow, that the last piece of another puzzled fell into place.

"Oh no... I know I'm not the quickest warrior you'll ever find, but I'm not completely stupid. Me... and that irritating old..."

"You're the best suited. A good warrior and a man who can handle a situation with tact and discretion." Daliel smiled wryly. "Your little adventure with Jenna showed me that."

"That's a completely different thing. Besides, how can I be a good warrior? I was captured and held prisoner."

"The vagaries of battle are no reflection on ability, son. Each nation state will be picking a bodyguard to shadow their Mage, to protect them from immediate physical harm. It takes a certain skill, a certain type of warrior. Certainly not a thick ear like me."

Simeon 7 stood five steps down from his friend. He knew that this was to be a turning point in his life. He wasn't sure if he was ready for it. He knew it was not his decision to make. Daliel had already made it for him.

"Come on, son. You've got to be properly introduced to your new assignment"

# CHAPTER THREE

## Signing Day – Year Zero

If the day itself had seemed unreal, then the evening was far beyond: it was something that Simeon would not have wished upon his worst enemy. For what would prove to be far from the last time, he found himself cursing his so-called friend Daliel for the position in which he had put him. Admittedly, he could have refused the offer to be a Mage's bodyguard: but at what cost? Having turned down a post that was to be considered an honour, he would have found himself discharged from active duty in the peace, with little chance of a reference to any future employer. In truth, the idea of any future employers queuing up for his services was little short of laughable.

So he had, less than graciously, accepted. The two warriors had then completed the walk to the Mage's bedchamber and awaited the return of Ramus-Bey. They didn't have to wait for long: like all the Mages present, he found little to interest him in the petty affairs of dullards and fools. A point he had made most forcefully on his return and at great length. At the same time, making it obvious that he included the two warriors in his scathing verdict upon his fellow countrymen.

Furthermore, he had been less than pleased with meeting his fellow Mages. They too were fools. Either that, or they cultivated an air of facile stupidity in order to try and deceive him as to the extent of their true knowledge. With the possible exception of that arrogant cretin from Praal. He was beyond any description... although this did not prevent Ramus-Bey from exercising his considerable vocabulary and talent in the art of scorn.

Simeon sat on the end of the Mage's bed while the small, wizened ball of vitriol strode up and down the chamber extolling his views at length. It was going to be a long night.

Eventually, the Mage calmed down enough to listen to Daliel explain why they were in his chamber and what Simeon's role was to be. As Simeon expected, the Mage was less than impressed. There followed a long diatribe on how it was absurd that anyone would want to kill a harmless Mage. This from the man who had, a few days before, explained equally how he could annihilate his bodyguard with a raise of the eyebrow. Apparently irony was lost on those of a magical bent.

Eventually the old man calmed down and it became apparent from the way that he spoke of the academy that he was homesick, and longed to be back at his studies. From the way in which his face softened as he talked of home, Simeon began to see that part of the old man's seeming irascibility was down to him being old, and a long way from home. He may be a master of his craft, but he was still a man.

Daliel left them to rejoin the peace festivities in the great hall. It was as much for the watching millions around Inan as it was for those who took part, and the old warrior was determined to enjoy himself. The tables piled with food may have been part of a show, but it still had to be consumed.

"It's like cleaning the sewers, son: you don't want to do it, but it has to be done... and you may as well enter it with relish!"

"Quite. I'll try and think of it that way, it may make me feel better," Simeon replied as he bade his friend farewell, glancing back at the resting Mage who lay on the bed, snoring softly.

So the remainder of the evening passed quietly. Praalian castle servants brought his sparse travelling pack when they came with the evening meal. Obviously they had been briefed about the change in circumstance. Simeon tried to ask the servant if the same procedure had been followed by all parties at the peace talks. Even as he heard the words come out of his mouth he knew that he would have, at best, a non-committal answer. In fact, all he received was a blank stare.

Inscrutable and discrete in all ways, the Praal.

All the way down the line Simeon felt as though he had been manipulated. Indeed, the idea of a guard must have been mooted from the moment the peace talks had been planned, as a cursory look around the Mage's room revealed an ante-room with bedding already prepared.

As they ate, Simeon made an attempt at conversation. After all, he was going to be in the old man's presence almost constantly. They hadn't got off to the best of starts. Despite Simeon's stumbling attempts, the old man made no attempt to meet him anywhere near halfway, and the meal finished in an uncomfortable silence.

The Mage meditated for a short while, humming tunelessly and making it hard for Simeon to concentrate on the story pamphlet he opted to hide behind to while away the time. Easily bored, Simeon always carried a few of the flimsy publications with him. They were almost juvenile in their simplicity, telling mostly of imaginary academies and the misadventures of junior adepts. However, it was this soothing simplicity that he sought at such times, and unlike the heavier tomes of adult storytelling, they were easy to carry in a light pack.

It was though, a bad choice to hide behind in front of a Mage. When the old man came out of his meditative trance and noticed what his bodyguard was reading, he sniffed heavily. Simeon elected to ignore him. So Ramus-Bey sniffed harder, and with a greater emphasis. Still Simeon ignored him. The Mage opted for a more direct approach.

"It's only fit for the dung-heap, you know," he murmured in a disparaging tone. "Nothing like real life at all," he added after a short pause in which he had been further ignored.

Simeon lowered the story pamphlet. "Probably not. But that isn't really the point of such stories. They're designed to provide a brief respite from the everyday, and as such are hardly likely to let the harsher truths of reality intrude... are they?"

He enjoyed the look of surprise on the old man's face.

"Hmm... I suppose not," the old man sniffed, then fell silent.

One-up to Simeon, the newly appointed guard thought, allowing himself some small degree of smugness. Certainly, if nothing else it kept the Mage quiet until the time came when he announced he wished to retire.

Simeon made a cursory examination of the chamber, checking the window and surrounding walls. In truth, he felt that the Praal would have the situation covered. There was no way that they would risk any transgressions on their territory. Still, it did no harm to get into the habit of security checks from the very beginning.

Once he was satisfied that the situation had been secured, he bade the Mage good night and retired to the ante-room. Light extinguished, the old man was soon softly snoring. Under a dim light Simeon attempted to read a little more, but now, without the need to distract himself from his charge, he felt his mind wandering.

It had been a strange day. Why had he been chosen? Because Daliel had spent time with him and considered him trustworthy and conscientious? He would like to think that was so, but there were two factors militating against this. One, that he had spent his time with Daliel as a war prisoner, and so the older man had never seen him in combat. Two, Simeon had shown a willingness to consort with the enemy. Admittedly his relationship with Ensign Jenna had been far from military. Nonetheless, she was from another land. One with which he had been, ostensibly, at war.

He knew he should feel flattered at being chosen. Yet there was something nagging at him, saying that he was supposed to feel this way because that was exactly how someone wanted him to feel.

He drifted into an uneasy sleep.

Bolt awake. Sitting up, eyes wide, brain lagging a fraction of a moment behind. Not good. Better reflexes.

Out of bed, blaster in hand. Still dark, faint light of the moons through the window. Enough to see. Cloudless.

Softly, careful tread. In faint light, doors are still closed. Ramus-Bey asleep, muttering. Turning over.

Can't feel anyone else. Hold breath. Hear the blood pounding in her ears.

Blink for the first time since coming upright. Breathe again, soft and even.

For the first time since rising, can actually feel limbs. Not moving on automatic.

Not good enough. If someone was here, probably be a heap on the floor by now, blood-soaked and beyond caring.

But if the sound isn't in here, then where...

Simeon blinked hard, looked down at the blaster in his hand, and shifted the balance, so that the butt of it sat more comfortably in his palm. The boards beneath his feet felt cold. Why was that? Oh – bare feet. Not the best way to face an intruder. He'd have to think about that, as he didn't feel too good about sleeping in his boots.

No matter: right now, everything was under control. The room was peaceful, the silence in here broken only by the murmurings of a dreaming old man.

Outside, though: that was another matter. Somewhere down the corridor there was a commotion. He could hear shouting: a mix of harsh, barking tones that he took to be the Mages – at least if they all sounded like his charge – and louder, gruffer tones, speaking more than one language. Something had bugged the hell out of everyone on this corridor, and if his surmise was right he wasn't the only guard who had been assigned as soon as the treaty was signed.

Simeon moved over to his Mage, and gently tapped the old man's shoulder. There was no response beyond the irritated twitching of the offended shoulder, and an increased level of muttering.

"Ramus... Ramus-Bey," Simeon hissed, with the kind of loud whisper used only by those who want to simultaneously shout and not shout.

The old man came awake with a yell, sitting upright for just a moment before sinking back into the blankets, clutching them to him and shaking, wide-eyed.

This terrified old man was the ultimate threat? Gods help them if all the Mages were this way and this was how they planned to keep the peace...

"It's alright, don't be alarmed," Simeon soothed. He followed the line of the old man's eyes, and could see they were focused on the blaster. Simeon holstered it.

"Don't worry," he continued. "I heard a noise, thought it was in here. That was just a precaution. There's nothing here."

"Then why are trying to scare me into a premature meeting with my other selves?" Ramus snapped, his earlier, peevish tones returning.

"There is some commotion outside," he explained. "Whatever's going on, I want you awake and aware. We need to be prepared."

"For what?"

"I don't know. That's why we need to be prepared."

It was Ramus-Bey's turn to be perplexed. He, however, was not one to let it pass. "How can I prepare if I have no notion of which preparations to make?" he began.

Simeon cut him short. "Any other time, but now... I need to check this out. We're secure in here. I want you go to that corner," he continued, indicating an alcove furthest from the door. "Hunker down there, and use your blankets."

"Why..."

"It's the least accessible point from the corridor, the deepest in shadow and the blankets will help obscure your form in that darkness. It won't save you if I'm taken out, but it'll keep you out of sight while I deal with whatever. Now do it! I'm not going to waste time explaining myself to you."

His tone was calm, firm: it had the desired effect. Without question, the Mage obeyed. When he was in position Simeon nodded his approval and approached the door.

The noises had not grown in volume. Whatever was happening, it hadn't moved closer.

With care, Simeon opened the door, standing behind and away from it as he did so: not in line of any fire, and not close enough to be hit if the door was forced. As the heavy door swung on its hinge, a line of soft light from the corridor beyond appeared down the hinged edge. It was enough for him to see that there was no-one immediately outside.

The sound increased. Simeon had a rough working knowledge of most of the tongues spoken on Inan, both in language and area dialect. Pausing behind the door to take stock, he could make out enough of the scrambled dialogue to figure that an attempt had been made on one of the Mages.

Where in the name of the Gods had the Praal warrior security been while this was happening? Had they decided that it was every man for himself now that individual guards had been appointed? Or was there something more insidious: what was it that could beat Praalian magic-powered security?

He needed to check this out. It could be a diversion, yet if he took his Mage with him, he was leaving him open to attack. He turned back to the room, closing the door briefly.

He beckoned to the Mage. "Listen to me, can you cast an invisibility charm?"

"You dare to impugn my power at a time like this..." an outraged Ramus-Bey began, his voice rising with his indignation.

Simeon clamped a hand over his mouth. "It was a simple question. Am I always going to have to explain myself? I need to leave you here while I check this out. I want you hidden away. Call it covering all my options."

The Mage bristled: "You think that I cannot protect myself, that I need a charm to hide, that any attempt at a magical..."

Simeon cut him short: "I don't care. This isn't about

you. It's about me. I've got a job to do and I don't know all your strengths. I'm just covering bases. I leave you here as you are right now and they can just blast you, for the Gods' sakes!"

Ramus squeaked behind Simeon's hand. Partly from fear, partly because Simeon had dragged him into the ante-room and was in no mood to be gentle for the sake of propriety.

"Get under the bed," Simeon said abruptly, releasing the Mage. "Cast the charm, and for the sake of your life, keep your mouth shut. Just this once."

Ramus-Bey shot him a look that was part outrage and part anger, but obeyed the injunction to silence. The old man got down on the floor and slithered under the bed.

"Good. Stay there 'til I return. I promise you I won't be long," he added, a qualm of guilt nagging him about leaving the old man. There had been something pathetic about the sight of him on his belly that stirred the warrior's conscience.

But better he be undignified than dead. For there was one other thing that was nagging at Simeon as he made his way back to the door. Any kind of attack that got past Praal security had to be magical. And it had to be strong magic to counter their undoubted skills. Which meant, that unless there were levels of skill that he wasn't aware of amongst the other warriors, politicians and diplomats gathered at the castle, then the only conclusion could be that another Mage was responsible.

He knew it wasn't his charge. But no-one else would know that, and anyone could be reaching the same conclusions right now. So even if Ramus-Bey wasn't the direct target, he – like all the others – could be under threat from a number of sources.

Great. First day on the job too.

He cracked the door carefully and made his way into the corridor. To defer any immediate attack, he kept his weapon holstered, but his hand hovered ready as he walked with a measured pace towards the sounds of conflagration.

He relaxed as he turned into the corridor. It had been scant moments since the uproar had started, even though time had seemed to slow immeasurably as he took precautions, and already it appeared that panic had given way to belligerence.

The corridor was filled with warriors. There were several Praalian guards attempting to find out what was occurring. Not a loud race by inclination, they were easily drowned out by the three Mage guards, and several other warriors of different races who had responded to the alarm as only a warrior could. There were three Kyas warriors, four from Varn and three also from Turith. Simeon could see only two black tunics of Bethel in the throng, gathered tight in a corridor not constructed for such activity. It seemed somehow significant to him that one of these belonged to Daliel.

As Simeon neared he heard a clear, fluting voice cut over the general noise, addressing him in a supercilious tone.

"Ah, a man of Bethel. Last on the scene, as ever."

It had the speaker's desired effect. The noise ceased, and all the warriors in the corridor turned to face him.

Simeon looked to see who had spoken. One of the Mages had dared to open his door, and the sardonic smile and icy, glittering eyes of Vixel, the Varnian Mage, met his.

"Shouldn't you be under cover? Your man's not doing a very good job, is he?" Simeon countered.

"Oh, if words could wound, I'd perhaps have a scratch. I can see I'd have nothing to fear from you."

One of the Varn warriors cut across the Mage's withering sarcasm. "Our guard cannot defend his charge. He's dead."

"How?" Simeon asked.

"It was a magic attack. There's not much of him left." The flatness of his tone belied the expression on his face. "Whoever's responsible can't be far from here. There is only a limited range for such power. We're going after him. Whoever attacks one attacks all!"

Simeon shook his head slowly and chose his words with care. "No... some of us have a greater responsibility now."

A Turith man, whose red face almost matched his scarlet jerkin and told of too long spent in taverns, flared up at the Bethel bodyguard. "These old men can take better care of themselves than we can. I am a bodyguard, but I put my fellow warriors first. If we no longer have to fight each other by command, then we are bound by the codes that kept us together with our fellows in time of war. Only a coward would say otherwise."

Inflammatory words, but Simeon kept his temper. "You have your view, I have mine." He could see Daliel nod, almost imperceptibly, in agreement.

Spitting on the floor in disgust, the Turith warrior turned away. The men began to discuss their course of action and Simeon returned to his charge, feeling the mocking gaze of Vixel follow him. The Varn Mage didn't seem that concerned.

Another thing: someone who had the power to almost obliterate a warrior so there 'wasn't much left' would not necessarily need to be in close range.

It was with a sense of unease that Simeon secured the chamber, beckoned Ramus-Bey and settled the old man, letting him run off at the mouth about having his rest disturbed. As his grumbling resolved into muttering sleep, Simeon stayed awake. He listened to the warriors blundering about the grounds. An attack on a Mage was no longer just a crime of war, it was an international crime under Inan global laws defined in the treaty. The warriors combing the grounds were an international force.

He could see why the man from Turith had spat: in one way, it seemed as though he were opting out of the fight. Yet, what could men of material force do against a magical intrusion? He also felt ill-at-ease with the manner in which Daliel had acknowledged his decision. He felt as though he were on the calm surface of the sea, only a touch away from the treacherous currents running beneath.

He sat in the old man's room, watching from the window as the night drew on. The blundering of the warriors grew less and less as they found nothing, dying down finally to one or two distant shouts before settling to silence. Even though he had been proved correct, there was still a part of him that felt as though he should have been with them. He looked over to the sleeping old man. He seemed so frail like that, his mortal shell so vulnerable.

It was while he was lost in such thoughts that he felt it. Not saw, or heard, but felt. The sparse hair on his head and down to the nape of his neck seemed to stand on end, his scalp tingling as though shocked.

He looked out of the window, straining his eyes. Nothing... except... it was the faintest flickering. A shape. Not any animal he recognised; seemingly not even fixed. Blurred at the edges, perhaps because of the poor light. But perhaps not...

No. Not that. It was moving swiftly across the land before the castle wall, and leaving no trail on the dusty earth.

Simeon rose slowly. It was coming again. A thought creature, shaped only by the aim of whoever created and controlled it. Maybe it wasn't coming for Ramus-Bey, in which case it was someone else's problem. But if it was, then meeting it head on may give him more of a chance. No... be honest: he wanted to atone for not going on the hunt earlier, even if no-one but he would know.

He turned to rouse Ramus: the Mage would be less than pleased to be dragged from his bed a second time, but... to his surprise he found the old man sitting up, watching him.

"I know. I can feel it," the Mage said simply. "And I know what you feel you must do, with your ridiculous pride. I shall crawl under that dusty bed, cursing the lazy servant who does not sweep there. Now go – but take care, I can feel great power."

Simeon assented without a word and followed the Mage into the ante-room: this time he would remember to pull on his boots. It would be stupid to loose a match because he was distracted by a stone in his foot.

He did not wish to arouse any suspicions or to wake any other warriors. Not until he had scoped the territory and observed the thought creature up close. So the corridor was a no-go. He hung his head out of the large window in the Mage's chamber: straight up and down, but plenty of hand and footholds if he could cope with the numbing cold of the stone. About eight to ten storeys down. A long way to fall. But at least the Praal surveillance wouldn't be expecting to monitor anyone going down.

Pulling on thin cured-hide gloves to give him a measure of protection from the cold whilst still allowing a sureness of feel, he took one last look to place the thought creature and heaved himself out.

The breeze around the sheer walls was almost as icy as the surface of the stone. Sooner he was down the better: feeling for protrusions with his right foot, he began to descend. The cold bit through the hide, but at least his fingers were aching rather than numb and it took his mind off falling. He reached the ground without once looking down or round, so focused had he become. He was breathing hard as he looked around to locate the shadowy, indistinct figure of the thought creature. He could only hope that he hadn't been spotted, or that Praal security were still wondering why someone was breaking out rather than in.

It was there. Over to the left, visible only as a darkening in a clump of bushes. There was no cover in-between himself and the creature. Had it seen him? Could it – or whoever had control over it – 'see'?

There was only one way to find out. He moved slowly, but with purpose, towards it.

It hovered, seemingly waiting for him.

Simeon drew his blaster, though he had no idea if it would have much effect. Thought creatures were energy based, and though large pulse-cannon could disrupt them, a hand blaster may not be enough.

He drew closer, sweat prickling in the small of his back. The thought creature lurked with what seemed like malevolence, though he knew it to have little sentience.

A rush of heat enveloped him, picking him off his feet and slamming him back into the dust. The hard-packed earth jarred his spine, driving the air from his lungs. He discharged his blaster, knowing the creature enveloped him. The very air crackled and sparked. A scream pierced his brain.

He could breathe again. Pulling himself up, fear

overcoming pain and fighting for breath, he could see the indistinct shape a short way off, hovering. It was smaller. With luck he had dissipated some of its energy field.

It came for him again. Once more he fired into it as he was driven backwards. He felt muscles tear as his torso was wrenched sideways; his black tunic ripped as sharp energy like claws scored his flesh.

Again he heard the unearthly scream. He fired again, and felt the weight lift from him as the air lit up with an energy charge.

Gasping for breath, aching all over, he saw the thought creature draw back. He tried to rise, but could not support his own weight. With a sickening plunge, blackness descended.

His last thought was of failure.


Simeon awoke with a jolt, then wished he hadn't as pain wracked him. He was in his bed, with Ramus-Bey watching over him.

"Brave... but pretty foolish. You took enough of its energy to force it to retreat, too weak for its task. I had to act pretty quickly, too, to get you up here before you were discovered. After all, I don't want to have to break in a new bodyguard already. People will talk. But really, you'll have to learn to do a lot better."

Ramus-Bey turned away, leaving Simeon to his agony. In as much pain as he was, Simeon couldn't help but notice that the old man's tone, mocking though it was, held something new. Something like respect?

Perhaps. But there were other things that as yet only nagged at the very edges of his consciousness. He had repelled a magical attack. That was not his job. He was employed to fight other flesh and blood creatures, not demons of the mind and magic. Why hadn't the Mage stepped in?

Maybe he was scared: for all his bravado and bluster, back in the bed chamber he had been a small, terrified old man. Frozen in fear.

If this was the case, then it was going to be a far greater task than Simeon had initially envisaged.

# CHAPTER FOUR

## Year Zero - Period Three

The sea beneath them was still flecked by white breakers, but the colour now became a pinkish grey as the sun began to rise. The pale beginnings of a new day caused Simeon to squint as he gazed at the sky.

"Daylight. We're losing time."

"Not necessarily. Remember that we're going into the day."

Simeon frowned. "You always had this way of making things sound complicated. What has 'going into the day' got to do with anything? What does it even mean, for the Gods' sakes?"

Jenna sighed. She was staring ahead – partly to judge the distance between their holoship and the coast of Varn, and partly so that Simeon wouldn't break her concentration – but she could imagine the vexed expression on his face. The fiery eyes staring down the aquiline nose, the long jaw, lean jowls and high cheekbones seeming to direct his gaze so that it had the burning intensity of a laser. When he wasn't happy, you sure as hell knew it.

"Look, stupid, it's really simple. We're not losing as much time as you think. We're heading towards the rising sun, so we're actually ahead of where time is in Bethel right now. Clear enough?"

"It'll have to do," Simeon grumbled.

"Hey, cut that out," Jenna said angrily, turning to face him and in the process causing the solidity of the holoship to flicker indistinctly for a fraction of a moment. She caught herself, brought her anger under control. If she lost it like that again, by the time she got it focused, they could find themselves embedded in the ship up to the knees.

Simeon had noticed this too, and he raised a placating hand. "S'ok, Jen. I didn't mean you weren't doing a good job. I just meant..."

"Yeah, well, you just remember that," she bristled, cutting him off.

He returned to looking out at the rising sun. He knew he'd been unfair and that he'd angered her. First rule, after all... Best to let her calm down and continue piloting the ship without interruption, at least until they were in sight of Varn.

Jenna had other ideas.

"Sim," she hadn't called him that for a long time, "why did you ask me? Why didn't you raise a general alarm?"

He chuckled. A deep, growling sound that seemed out of place in such a slim frame. It also had the bitter edge of irony. Without turning around he said: "You think I was going to admit my failure? I was hand-picked for this job, and I messed up. Me. No-one else. So if anyone was going to put it right, it had to be me. How could I tell anyone what had happened, admit my stupidity? You were right about me just now... a stupid grunt from the ranks. Blaster fodder with no place in a world without war." He gave a short, barking laugh. "Thinking about it, I wasn't even much good, then... and maybe that's why they picked me."

"I don't follow," Jenna said softly. She'd always hated the streak of self-doubt in him, and she wasn't sure she wanted to hear about it when they were more than half-way to a foreign shore in what was – for want of a better term – a combat situation. But she knew him: he had to say it.

"Think about it, Jen. You've got a formula for Inan-wide peace that means dragging these old guys out of their academies and touting them as super-weapons. Which they are. But they're also frail old guys who could be taken out long-range by a sniper without warning. They're Mages, not seers, right? Wrapped up in their own little worlds. So you give them bodyguards."

"Makes sense to me."

"Yeah, except then why would you then appoint someone who had spent most of their war service on a prison farm? I can grow crops... combat experience doesn't include a shovel and a bucket of animal shit."

"They must have seen something in you," she said, groping for the right words.

He laughed that bitter growl once more. "Oh yeah..."

They continued in silence. He stared out of the port, not even seeing the sea as it reddened in the rising sun, lost in a private hell of doubt. Jenna stared straight ahead, willing the ship to move faster. Despite herself, she wished he hadn't come to her. Wished that she had been posted anywhere but Bethel as an assistant envoy. Wished that she had never met Simeon 7.

As the ship slowly progressed, she had little else to do but think of how their paths had crossed, back in the last days of the war.

*Kyas was a small nation state. The terrain was rough around the coast, hard to penetrate without a concerted bridgehead. This had been their protection in times of war. Situated close to Bethel yet choosing to ally themselves to Varn, they would have been in a vulnerable position if not for the rocky lands that kept the seas at bay. Only some sparse vegetation and the rangy Anlo could survive. The Anlo, a horned, furry, stringy creature – waist-high to the average Kyan – was a hardy survivor, and its image had come to represent the Kyans, taking prominence on their nation state emblem.*

*Inland, the soil was richer, made up of equal parts loam and clay. Some areas were easier to farm than others, and although the terrain was still hilly, there were large tracts of plain which were used for arable farming. In these areas most of the cities and towns had been settled. The only habitable areas around the coast were those inlets where port settlements had sprung up, serving as the sole trading areas before the advent of technological and magical air travel.*

*The difficulty of access by sea had isolated the people for much of Inan's history. Walls of rock, jagged and hard to get past, claimed much of the coastline. Only in a few places did the landscape sink down to sea level. These rocks also extended out under the water, forming reefs of sharp, sudden death for those who dared to sail over them. Only in few places did these natural defences subside sufficiently for the people to build small towns and ports, and for them to dare to venture out and find channels through which they could pilot sea traffic.*

*Through necessity, they had developed holoship magic to a much stronger degree than any other nation state. It served as a defence – how much harder to attack a land by air that had a better air fleet than you – and as a bargaining tool. Aerial warfare had grown with the years, and the magic and tech born of necessity had made them an ally for whom others would pay well.*

*It also gave them the perfect territory for containing enemy prisoners. To escape by air was virtually impossible. The port settlements were tightly sewn up, and to risk the inhospitable terrain that ringed the rest of the nation-state was to invite an almost certain death. Perhaps there were* those prisoners who would prefer this to a life subjugated as a farm labourer: they were in the minority. For the most part, any prisoner taken and shipped to Kyas was content to settle into the well-established system that allowed the Kyans to concentrate on war and trade, using a virtual slave labour force to farm the nation's food crop.

It was a part of any Kyan's military training that they serve time as prison farm security. A tedious task, part-farmer, part warden, it served some well as it kept them from active service and the risk of death. Others felt constrained, and that their talents were wasted.

Ensign Jenna Eslo was one of the latter. Her father had been a holoship engineer, killed in the great battle of Tempus Peak when she was only a small child. He was a hero and, as a result, she had been brought up on tales of his skill, bravery, and selfless devotion to the cause of Kyas. It was no surprise then that the impressionable child had grown into a dedicated adult. She had entered the holoship academy as soon as she was eligible for military service, determined to develop her magical skills and continue in the noble tradition of her father.

Despite the equality in other fighting units of the military, the holoships were regarded as a specialist skill and still mostly the preserve of the male. She encountered hostility from other grunts, and some prejudice from the minor Mages who instructed the raw recruits on the finer points of constructing and piloting the mind-based warships. Her father's reputation smoothed some of this, and she stayed the course as the few other female recruits fell by the way, transferring to other branches of the military.

Jenna Eslo graduated with honours, attaining the rank of Ensign at a younger age than any of her peers – male or female. Yet she would never achieve her ambition. The

*only thing she wanted was to honour her father's memory
by being like him. Perhaps, in some darker recess of her
mind, she was driven by the thought that only in self-
sacrifice could she be worthy of him.*

*That cankerous thought may have been the thing that
nagged and itched at her as fate denied its fruition. Her
timing was bad: as she graduated, the war was drawing
to a close, though none but the higher echelons of each
nation state were aware of this. Moreover, she had first
to serve out her time as prison farm security. A tour of
duty in such a service was the fate of a Kyan at the start
of their military career, and as a career break every five
years – assuming they survived that long.*

*Jenna was at the very beginning of her career, straining
to go out and prove herself. It was considerably more than
frustrating to have to sit out six periods on a prison farm.
Furthermore, she was from the south: those in authority
had directed that her time be served in the north, where the
nights and winters were inhospitable. Kyas was not a large
nation state, but large enough for there to be differences
in the people of the north and those of the south. The
taciturn northerners were loath to mix with southerners,
even if they wore the same uniform of military service. So
she was not even granted the consolation of serving her
time near to friends and family.*

*She found it grimly funny that she felt less at home
than the men of Bethel she had to guard. In the north
of Kyas they said that if you sniffed the air you could
smell Bethel. Many of the male guards would use this as
an excuse for a series of coarse jokes involving the dung
heaps and organic matter used to feed the crops.*

*At the farm prisoners were kept segregated for the
purpose of avoiding cohabitation: after all, which nation
state would wish to pay for the offspring of those it was*

keeping confined? By the same token, guards were usually allocated on a same-sex basis, to avoid any relationships that could be looked upon as detrimental to the cause of war.

Usually.

Sometimes the numbers would not add up, and so there was some mixing of the sexes between guards and prisoners. It was rare, but the fact that it had precedent meant that her complaints were dismissed. So she settled spikily to her six period stint, willing it to end quickly so that she could be off to war.

She was not to know that at the end of the six periods, with just weeks till her deployment, the peace was to be declared. She would not get her chance to fight and her chance, perhaps, to be a martyr.

Yet, by the time that this happened, her views had changed in a way that she had not expected. The men of Bethel who came under her charge had not been the black hearted enemy she had expected. Not monsters. Merely men. She had begun to realise that the myths with which she had been raised were simplifications. She was now well out of adolescence, into her twenty-fifth anum, and all her life she had been either focused on her dead father or, or on her holoship training. It had been tunnel vision.

The harsh weather, hard outdoor slog, and the phlegmatic attitude of the men to whom she acted as overseer were, perhaps, an unlikely catalyst. She felt her attitudes begin to change. They became deeper, more complex and less immediately understandable

At least, it was on this that she blamed the action that could have seen her instant dismissal and the execution of another.

She had first noticed Simeon 7 about three weeks

*after her arrival. The first week had been induction, and the second had been spent in getting to know the territory to which she had been sent. The prison farm covered a vast area – with at least a hundred and twenty enclosures, growing seventeen different crops in rotation. The prisoner's barrack blocks were located at the north-western tip. This put them as far away as was possible from the nearest town and although they were near to the coast, the forbidding rocks and the reputation of the Anlo for feeding on those foolish enough to make a break for it were enough to discourage any escape.*

*Third week. Enclosure Seventeen/One. Sweet Bagas, a root crop. A seven-man party, including two who were obviously firm friends. A squat, heavily scarred man running to fat, and a tall, lean warrior worked slightly apart from the others, joining in conversation with them on occasion, but obviously continuing some debate of their own.*

*To the new, keen eyes of Ensign Jenna Eslo, this was obviously suspicious, and a chance for her to stamp her authority on the prisoners. Gods alone knew that she was failing in that with her fellow guards.*

*"You – what are you doing?" she yelled from atop the sixteen-hand Tallus. The creature snorted, breath misting on the cold air, and shifted under her tense grip.*

*"Digging. As you want," replied the squat man blandly. The other looked at her. He was trying to keep his expression neutral, but anger bubbled close to the surface.*

*"The talking. What were you talking about?" she asked. From the corner of her eye, she could see that the others in the enclosure had ceased work, and were watching with interest. Unconsciously, her hand strayed towards her blaster.*

"Typical," spat the tall prisoner. "We're held here, we do what you want, and because you feel like it you pick on us."

She was torn. He was, of course, correct. She was using them to assert her authority for no other reason than... well, to assert her authority. But now she had started she could not back down. To take no further action would be seen as weakness. It would cause problems with the prisoners. It would get back to her fellow guards.

The squat one had thrown down the tool with which he had been turning organic matter into the soil. He addressed the tall warrior.

"What did you do that for, Sim? You know she's gonna have to take some kind of action."

Anger blazed in her. From the way in which he had said it, she could feel that he was mocking her. She drew her blaster and fired at his feet. The wooden haft spluttered and burnt, turning to ash in the intense heat. The metal head buckled and melted, spreading across the soil.

"That will come out of your credit," she said, trying hard to stop her voice shaking with anger. It was a good punishment: the credit system acted as an incentive for the prisoners to work harder, allowing them a small measure of luxuries from prison farm stores. To take this away was to take away some semblance of being a man.

"As for you," she continued, directing her gaze to the tall warrior, who watched her unblinking, "you will come to the main admin block at sundown, where you will be punished.'

"For what?"

"For daring to ask."

She turned the Tallus and dug her heels into its flanks. It's long, spindly legs loped awkwardly over the soil, breath whinnying in its throat. She did not look back, but *she was sure she could hear some faint laughter.*

*It was only when she was some distance away that she recalled: she had forgotten to get the squat prisoner's name or number.*


*The tall one turned up at sundown. She expressed her surprise.*

*"You'd only come and find me on the morrow," he shrugged. And when she asked the name and number of his squat companion, he shrugged once more. "That I couldn't tell you. War wound... bad memory. You should have asked."*

*It was then that her temper snapped and she did something she should never have even contemplated: she came round the desk and hit him. A roundhouse punch. She had gone through basic combat training, but as a holoship trainee she had not been through bodybulk training. She was slow, weak compared to others on the farm. The tall warrior caught her arm with ease and used her own momentum to turn her, pinning her to the wall. He looked down into her face. She knew he could see the sudden fear in her eyes.*

*"That was really, really stupid. Even for a Kyan," he said quietly. "I know the routine here. We all do. Just because we know escape would be futile, don't think we pay you no attention. This is the admin block. It has eight admin rooms and three sleeping quarters for those on night duties. The dorm block is to our left, the recreation and repast hall to the right. Both of them are too far for any noise to carry. At sundown, everyone will be either sleeping or eating, ready to change watch. You're the only one here. And you've nowhere near the experience or strength to break the rules by striking a prisoner and*

expect him not to retaliate." He let her go and stepped back. "We get by here... all of us. Mostly by giving and taking. Prisoners would rather be home: maybe we get picked for repatriation swaps, maybe we die here. But at least we can live with some dignity... all of us."

Her breath was tight in her chest. Partly from fear, partly from the pressure of his body against hers, crushing her. She was petrified of being brought face-to-face - literally - with her own limitations. So she did the last thing in the world she should have done.

She kissed him.

By necessity, they had to be furtive about what came next. She discovered that the squat warrior's name was Daliel, but she never did get around to punishing him. How could she, when he was to collude with the tall one – she found out his name was Simeon 7 after she jumped him - in helping them to get time together?

Of course, he wasn't helping them purely from a sense of altruism. Like Simeon, he found the credit he was accruing had a certain capacity for growth that it had not had before. He was also discrete, which was another advantage, and smart. A back injury which came to him suddenly caused a switch in duties. A switch to a two man checking shed for stored and harvested crops. A checking shed near the admin block. Oh yes, Daliel was smart: beyond lighter duties and more credit, it was hard to see what he gained, but perhaps any gain was better than none in such a situation.

Jenna didn't care. Neither did Simeon. For his part, he had been alone too long as a prisoner. If there was anything else, he was careful not to give it away. For her part, a more complex set of emotions coursed through her.

*All of her life Jenna had been dedicated to the ideal of military service. There had been no room for thoughts of the opposite sex except as those she would serve alongside. Anything else had been repressed: if not consciously, then certainly by her subconscious as something that would only obscure the goal. Maybe there was something in there, too, that related to her father. How could anyone live up to the god-like creature she had created from her imaginings and the stimulus of the stories she had been told?*

*Now it had been unleashed: all that had been pent-up and contained. On not just a man, but a warrior; not just a warrior, but a prisoner of war. A man who should be her enemy. A man who, despite having been captured rather than shot down in flames, still had dignity and nobility.*

*She realised that she had considered prisoners to be cowards merely because they had not perished in battle like her father. But now she wondered if her father had perished from chance rather than choice; from stupidity rather than bravery? To question, in such a manner, the things that had driven her life and given her purpose up to this point left her in a whirl of confusion.*

*This was not aided by the fact that Simeon's base desire soon transmuted into the gold of a finer feeling. The tall warrior fell in love and made no secret to her of the fact. It was an impossible situation, made the more difficult by the fact that their fledgling relationship had no avenue for progress.*

*Perversely, her own feelings – which had started as a complete infatuation – began to cool as his heated. There were things going on in her head that she couldn't even begin to assimilate. Had her feelings for the warrior been stimulated because he represented her dead father? Or were they an insult to that worthy's memory? In a more practical manner, how could she allow this to continue, to put her life at risk for sexual gratification? Gods alone knew she had left it long enough, but did she need this much danger?*

For her, the peace had been more welcome than she would have allowed only a few periods previously. Where it would once have frustrated her need to join a combat squad and prove herself, now it signalled an arbitrary – and thus easier – end to her relationship with Simeon. He was to be repatriated along with the rest of the farm. Sent back to Bethel. Allied nation state personnel were kept on separate farms. Segregation such as this was intended to make the running of the farms a simple matter.

If only it had been that simple.

It should have been. The northern farms were to be repatriated first. They were nearest to Bethel, so it made sense to begin there. Simeon was a man torn. He was happy to be going home, but was unhappy about leaving Jenna. She said she would keep in contact as much as possible: she did not know what the terms of the peace were to be. Enlisted as a holoship ensign, she could be sent anywhere, deployed in a number of ways.

In truth, she had no intention of contacting him. It would be for the best, she was sure. Consequently, she had been appalled at her posting to Bethel. However, it was a vast continent. The chances of running across one man were minute. She had not tried to contact him. She assumed he would forget her once he was home. She thought he would have no idea she had been deployed in his home land. She heard nothing from him.

Until he turned up in her sleeping quarters one night, begging her help.

"Jen – are you listening?"

She snapped out of her reverie, aware that she had been keeping a section of her mind – that which had been trained for such a purpose – focused on the holoship, while her memory had led her astray. Simeon had been talking the while, and she was unaware of a single word.

"No," she answered honestly. "Whatever it was you were droning on about, I neither know nor care."

"Fine. You want us to walk into a trap then."

"Trap? What trap?"

"There... may be one," he said with emphasis. "I was trying to plan for all eventualities. This is my mess, and I don't want you to get in too deep."

She turned and looked at him. "Hello? Inan to Planet Simeon – you're in my holoship about to cross a nation state border in peacetime with an intent to break that peace. How deep is that? Or do you consider 'too deep' to be... oh, I dunno... how far exactly?"

"You said it – this is a holoship. Invisible to scanner tech. You can also make it invisible to the eye. No-one need ever know you're there. You can stay in the ship while I go and get Ramus. But if you do, then you need to have a contingency plan for if some Varnian warrior smacks his head on the side and stumbles onto you."

She shook her head. "You're a cretin, you know that? You think I would have piloted you all the way across the seas just to leave you and cower here while you do the hard bit? You don't know me at all do you?"

"I do... I know you'd risk your life. But I don't want you to. It isn't your fight. I wish it was. I wish I hadn't had to find you... for so many reasons. But I did, and it's up to me to keep your risk to a minimum."

"Stubborn bastard. You also know I couldn't let you do that."

Beneath every word, there was something else flying between them. Three periods had made no difference: no matter how much she ignored it, it was still there. Obviously, it was too for Simeon: why else would he have sought her out?

"When this is over," he began hesitantly, "assuming we make it back, then..."

"It'll have to wait," she said, turning to face the view screen. She didn't need it – her trained magic sense gave her a three dimensional sense of space – but she wanted to show him. "We've got work to do."

Ahead of them was the coast of Varn.

# CHAPTER FIVE

## Year Zero – Period One

"I don't see why you're being so difficult about this. It's obvious that there will be danger. That's why I'm here! In the name of the Gods, can't you grasp that? I thought you were supposed to be intelligent beyond the bounds of most men?" Simeon shivered. "And why is it that you can't feel the cold? It must be close to freezing in here."

Ramus-Bey sighed heavily, finished scratching on thick parchment with thin, watery ink and turned to face his bodyguard. He slipped the small half-moon spectacles from the bridge of his nose and gave Simeon his best 'I-hate-being-disturbed' stare.

"You wanted something?"

Simeon waited a beat, calmed himself, then said: "You haven't heard a word I've said, have you?"

Ramus raised an eyebrow. "I think, my dear man, it would be almost impossible for me not to have heard your words," he intoned with a heavy emphasis. "The point, rather, is what point there was to them?"

Simeon said nothing for a moment. It had been this way since their return. Finally: "There is an ever-present danger. You saw what happened the night of the signing. We've been back here for almost a whole period and in that time it seems to me that you've almost gone out of your way to prevent the implementation of any security measures at the academy. How can I do my job properly when I get no co-operation?"

"Simeon, you have to understand one thing," Ramus-Bey began, standing and shuffling to the stone mullioned window, staring out over the lush grounds. An artful use of topiary around the boundaries kept the glass and steel erections of the city at bay. In a similar way, Ramus-Bey wished to keep everything else from the outside at a remove. He turned back to face his perplexed guardian before continuing. "The work of the academy – researches into the very fabric of being and the ability to transmute that via the power of the mind and the strength of the will – is something that not even half a millennium of war was able to deflect from its path. Why then, should I be the one to disrupt the lives of the Mages and wizards, and the work of the adepts who wish to further those studies by their own education, in order that I may be able to fend off some *mythical* attack from the outside?"

Simeon blinked, took a deep breath. It was the same argument he had heard since their arrival. His retort was so polished he felt as though he could recite it word perfect without even thinking.

"You saw what happened the night of the treaty signing. An attack was made. Not upon you perhaps, but certainly on at least one Mage. By an unknown enemy. A magical attack. There has to be a contingency for that. But you are physically frail, so we have to ensure that your corporeal body is as protected as is possible. Which cannot be done while the surrounding area is not secured by the measures which I have suggested."

Ramus-Bey smiled wryly, and with tongue in cheek replied: "Very good. Your timing gets better with each delivery. If the live entertainments still existed, as they did when I was young, you could have made a fair career for yourself. However, mine own memory fades a little with the passing of the anum, and so I cannot be as correct. But the substance of my answer remains as before. That attack was more than likely the result of a rogue element who wished war to resume. They had a window – a moment of 'optimum opportunity', as you military types may phrase it – and they took it. Now it no longer exists. Long-distance magic of great threat is something only Mages can achieve, and as we were the targets, we're hardly likely to be the ones to launch attacks against ourselves. We're academics for the Gods' sakes, not soldiers. As for the physical: who is going to risk sending a force into the heart of another territory and break all treaty conditions?"

"Anyone who feels that a nation state without a Mage is a tempting target," Simeon answered. "Once one is down, then don't think that everyone else wouldn't start to talk of alliances and co-opting the weaker territory."

Ramus-Bey chewed his lip thoughtfully. "It saddens me that the military teach a man to think that way... I will have no more discussion on this, I have work to do."

With which, he dismissed Simeon 7 with a half-wave of his hand, as though he could not even be bothered to complete the dismissal. However, as a furious Simeon turned to go, he attempted to make amends.

"I will tell you one thing. The cold. Magic causes spatial disruption, affecting the pressures within localised areas. This has a direct affect on currents of hot or cold air. The kinds of pressures generated by the disruptions of magic differ according to how adept the practitioner may be. For example, a junior may be able only to cause small disruptions, and so the temperature fluctuations may be slight. But someone such as myself, in the course of everyday study, is generating an immense amount of almost permanent disruption. Resultantly, it's almost permanently cold around these centres of the academy. Hence, one would assume, the expression cold as a witch's teat. Although, I should point out, that it is most unfair to blame the female of the species alone."

Simeon looked at him, baffled. "Thanks for that," he murmured. "But it still doesn't explain why there's no heating."

Ramus-Bey chuckled and shook his head. "Because any heat produced would be instantly sucked up and dispersed by the pressure fluctuations. They don't teach you science in the military, obviously."

"Only if it involves killing the enemy," Simeon conceded. "So what do you suggest I do, if you're so smart?"

"Purchase warmer clothes, dear boy."

It had been this way since the journey back to Bethel. The Mage had seemed to warm to the man who was to be his bodyguard, and on the ship that took them back he waxed at length about the Bethel Institute – the correct name for the academy, although it was rarely referred to in any other way – and the beauty of it's grounds. A millennium old stone castle construction, complete with keep and moat, it was protected from the rest of the city which had grown around it by a weak magical barrier as well as by a stone wall.

The magical barrier was not intended to keep out intruders, but rather to keep in the fauna that wandered free in the grounds. Several different breeds of Tallus, small mammalian creatures that lived in the trees and shrubs, and a number of giant reptilian birds – that were the result of a resurrectionist spell involving a clutch of fossilised eggs from Inan pre-history that had gone slightly awry – all roamed free. They were of no danger to the outside city, but were distinctly rural. The thought of a Tallus herd wandering onto the streets, causing chaos in the busy traffic system, was not one to idly contemplate.

To Simeon, as he listened to the old man happily talk of home, it sounded like a security nightmare. Wandering creatures, some of whom could inflict a lot of damage if angered, could easily trip any warning devices he chose to install. Moreover, the magic was only one-way: anyone could easily scale the wall.

Also, there was the matter of the castle itself. A vast, ancient stone building that bore more than a little resemblance to the castle in Praal where the treaty had been signed. But, whereas that building had been about spirals and staircases that seemed to go on forever, the interior construction of this building was based around rectangles: the staircases had sharply angled turns, and all ran through the centre of the building, corridors radiating off from this central hub to allow access to the rooms on several levels. Eight storeys in height, the castle had not a single room that was without a window, allowing a view of the brightly coloured fauna where trees and shrubs in greens and yellows clashed with the vibrant turquoise, pink, purple, and magenta of the flowering plants. The wildly varying colours of the fauna's pelts – broken only by the dull black sheen of the reptilian birds – added to the riot of colour.

It was an oasis of the old ways in the city. Belthan was the ancient capital of Bethel, on the western side of the continent. It lay well inland, away from the port towns and on the edge of the wasteland known as the Deadlands. This extent of barren land formed the centre of the continent. Winds howled across the arid plains, bringing their freezing cargo to the edge of the city, where giant reflectors kept the worst of the gales, snow and sleet at bay during the long winters.

Belthan was a monolithic city of dark stone buildings from across the ages, with a predominance of glass and

steel constructions in the centre. The jumble of styles
and ages gave the city a strange, lop-sided feel that was
also a trademark of their anums long rival, Varn. As the
richest nation states, they had the largest concentrations
of population and wealth in their capitals, enabling them
to build more. Yet a respect for their history – it had taken
them a long, hard slog to amass their wealth – ensured
that the old was revered alongside the new. Where other
towns, other nation states would clear vast tracts and
begin again, the capitals of these great rivals ironically
echoed each other in their desire to preserve – and thus
flaunt – their history.

It should be noted, too, that their ability to contain
both old and new was because of their ability to repel
aerial attack: a luxury in which less privileged towns and
nation states could not share.

The people of Bethel lived on a land-mass that was
apt to be severe in weather conditions, suffering from
no night-time during the high season, with overcast and
dark conditions determining the rest of the year. Colour
was either bleached from the landscape or driven deep by
snow and wind, and this was reflected in the colouring
they chose for their clothing and for their buildings.
Greys, whites and blacks predominated, with a preference
for the darker end of the scale.

Simeon 7. was from the east. He was a small-town boy
who had grown to adulthood and the military without
going outside the immediate area of his town. Air-raids
had reduced much of the town to rubble before he was
born, and he was familiar only with the newer styles of
architecture. On his trips overseas with the military he
had seen little save the Bethelians' own encampments,
established in the steamy jungles of south-western Varn
before his capture. His overwhelming impression of those

few weeks attempting to encroach enemy land was of damp, the smell of rotting vegetation and a green that made the skies dance when you looked up. After that, there were the harsh lands of the Kyan prison farm. It was almost like being on the farmlands near his home town.

The castle and surrounds in Praal had been strange enough to him. But now, to see the whole of Bethelian history laid out in the jumbled design of one city, with the seemingly bizarre contrast of the riot of colour that was the Institute sitting as an island in the centre, was almost overwhelming. He was finding great difficulty in assimilating the presence of the city, while at the same time attempting to work out a strategy for the defence of his charge.

In the end, he adopted a simple strategy of his own. He elected to ignore anything beyond the gates of the academy, choosing the walls as his own boundaries. By ignoring what was beyond, he was able to focus on the interior of the grounds and the castle itself. The adepts, wizards and Mages within the castle walls acted as though the city beyond was not there; as though the wider world of Inan was not there. They existed only within the world of the Institute. Magic – and the study thereof – may have made their interior world richer, but it was at the expense of acknowledging the material world.

However, it did amuse Simeon to note that although all within the academy made a big thing of rejecting the outside world, they were not averse to bending their self-imposed rule. Although much of their food was grown in vegetable patches in the grounds, and some of the smaller fauna were farmed for slaughter, many of those in the academy had a weakness for confections that were delivered on a weekly basis.

Step one: monitor delivery vehicles regularly, establish relations with delivery staff, carry out routine security checks on said vehicles.

Another concession to the modern world was that the kitchens relied on tech-powered ovens and refrigeration (though he bitterly considered this a waste: put the frozen and chilled foods in Ramus' rooms, and you would alleviate this need). Partly practical – fossil fuels would soon run out unless magically replenished in the relatively limited castle grounds – the tech also enabled them to feed themselves faster and with less work.

Finally, as many of the new adepts had grown up in the outside world of tech before entering the Institute, a concession to the age was made in the shape of an entertainment room with holovid displays and comm-gear.

Step two: monitor these for bugs, for signals sent or received, and also vet any repair/maintenance personnel who should call. All new and replacement equipment to be vetted on arrival, delivery vehicles checked.

For his own part, Simeon had his own comm and holovid equipment, as well as surveillance and observation tech supplied by Daliel, who had arrived almost simultaneously with Simeon and Ramus-Bey. This, too, was regularly checked, vetted and maintained.

With this, and the regular patrols on foot around the academy that he undertook, Simeon found his time more than adequately filled. It would have been easy to fall into a routine within a matter of weeks, but he was determined to stay out of this trap. He varied his routes and times around the grounds, aware all the while that the adepts mocked him. Young believers in the power of magic, they could not understand the use of a military man within the grounds of the castle. It was not difficult for them to see that Simeon was a man whose nerves were on a razors edge: determined to get it right, still familiarising himself with the surroundings. He was seeing danger in every shadow. Although aware that this was the attitude he would need to adopt, he also wondered how long it would be before it burnt him out?

As a result, it was easy for a mischievous young adept to conjure up a simple thought form in the shape of a shadow, then laugh as the warrior gave chase, stalking the mind construct until he was within range only to be foiled as the adept simply let the image go, leaving him with nothing to attack.

It became a game for the adepts. The problem was that some of them were nowhere near as skilled as they believed themselves to be, and so the thought forms, when let go, did not dissipate: rather, they wandered off to roam the grounds, mindless and directionless energy in search of a task. Joining, as they did, with other thought forms that appeared and disappeared with regularity as the by-products of magical experiments, they littered the grounds, moving amongst the cover of the flora, setting off security alarms with regularity.

Simeon found this irritating as it was, but it was made worse by the insistence of Ramus-Bey that these alarms were disturbing the studies of the academy, and he would go directly to the Chief Minister if such interruptions continued.

There were times when it seemed like an impossible job from the very beginning. Encounters such as the one that very morning with the Mage made things no better.

But worse was to come.

Dusk fell over the city. Outside the walls of the castle, traffic noise rose and then receded as the city ended its working day and began the leisure of the evening. Inside the walls, the animals responded to the darkening skies by searching for food, retreating to favoured corners. Even the reptilian birds hunkered in the trees, malevolently surveying the skies and waiting for the light to come once more so that they could continue their ceaseless vigilance.

In the same way, Simeon was preparing to step up in his own ceaseless vigilance. During the day, following his latest fruitless exchange with the Mage, he had returned to his room and checked his schedule. There was little to be done on this day: a routine delivery, which was only a short time away. After that, nothing. Usually, the hi-tech surveillance equipment came into its own once darkness fell. For once, though, he wanted to be out there in the night, to get a feel for the area. The city provided ambient light to stop the grounds becoming too impenetrable to ordinary vision. He also had infra-red night vision goggles which connected to the surveillance tech in his room.

He hadn't had the chance to try them out. Simeon became inordinately excited, and then caught himself. He was beginning to feel that glorying in the tech was the only pleasure he would get for a long time to come. Which, he had to admit, was not the greatest feeling.

He ate alone in his room, not wanting to mix with the adepts after the last few days of thought form teasing. The wizards were apt to dismiss them as harmless pranks – even as good practice – yet Simeon had the nasty feeling that one day soon he may (accidentally?) shoot an adept, such was the tension he felt. He wished he could communicate this, but there was a gulf between the academics and the military that seemed too great to cross. As well as his current desire to hit an adept if one so much as looked at him wrong, he knew that if they realised he was embarking on night patrol, it would be too great a temptation for them.

Perhaps for him, too: something he wished to avoid.

He waited in his quarters, keeping half an eye on the surveillance equipment, which was registering normally. There were minor fluctuations in readings, but to the degree he could tell when these were the weak thought creatures that still roamed loose. They showed as little more than blips in the energy detectors. Similarly, he was becoming something of an adept himself when it came to reading the register on other surveillance equipment. The shapes, footfalls, and rustlings of the fauna were becoming both familiar and distinguishable to him.

Ramus-Bey had a regular hour at which he retired for the night. Others in the academy were tempted sometimes by their studies to ignore the passing of the night, but the Mage had disciplined himself over the years. He knew the limits of his own body: magic may have prolonged his life, but only by slowing its decline. He had learned to work within those limits.

So, at that time, Simeon made a last check. They exchanged a few words, the coolness of earlier still between them. That suited Simeon fine. He had work to do, and had no wish to waste time in idle conversation.

He returned to his room and prepared for his patrol. Slipping out of the castle, avoiding those wizards and adepts who were still in the entertainment room or the kitchens, he began to follow the route he had prescribed for himself.

It was odd how different the castle grounds seemed by nightfall. It had taken him some time to get used to their strangeness by day. Now it was as though he had to re-learn everything. He knew from his brief experiences of combat how alien an environment could be by night, but the flora was causing problems: shrubs with raised root systems that conspired to catch at his ankles; overhanging branches shaded by the lack of light that suddenly loomed at him; the way in which many of the flowering plants changed their scent in the darkness, as petals and stamen closed themselves to the cold night air. His portable tracker told him one thing, his senses another.

The wildlife didn't help either. Snuffling, whining sounds caught his attention and made him turn. Leathery wings beat above his head as his wanderings disturbed the irritable reptilian birds. Tallus dung lay treacherously and thickly in his path.

Just as he was beginning to think that a night patrol was a really bad idea, his tracker went wild. Looking down at the small screen, he could see that a large surge of energy had appeared, breaking near the southernmost wall. He flicked a switch, transfering the signal to a small reflective screen in the night vision goggles. He holstered the tracker and drew his blaster, moving as fast as he dare towards the source of the disturbance. The last thing he wanted was to stumble and fall on the treacherous surface. It was an uneasy compromise between the need for speed and the need for caution.

He glanced towards the castle. As he circled towards the energy source, he noted that very few lights were ablaze in the building. Good, he didn't want anyone wandering into what may be a combat situation.

As he approached, his task was made harder by a sudden rush of creatures making their way in the opposite direction. Panicked by the energy source, the Tallus herd has started a stampede of the smaller creatures. This in turn had stirred the birds, which were circling for prey. The air was filled with their harsh, cracked cries.

In the dark, even with the aid of night vision, it was difficult to pick his way past the panicked fauna. He slowed, having to side-step Tallus that galloped sightlessly, to stop the smaller creatures from tripping him, biting or scratching him as he tried to avoid treading on them, or kicking them.

He soon discovered why they were so terrified. The thought creature came into view: it was almost twice his height and width, and a Tallus hung from within its centre. He could not see the front of the animal, only the flailing rear legs, and the shower of blood and meat disgorging from surrounding area. The thought creature was shredding the animal.

Above him, reptilian birds attracted by the scent of blood homed-in on the thought creature, tiny brains focused only on the Tallus. They screeched in agony as they hit the energy form, their leathery skin frying on contact, the ground reverberating at his feet to their falling deadweight.

Simeon cursed. This was a big bastard. No adept had made this as a joke. Serious magic was required for this amount of power. But how the hell was he going to engage a thought? On his previous encounter, he had blasted into its centre, dissipated it. He doubted whether he could get close enough to do that without being chewed up like the Tallus.

It was headed for the castle, but had been distracted by the Tallus and the birds. One good thing about thought creatures: none too bright. Perhaps...

He circled it, hoping to draw it towards him by firing into it, hoping the irritation of the blaster energy would distract it further. He had no real plan beyond that, but a notion that if he could guide it to the area where the other stray thought forms clustered – he checked this on the tracker screen – then perhaps the thought creatures would attack each other, overload and burst; like a balloon that has been overblown.

Simeon was about to fire when he saw him: Tamlin, the youngest of the adepts in the castle, and the one who was most likely to tease him. Why the adept was there he didn't know, only that the fool was walking straight towards the thought creature.

"Tamlin – go back now!" he yelled, knowing even as he did that the boy would not hear him above the cries of the birds.

"Woah... power... some kinda... mazing..." He could hear scattered words from the boy. The stupid lad thought that the creature was another of the adept's tricks on the warrior security. Instead of going back, he was moving towards it. He was saying something, looking at Simeon, but the warrior could not hear him.

The bulk of the thought creature shifted. It's head – if it could be said to have one – turned to the adept. His expression changed to one of frozen fear. He couldn't move as the hazy limb of the creature reached out and drew him up.

Simeon fired into the creature to try and distract it. It was no use. Too little, too late: the boy was shredded in a shower of flesh and blood like the Tallus before him.

What little was left fell to the ground with a wet noise as the creature dissipated.

"I'm telling you, it was sent to hunt you down. I'm sure it vanished after Tamlin was dead because it thought it had fulfilled its task. It sensed the magic in the boy, and knew it had annihilated a magic soul. We were just lucky that a thought creature isn't created with enough intellect to detect degrees of magic. That lad should have been you!"

It was the following morning, and the exhausted warrior was in the Mage's chambers. Absurdly, as it seemed to him, having trouble convincing the Mage of the reality of the threat.

"No – no, I won't have it," Ramus-Bey yelled at the guard. "It was some stupid experiment that got out of hand. I will conduct an enquiry and the culprit will be reprimanded. You do not know magic as I do... accidents occur. It is the nature of the practice. Regrettable, but..."

The Mage tailed off as he looked out of the window. He had not met Simeon's gaze. Prior to this he had not wanted to acknowledge a threat, and the guard had put this down to an unworldly stubbornness.

Now he was not so sure. Was the denial at least in part fuelled by fear?

Was Ramus-Bey – the peace talisman of his people – scared?

# CHAPTER SIX

## Year Zero – Period One

The two men sat in shadow. Before them images of the thought creature's attempt to gain access to Ramus-Bey played out.

They watched as the Tallus was destroyed. They watched the young adept Tamlin enter the frame and then he too was shredded.

One of them also kept a watch on Simeon 7, bumbling and stumbling in the presence of the thought creature. He looked completely out of his depth. This was good.

With a heavy sigh, one of the men paused the recording as the thought creature began to fade.

"There has to be a better way. Just send a detachment in there and blast the old man to the Gods he swears by. It'll be quicker."

"And traceable. Very traceable. A detachment is a lot of people to hide in plain sight. Even though Simeon has been picked because of his unsuitability, he's still a warrior. He could take some of them out before they took him. Leaves evidence. You don't want evidence."

His hand hovering over the control, the second man pondered this for some time before decisively erasing the recording. With a brief movement of his hand he brought up the lights. He rose from his chair, long black robes flowing as he moved over to pour them each a glass of the wine that stood on a side table. It came from a decanter, the top of the liquid rose pink, the lower half a deep purple. It mixed in swirls as he poured, before settling and separating once again in the glass. He handed one to his companion before returning to his seat, robes rustling softly as the thick material brushed the floor.

Every move was deliberate, considered. It was a few moments more before he spoke.

"That's the problem with magic. It has too many unknown factors. You know where you are with a detachment of elite warriors."

"Warriors screw up too," the man seated opposite pointed out. He was dressed in a black military tunic, and was obviously coarser. Where one was tall, blond and lean, the other was squat, dark and scarred.

"I wouldn't have expected you to prefer magic over military hardware."

The squat man drained his glass in one, then shrugged. "Minister, I'm from Intel, not just a grunt. I've examined the capabilities of both. Nothing is perfect, and there's always the possibility of a screw-up. All I'm saying is that if you match the capability to the task, then you reduce those possibilities to a minimum."

"And your opinion of our – ah – 'weapon' in this instance?"

The squat man grinned mirthlessly. "The term loose cannon could have been invented for him. He is, of course, completely unreliable. We would be stupid to dismiss out of hand the possibility of his being or becoming a double agent."

"It must be said in his favour that I approached him, and he is one of our own."

"Yes. But an ambitious man knows no boundaries. He may also be recruited by another nation state. Though I suspect not, as not even our own academy know of his powers. His ambitions are academic, and with Ramus-Bey removed, he can ascend to the chair he feels is rightly his. The chances of another Intel organisation knowing of him are small. His own ambitions, and their tunnel vision, reduce further the chance of his being recruited by an enemy. Their means may match ours, but we cannot risk their ends."

The tall man smiled wryly. "How refreshing to hear the word 'enemy' used again. I have to pretend to like them. I shall relish the chance to denounce them for what they will – ah – do."

"We all have to pretend we're one world, Minister. But we aren't. This peace is a sham, but it does offer the chance to finally gain ascendancy and end the conflict once and for all."

"Just a pity that these thought creatures cannot be better controlled."

The squat man stood up, flexing bones stiffened by old wounds, and helped himself to another glass of wine. He carried it over to the desk, placing it between himself and the man he called Minister. This gave him the opportunity to lean over so that he was able to stare directly into the face of his fellow conspirator. His voice, when he spoke, was hushed.

"It did as it was commanded. It terminated a man with a magic aura. The fact that it has no degree of subtlety or finesse is simply one of those variables. We can learn from this. The next attack will have that required subtlety."

"I wouldn't like to gamble against you," the Minister said softly as the squat man seated himself.

An ugly grin broke on the scarred visage. "I never gamble. I make sure there can be only the one outcome. That's why I'm still alive. That's why you came to me when you hatched this little plot. That's why I shall be the military chief to the next Chief Minister of Bethel."

"Of Inan," the blond man corrected, pouring them another drink.

"Why stop at conquering the planet? Why not re-name

it after the greatest nation state?"

The Minister paused, glass half-filled.

"Truly, you are a man of rare vision, Daliel."

A few days later, in the castle grounds, the mortal remains of Tamlin were laid to rest with a ceremony befitting an adept. His soul was consigned to the Gods by his wizard master. Ramus-Bey completed the blessing. The magicians drank a ceremonial salute to the departing adept. Finally, they sang him to the afterworld with an ancient chant. The harmonies, in fours and fives, sounded old and strange to Simeon as he stood slightly apart from the magicians, observing. Yet there was something about the song that touched him inside. It was as if the sound reverberated in his own soul.

When the ceremony was complete, and the academics returned to the castle to begin their daily rituals, Simeon remained by the grave.

He felt, rather than heard, the Mage approach.

"You must not blame yourself. You tried to aid him."

"But I failed."

"That is neither here nor there. You did all that you could. Tamlin made his own choice not to turn and run."

"Is fear a choice?"

Ramus-Bey shook his head. "He wasn't scared. You know this because you saw him. He was in full possession of himself, and he made a decision. It was wrong. That is all."

With an infinite tenderness, the old man turned Simeon and led him back to the castle. As he let the Mage do this, Simeon was in inner turmoil. There were so many things about the previous night, and about the Mage's reaction to events that he had so far failed to resolve.

He declined the old man's offer that he join the magicians for their mid-day repast, which would be a celebration of the young adept's life. It was better that they celebrate his existence than mourn his decline. Ramus-Bey was convinced that it would make Simeon feel better. Indeed, the warrior was almost convinced by the old man's arguments. But there was too much he needed to ponder, to work out for himself. He politely declined and retired to his rooms.

Once there, he went over the recording and logs of the previous night. To watch the recording made by the trackers was painful, but he made himself do it. He was spared the worst: the recorder nearest to the thought form had been disrupted by the burst of energy when it first materialised. There were a few moments of images broken by static and disturbance before the tracker shorted from a power overload.

He studied, over and over, the images of the attack. Studied them from every angle. He could only conclude that Ramus-Bey was correct: there was nothing he could have done. He had warned the young adept, but still he came forward. His weaponry, up against magical power, was next to useless. He could only use his mind. Maybe the notion of luring the mind construct to where the strays lingered would have worked?

There was something that was nagging at him. The more he looked, the nearer it seemed to get, and yet stayed frustratingly out of reach.

Simeon tried to contact Daliel. He was unsure of his friend's exact position in Intel and Security. He knew only that the man had a cloaked comm-code: a sign of some authority. There were things about the squat, scarred warrior that baffled Simeon. It was as though the man he had spent so long with on the prison farm did not exist: that man had been a construct as much as any thought form. Regardless, Simeon clung to the persona he had known. Whatever else, Daliel was his point of contact.

The comm-device did not pick up. There was no redirection, no message pick-up, no-one on the other end. Just a continuous bleep as the comm-link registered, but was not answered.

There was much to report and Simeon would feel his duty had been better discharged if he reported to his superior as soon as was possible.

Cursing, he disconnected. He would have to find something to fill the time with until he could make the connection, or else the waiting would turn his mind. Already he felt like a wire, singing at the point of over-extension. While the entire Institute was gathered in the main hall, and the trackers and surveillance were up, running and checked, he should take the chance to relax. He hadn't been able to sleep, that was for sure.

Simeon left the room he had set up as the surveillance centre and went into the smaller bed-chamber. He lay on the bed and stared at the ceiling. He needed something to unwind; something that would completely take him out of his own problems.

He opened a cabinet by the bedside, and rummaged inside, drawing out a story pamphlet at random. Smiling to himself, he saw that it was one that he had read many times before. It would comfort rather than tax him to visit there again. The world of story pamphlets was a simple world, easier to understand. To escape for a while would be a relief.

His eyes skimmed the text, barely registering the words. He bathed in the familiarity, letting his mind drift.

With a barely suppressed cry he sat bolt upright. Escaping

the present had certainly helped in one way: while he paddled in the shallows of the story, his subconscious had delved deep. He sprang from the bed and returned to the trackers, where he called up the recordings of the previous night. He played it over, maybe three or four times, just to check.

That was it. The thing that had been irritating him like an itch that couldn't be scratched. Not that it was a relief. If anything, it caused him more disquiet.

The thought form appeared in the same way, no matter how many times he replayed it. It materialised in the middle of the castle grounds.

Thought forms could be made to travel over distances. But they moved like living creatures – which, in a sense, they were once they had been conjured – they had to ambulate. By their very nature they could be sent vast distances once formed, but had to be materialised close to the wizard who created them. Which is why the thought creatures charmed by the adepts had always appeared on the internal trackers, and had never breached the surveillance around the castle walls.

He checked the tracker records. Double-checked on the perimeter surveillance.

When the surge had appeared the previous night he had not had time to register that it was not a wall breach on the screen, but a surge from within the internal trackers. He could see how this had happened. The surge had occurred just inside the southern most wall. At the time, he had assumed that he had picked up the signal as it breached the wall surveillance.

Not so. The thought creature had been cast as near to the wall as possible (to make him think it had come from outside?) but had materialised within the walls. Which meant that the wizard casting the thought form had to be nearby. It was a strong thought form; would need a wizard of immense power to cast it. The likelihood of one of those hanging around on a city street unnoticed was remote, particularly an out of state wizard.

Much more likely that it came from inside.

Ramus would use this to point out that it was an accident, an experiment gone wrong. But Simeon had already made up his mind. To conjure a thought form that powerful demanded deliberation. Whoever cast it knew what they were doing.

Which was unfortunate.

It meant that the enemy was within.

# Year Zero - Period Two

Ilvarn. The capital of Varn. Like the continent itself, a place of colour, clash and contrast. As with Bethel, it was the only city of it's nation state to escape wholesale aerial warfare, and so was the only part of the continent where the old and new rubbed together, with white stone buildings from the ancient times sitting uncomfortably next to chrome and glass skyscrapers and with brightly coloured canopies and awnings that fluttered against the blue sky. It was a warmer climate than Bethel, and this reflected in the temperament of those who lived within the city's bounds.    Two men were sitting in the grounds of the Ilvarn Institute. Spiky fronds screened them from the excesses of the heat, and they sipped at an iced tea made from herbs grown in the Institute's gardens. Both were dressed in colourful robes. The younger man had heavy, rich materials despite the weather. The other had a looser robe of lighter weave. It looked faded, almost as old as the man wearing it. It was the latter who spoke first.

"I would assume that you were paying your respects, if not for the fact that you've never had the grace to do so before."

"You are, as ever, as charming as a wart on the posterior, Vixel. Possibly the least likeable man I have ever met."

"I could say the same of you. Which suggests that we are well matched, my dear Minister. So, now we have dispensed with the niceties, why don't you tell me why you are here?"

"Our spies in Bethel..."

"Spies, when the war is over? Tut-tut," the Mage interrupted archly.

The Minister ignored this interruption. "Our spies have supplied us with some fascinating intelligence. Something that I feel is a little more in your line than in mine."

He paused, waiting for a response. The Mage enjoyed keeping him waiting, before saying: "If you tell me what it is, then perhaps I can agree or disagree with you..."

And so, despite the apparent cessation of hostilities and the subsequent treaty, the Chief Minister of Varn delivered a report of what had occurred in Belthan the night before. The Mage listened in silence. When he had finished, the Minister waited for the Mage to comment. Waited for what seemed like an age.

"Well?" he prompted finally. "What do you think?"

"I think it's very interesting that Bethel should receive back what they send," the Mage began, sipping at his iced tea. "I have little doubt that they were behind the attempt to take me in Praal. I wonder then, who would try to snatch that pompous old fool Bey? Not us, I take it?"

The Minister raised an eyebrow. "Magic of such strength could only come from you," he said blandly.

"I wonder... I ask because it wouldn't surprise me if you

had an adept hidden away with such skills. Not everyone is suited to the academy life. And for certain it was not Bey who conjured the thought form that terminated my guard so abruptly."

"Who, then? Kyas or Turith?"

The Mage shook his head, after some consideration. "No. Not them. They're quite a way behind myself and Bey, even though the old fool is senile."

"Praal, then?"

This time the decision was instant. "No. Certainly not. Oh, they have the capability, I grant you. They are a spiritual people, almost to the point of sanctimony. Beyond, perhaps. And, much as I would like to believe that I am the strongest Mage on Inan, I know that Kathel is far superior in knowledge and ability. But he would not sully his hands by taking part in such a sordid manoeuvre."

"And you?"

The Mage smiled. It was like seeing a Sea Tallus grin before it ripped off your leg.

"I'm far too worldly to attain that level of skill. But that, on the other hand, has its advantages. For instance, I would find it amusing to sully my hands in such a matter. It would certainly muddy the waters of whatever little plot they have in Bethel. Such a labyrinthine mind as a race. Study of them would yield interesting results, I think."

The Minister picked at his robe, looked thoughtful. "Are you saying that the attack on Ramus-Bey did not come from another nation state? It came from within?"

"You're quicker than I would have expected, dear Minister. What I'm saying is that the thought form you describe is like a more powerful casting of the creature that tried to take me. I believe that came from Bethel, but not from Bey. It would be simple, would it not, for an ambitious magician and an ambitious Minister to conspire for the removal of a Mage, looking to effect substitution and also to place blame on another, in order to stir up a new conflict?"

"Then the attack on you..."

"Was an experiment. If it worked, then all very well. If not, then nothing lost. Rather, a lesson learned."

"And my lesson?"

Vixel's smile was as warm as winter in the Deadlands. "Is to use your enemies plans against them. Now, as for ours..."

The sun beat down. The Mage's bodyguard was despatched for more iced tea. There was much to discuss.

The days of this period passed slowly, or so it seemed at the time. Nothing much happened at the Institute in Bethel. Simeon finally made contact with Daliel, who listened with care, and then dismissed his suspicions. Intel reports had placed a rogue wizard from Kyas in Belthan at around that time. He had also caused trouble in Turith. Exiled from his Institute for practices that went against the spiritual laws of that nation state, he now held a grudge against the academies. Intel placed him leaving the nation state by boat the day after the attack. Tamlin was not a mistaken target per se: the wizard had a grudge against any academic. Anyone in an academy who was unfortunate enough to get in the way would likewise have suffered.

It sounded reasonable enough. Certainly, it satisfied Ramus-Bey. He was relieved that the death of Tamlin was not an internal accident, and crowed over the fact that he had been correct in maintaining that there was no attack intended on his person. But still Simeon found it hard to calm his nerves. He no longer felt like a stretched wire, but relaxing into his tasks was another matter.

Maybe that was why he was ready when it happened.

What it was exactly he was loath to say. Something beyond his understanding. Beyond, he suspected, that of Ramus-Bey, although the old man would never admit this.

It started on the fifth evening after the death of Tamlin. An ordinary day, coming slowly to an ordinary conclusion. Simeon was checking the trackers and surveillance when they flickered, then died. He cursed, checked the power and power back-up: they were functioning. Something had blocked the signals. Frowning, Simeon realised that there was no tech strong enough to block every single piece of equipment around the academy. It had to be magic.

First thing: check his charge.

Ramus-Bey looked up from his books when Simeon entered without knocking. "I hope there is..."

"No time. Just needed to check you were all right. Something's happening. I think it's magical." The warrior shivered involuntarily: partly at the drop in temperature in the room, partly at the thought of swimming once more out of his depth.

Ramus sighed heavily. "Not that again. I'm growing weary of this constant... I take it back. You may be right. I can feel something. Something not quite... how odd!"

Simeon waited for him to elaborate. Infuriatingly he did not, merely stood there, sniffing the air like a hunting beast.

The room seemed to close about them. Simeon felt a sickening lurch in his stomach, his balance upset as the floor seemed to move beneath him. His head began to spin, and he felt as though he might vomit. Yet when he looked straight down, all was as before. Strange whispers crept into his head – heard yet not heard – distinct, yet just beyond the grasp of understanding. His skin felt as though it was being pricked in a thousand – no, a hundred thousand – places. He looked around. The edges of the room were in darkness, closing in. Not a complete black, but the black of a million shifting shadows, threatening to engulf him.

He tried to move, but it was as though he were buried in peat, with only the merest give in any of his limbs. The blackness was reaching out tendrils to Ramus-Bey, trying to take him, and his guard was helpless. In fact, his guard was about to vomit. He finished retching, only to look up and see Ramus examining the tendrils as they twisted about his arm. He raised a finger, then looked perplexed when the tendrils failed to retreat.

Then it happened. That which made the strange become the truly bizarre. The tendrils began to fight each other. They twisted around themselves. The sounds in his head had two distinct accents, although the words, beyond random syllables, were still indistinct. The room spiralled back and forth before him, making the urge to vomit again stronger than before. He felt on the edge of consciousness.

Ramus gestured again. This time it seemed to have effect. The darkness began to retreat, seeming to separate as it did so. As another kind of blackness came over him, it occurred to Simeon that there was not a single attack taking place here: there were two, in direct competition with each other. And it was only their conflict that enabled the Mage to gain the upper hand.

How long was he out? It seemed like an eternity, but

could only have been a few moments. The cold water, chilled by the room, was sweet in his throat, washing away the sour taste of his own vomit. Blurry vision resolved into the Mage, kneeling over him and cradling his head.

"Magic attack," Simeon husked in a cracked voice. "Looked like more than one... this is getting serious. I need help. Can't..."

"You foolish, foolish boy," the Mage snapped. He let Simeon's head drop, his anger needing an outlet. "You are here for corporeal menaces. I am a Mage. Nothing magical can touch me, for am I not one of the most powerful wizards in Inan? You think I have wasted my life so that a mere shadow charm can harm me? You concern yourself with a physical threat. I will deal with anyone fool enough to tackle me on my own ground."

The Mage returned to his books, pointedly ignoring his bodyguard as Simeon slowly got to his feet. All the while that Simeon cleaned up the vomit, mopping down the floor, the Mage kept his back to him. Like a spoilt, petulant child.

Why? Because Simeon had dared to question him?

No. Rather, Simeon suspected, because the Mage had been shaken by his inability to instantly repel the attack with the first charm. He didn't need a bodyguard to question his ability: he was only too well aware of the questions he must ask himself.

# CHAPTER SEVEN

## Year Zero - Period Three

"If you say 'are we there yet' one more time, then I will, of course, be forced to kill you before we reach the target area."

"I would never say that... but are we?"

Jenna turned, pulling a face halfway between irritation and amusement. "No, of course we aren't. The *Peta* is a holoship, not a battle cruiser."

"Pity. It'd be a damn sight quicker." But he said it with a smile on his face.

There was no doubt that Simeon's mood had improved no end since they had passed over the coast of Varn. They were now in enemy airspace – or, at least, what had once been enemy airspace – and so that much nearer to their target. He was flexing himself mentally, thinking through strategies for when they hit Ilvarn. It gave him something to do rather than just pace the deck and stare out at the ground below, brooding.

Of this, Jenna was relieved. His tension had been getting to her, distracting her to the point where the speed of the *Peta* – by its very nature slow at the best of times – had been reduced to a near-crawl. Holoships had the advantage of being invisible to surveillance tech, and at times invisible to the naked eye (if the Ensign whose construct that ship may be had sufficient skill), but they could be incredibly slow. Thus, the very thing that had made Simeon approach Jenna for help was that which also frustrated his aim.

But now, as the pink sun cast its early morning glow over the dense undergrowth beneath them, he could feel that progress was being made. True, Varn was a vast continent, but it was some comfort that they were now over land and not sea.

While Simeon occupied his mind with exploring every possible scenario he could conjure, Jenna concentrated on extracting the maximum speed from her craft. It was far from easy: the construction of holoships and their projection through the skies demanded much mental energy from those who were trained in the arcane art. It had not helped that she had been dragged from her bed in order to make this flight. In its favour, it had to be said that this unorthodox mission was under-manned compared with the usual flight. Holoships had a history of either merchant flight, or undercover troop missions. Ensigns were trained to carry weight: two people in a holoship meant that greater speed could be achieved. Nonetheless, she could feel a pricking at the back of her eyes that indicated a need to sleep.

She willed herself to stay focused, to stay awake. The last thing she wanted was to fade out and plunge them into the jungles beneath. It would be an ignominious end.

Balance. Should she force herself to extract maximum speed and get there quickly; or should she hold back and save energy by reducing speed? Unable to decide, she kept the ship moving in a series of lurches.

If Simeon noticed this, he held his own counsel. In truth, his mind was in another place. The ship was Jenna's responsibility. His work would begin when they landed.

They gained from the change in climate as they travelled further inland, heading towards the centre of the continent. Beneath them, the lush jungle lands gave way to plains and plateaux of veldt, where muscular quadrupeds in spotted hues of red and orange roamed in packs. Scattered in these regions were modern towns with skyscrapers and aerial shuttle services running between them. These ran at a low level, and it was easy for Jenna to lift the *Peta* above the scattered clouds, out of their flight paths.

The veldt lands were speckled with blue and green lakes that served as leisure resorts, with sprawling accommodation blocks around the edges. Once again, aerial shuttles serviced the settlements, and Jenna found herself lifting the holoship above them. She opted to stay above the cloud cover: although it was not necessary for concealment, she found that the air current resistance was easier to handle at this height. The adjustment in the ships' pressure resistance for those within demanded the lesser exertion.

The atmosphere within the holoship grew warmer as they reached the interior of the continent. Here, close to the equator of Inan, the land beneath them began to change. The plains gave way to a series of small hills, gradually rising until they became ranges of mountainous territory. The towns beneath them became less spread out, more and more concentrated into clusters that nestled in valleys. The mountains around shaded them from the worst excesses of the sun, yet kept them isolated. The need for aerial shuttles became more apparent to Jenna as she looked down on the small clusters, buzzing with shuttles and personal aerial transporters.

They must be near to their target. She had never been to the continent of Varn, despite their military alliance with Kyas. It had always been a shining, golden land of legend. The place where those who excelled in military service would receive recognition. She had seen holovid images of the land, of course, but it was not the same. Despite their mission, she was still filled with a sense of awe. It amazed her that these towns and cities could exist in this sun-scorched and seemingly inaccessible territory.

The rocks were bleached white by centuries of exposure to the pink sun. Yet their outcrops provided enough shelter from the heat, and from the rains when they came in the winter months, to allow the settlements to have flourished. There was enough farmable land to initially support the population, and with the advent of technological advances the aerial routes had rendered the need to farm obsolete. Now the thin soil supported trees and shrubs that were grown purely for decoration.

The location of these towns and cities had been less obtuse than might be supposed. Their locations nestled within the shadows of such forbidding rocks had made them almost invulnerable to attack, with the result that – unlike in other parts of the continent – all of these ancient settlements still betrayed their roots, with a seemingly random mix of the old and the new. It was easy to see why Ramus-Bey had been brought here, just as it was easy to see why this was where the elite of Varn would make their base. Difficult to bomb, almost impossible to invade, it was a fortress made by nature.

There were several towns and cities scattered amongst the hills, but only one that was large enough to be Ilvarn.

Jenna shook herself from her reverie, and focused on making the *Peta* invisible. She would have to take it down beneath the clouds and into the heart of the city. She could feel Simeon at her back, his breath hot against her neck. When he spoke it was almost in a whisper.

"This is it. Are you ready?"

"No," she replied truthfully. "But it doesn't matter, does it?"

The holoship descended into the airspace of the capital. It was well into morning and the residents of Ilvarn were going about their everyday business. As he stared out of portside, the holoship dropping swiftly, he could see vehicles on the roads, people in markets and trudging in and out of buildings. Everywhere was colour: unlike Belthan, this was a place where people would rather be terminated than wear black and grey.

Yet, despite this superficial difference, it struck him that they were exactly like the people he had left behind. Why they should be any different was a notion that he could not explain. In his imaginings during their journey, he had pictured the Varn capital in a state of siege, waiting for the Bethelian forces to descend. And now they looked as though they had no notion of the planet-changing events taking place in their midst.

Why should they? He realised he had assumed that everyone in the world shared his troubles. In truth, the average citizen of Ilvarn neither knew nor cared. Like everyone else on the planet, they were oblivious to what happened, nominally at least, in their name. Like himself, they were all toys in someone else's game.

But now was not the time to ponder such matters. Enough to know that it should make his immediate task easier.

Some cold comfort as Jenna brought the *Peta* in to land.

The main centres of Ilvarn were not something that Simeon had ever been called upon to investigate. However, even the dumbest of grunts knew that there were three old buildings in the centre that formed the hub of the capital. One was the Institute; a second was the Ministry building from which the governing body operated and the third was the Central Fortress, which had been, in ancient times, the seat of the old Regent and was now the hub of the military organisation. In the Fortress, the military leaders held council, planned strategy and held and interrogated prisoners of note.

Playing it like a gambler, Simeon figured it this way; if you captured a Mage, then you'd want to secrete him away as fast as possible. Somewhere secure. Somewhere he wouldn't be noticed. As there were representatives of all nation states in the Ministry building as a condition of the peace treaty – an opening of archives and files, a sharing of information that was supposed to promote trust and eliminate the need for further secrecy – then it was unlikely that any prisoner could be risked there for discovery.

So it was the Central Fortress or the Institute. Both had points in their favour: in the Institute a Mage could blend in magically and not be noticed; in the Fortress, he could be secured in a dungeon cell, out of sight and possibly out of mind. In the Institute, the mind of another Mage could cage him; in the Fortress, a frail old man could be physically shackled and tortured so that his mind could not focus on his magic. At the Institute, there was less likely to be an increase in warrior security without it being noticed; at the Fortress, any increase in magical activity would stand out.

It was hard to decide which was the more likely. In the end, these factors had no bearing on Jenna's decision. The truth was that she needed somewhere large enough to put down a holoship. It was in the nature of the craft that they were solid enough to occupy three dimensions when shaped by a trained mind. Their dimensions could be shrunk or enlarged up to a point but – and this was the crucial factor – they were very much 'real' up until the point when an Ensign relaxed enough to make them dissipate. To land one when laden with trade or troops demanded the same physical space as any aerial craft.

If Jenna was to land the *Peta* before dissipating it so that she and Simeon could simply walk free, then it was vital she find a space large enough to set down without displacing stone or glass and metal, thus giving them away.

The roofs of the skyscrapers gave no space. They were cluttered with roof gardens, observations posts or other constructions that would be crushed beneath the initial descent, so revealing their presence.

The turret, footway and walled surfaces on top of the castles also posed a similar problem. There was only one clear space large enough to take the initial descent in the whole of Ilvarn: the keep area of the Central Fortress.

Never let it be thought that I like to do things the easy way, Jenna thought to herself as she guided the holoship down. Each Ensign had a name assigned to their mental constructs, even though it could be argued by a metaphysicist that the 'ship', as such, had no *a priori* existence. Not that a metaphysicist would be tempted to say this if a holoship should choose to land upon them. However, the notion of giving these occasional constructions a name was to help the Ensign to focus, identify with them, and treat them with care whilst in operation. Jenna, for instance, had chosen to name hers after Peta, her first pet. She had even considered changing the name to Fermy after her current pet, in order to reinforce such identification.

Certainly, a psychologist watching the infinite care with which she manoeuvred her craft through the upward thrust of metal and glass, angling it to avoid contact, spinning it through ninety degrees so that it lay at a diagonal to the corners of the keep area as it settled, avoiding the slightest disturbance, would have found grounds for insulting those metaphysicists who had poured scorn on their reasons for encouraging the naming of holoships.

For Simeon, watching through the view screen as the city span around him, and as the cushioned fall of the *Peta* took them to their goal, such thoughts were irrelevant. Instead, he marvelled at the skill of the Ensign, and wondered once more about the stupidity of the military minds who had consigned her to prison farm duties instead of the realisations of her talents. Though, given that he would not have met her otherwise, and that he would not have been in a position to call upon her help, perhaps he should be grateful.

As the holoship descended into the keep area, down below the level of the old defensive walls around the castle roof, he felt his feet sink slightly into the surface of the holoship's floor. Simultaneously, the interior walls of the *Peta* shimmered as though in a heat haze and became transparent. He could see the floor of the keep, and the stone walls that surrounded them. He could also see the surveillance imagers mounted on each corner.

The interior of the holoship seemed to expand, appearing to rush outwards towards the stone walls, to meld in with them before finally vanishing from view. He felt his feet give way to the emptiness beneath them, falling just a short space before thumping gracelessly onto the stone floor. He had made only a few trips by holoship during his short military career, and found the adjustment to landing still a little strange. Having brought the holoship to within a fraction of the landing area's ground, Jenna had finally let go of the mental construct. Falling for a very short distance meant that the seemingly physical mass of the holoship would not create noise or disturbance beneath the castle roof.

In all, a landing that had been achieved with little to give them away. Except for the surveillance imagers, that must surely have picked up their presence as the invisibility of the holoship dissipated to reveal the two warriors.

Simeon grabbed Jenna and tried to pull her into a shadow beneath an imager.

"What are you doing?" she questioned, pulling herself away. He didn't reply, merely gestured to the imagers. She followed the line of his arm. "Ah, those... I shouldn't worry about them," she said with a baffling lack of concern.

"Either you've had a complete cretin attack, or you know something I don't," he remarked. He knew it was the latter as a sly grin crossed her face.

"Just a little trick you can master with a touch more effort: when I dispersed the *Peta*'s energy, I sent it – along with the invisibility field – out to the walls surrounding us. Any warriors who set foot up here won't be able to see or hear us."

"Can you extend it anywhere we go?" Simeon asked hopefully.

"I can maybe cast a short term charm around us when we step outside of this energy field"

"Anything we can get is a bonus."

"So this is the Central Fortress," Jenna said. "I suspect that getting off the roof will be a lot harder than it was getting down onto it."

Simeon assented. "This place is going to be crawling with warrior security and advanced surveillance tech.

There's no way we can avoid detection for long. What I need to do is get out of here and still give myself the best chance of making it in one piece."

"Woah there," she exclaimed, "what's this change from 'we' to 'I'?"

Simeon looked at her. His lips pursed, his eyes bore into her. "I told you. This is *my* fight. You can stay here. Maybe even use the holoship to get out quick. No-one has to know you're here."

"And I suppose they won't be able to work it out if they take you?"

"I wouldn't say."

"Sim, you'd be terminated. You wouldn't have to say. They'd soon trace your movements back, and that'd lead right to me. As soon as I said yes, I was in this for the long haul. Whether I really wanted to be or not. So stop trying to be noble. It's not the time for that."

He nodded. "If that's the way it is. Tell me, how far does the invisibility field spread?"

"Covers the whole of this area," she replied, indicating the sun-blasted stone roof. "Right to the edges. Where those doorways are," she continued, indicating the four – one in each wall – that broke the monotony of stone. "Then anyone staring in from the other side would be unable to see us, although we could see them."

"Okay... so if we open the doors ourselves, then..."

"Then we cannot be seen or registered on surveillance equipment as long as we stay on this side of the door."

"Would that be suspicious?" he said with humour. "Maybe not – not if there was nothing registering on the other side. Figure it's an advantage... I'll take these two, you take those," he continued, indicating that she take the south and east walls, while he took north and west.

Moving easily, knowing that they could not be seen, they conducted their initial reconnaissance. Simeon, for one, felt on safer ground. All the way along, the way that magic had overtaken conventional warrior codes had unsettled him. Despite the things he had learned from Ramus-Bey, he was still in essence a warrior, more used to dealing with tech and weaponry than charms and spells. Now, in having to tackle their exit from the Central Fortress, he was squarely in territory he knew.

Each of the two corridors he recce'd revealed the same thing: old stone passages and stairwells were lit by fluorescent tech, each with imagers on the bends. It was easy to guess that the imagers continued the length of the stairwells. Furthermore, he could see small studs set into the stone steps. They had no obvious means of operation, but he had little doubt that they were motion detectors, triggered either by the disturbance of light beams or by changes in weight on the stairs themselves. The actual walls seemed untouched, so it was unlikely that there were any defensive weapons inset. In truth, there was little need: if they knew you were coming, all they had to do was wait for you to get to the bottom. There you were either terminated, or you went back up 'til you were trapped on the roof.

He and Jenna met up back in the middle of the keep roof. She reported the same as he had observed, which was no more than he expected. Their next step was to look over the sides of the walls, to see exactly what lay beneath.

This was a trickier proposition. In order to get to the top of the old battlement walls they would have to climb up steep ladders. Once at the top, the walkways were narrow. Simeon was concerned that they would be seen from below. It would be considerably more than an irritation to throw away their advantage, yet he could see no way of avoiding breaking through the invisibility field in order to survey the ground.

"Right... let's do it," he said finally

Once more they parted company, each heading for a diametrically opposed ladder. Simeon scaled his swiftly and looked back to see Jenna ascending more slowly. Smiling to himself, he stalked the walkways, tentatively peering over the edge to see what lay beneath. His biggest fear would be imagers facing up. He knew that if he had been in charge of warrior security for such a building, he would have played it safe in this way. Imagine looking over the edge, right into the unblinking eye of a prime piece of surveillance tech. It would be funny any other time.

He thanked the Gods that whoever was in charge of equipping this castle had shown a flawed imagination. There were no imagers trained up, although there were several looking down on the walkways between the turrets and the keep building. These walkways were a long way down, and there was little in the way of footholds to assist any descent that was other than uncontrollably swift. The white stone was smooth and reflective, suggesting that it had been treated with an anti-climb agent.

Beneath, the castle seemed deserted. As he extended himself beyond the edge of the walkway, he became aware of the increase in temperature: it seemed that the invisibility charm acted as a shield against heat too. This was an excellent discovery. There was little chance that there would be too many guards who would venture out in the heat of the middle of the day.

Less chance of stumbling on any then, assuming that they could find some way off...

Moving round, he could see that on the next wall, it was much the same. A steep, anti-climb descent to the walkways between turrets and the keep below. Imagers pointed down. No guards. In the distance he could see, oblivious to what was going on above, ordinary citizens in the streets below. Looking around, he could see the glass walls of buildings surrounding the old castle, looking down on it from all sides. Idly, he wondered what it would be like to see a disembodied head appear over the side of the keep, and then disappear as suddenly. Would anyone report it, or keep quiet for fear of ridicule?

No point in worrying about that. The design of the old building meant that there was no other method of descent other than through the stairwells.

By now he had covered three of the four walls, and had come round to where Jenna was sitting down, back to the battlement baffle.

"Tell me what you saw," Simeon said.

She told him. He nodded briefly. "Same on all sides. No one charging up here to meet us, so I'm thinking that we weren't spotted. That's something. Looks like we're going to have to try and get down through one of the stairwells."

"Think I'd prefer that," she said.

"Tell you the truth, so would I," he replied. "Come on, let's get down to the level, and then work out which one..."

"Is he here, or at the Institute?" Jenna asked finally.

"One way to know..." Simeon took the amulet that he had secreted in his belt, and exposed the face of it to the sun. It was of a heavy metal, with a purple stone set in the centre. The stone had a pulsing surface that remained steady and rhythmic.

"He's not. It would have changed colour if he was near. That's what Vandyne told me when he gave it to me," and Simeon had no reason to doubt the adept would.

Slipping it back into his belt and securing it safely, he took out his hand blaster and checked the charge.

"Okay. Are you ready for this?"

"Like I told you, no, but we don't have a choice," she smiled. She took out her own blaster, feeling the weight. It would be the first time she had ever used it outside of training. This would be a proving ground.

"Each stairwell is equally protected... pick one," he said. Jenna indicated the door in the west wall. "That one it is then."

They moved towards the door. He felt the heat of the sun increase as she dismissed the invisibility field and then the temperature dropped again as she cast a temporary invisibility charm. As he took his first step beyond the door he felt he was entering into the world that he better knew.

Time to fight a real enemy. Not shadows.

# CHAPTER EIGHT

## Year Zero - Period Two.

Routine. The curse of the warrior. Yet, if Simeon stopped to think about it, something that could also be a blessing. For while he was engaged in the daily round of boring tasks, he wasn't in any danger of termination – and neither, more to the point, was his charge. Against this, the longer that things continued in this humdrum manner, the more lax he could be. Without even realising it, he was slipping into automatic. His mind was not on his work. Simeon would spend the night with the surveillance tech on full scan, letting it bleep to itself in the background, alerted only to any changes by the alarm (in the last half-period, attributable to three furry creatures in search of trash scraps and one reptilian bird that had somehow lost its way back to the nest). The days he spent in patrol. The beauty of the Institute grounds, which had so entranced him when he first arrived, were now nothing more than a gaudy backdrop, barely noticed.

It would be easy enough to snap out of this frame of mind though, to renew his dedication to the task and to become the guard he had set out to be. But if he did this, he would also become conscious of a few other matters: matters to which he did not wish to devote too much thought.

Firstly, he was still unsure of his own capabilities. His reaction to the two attacks that had so far occurred had done little to alleviate these feelings. He had spent most of the war inactive, and on the two occasions that he had been called upon to act, nothing more than blind luck had saved him from a terminal screw up. He had been tested magically and found more than wanting. His only consolation was that he had been employed for physical attack. But even this held doubts. Until he was actually tested, he would not know if he was up to the task. If he wasn't, it would be too late for amends.

His second problem, which was closely allied, was that of the chain of command. He was answerable to Daliel. The Intel warrior said that he had picked him personally, had great faith in him, trusted his judgement. Why, then, had Daliel done nothing after the two attacks had been reported? Was it because he agreed with the Mage's opinion that the attacks had been of no real threat? Was it because they had not been physical attacks, and so came under some other department's jurisdiction? Or was there some other, darker reason? Had Simeon 7, for some reason that he did not as yet comprehend, been set up to fail? If this was the case, then the warrior did not feel equipped to consider the consequences.

Finally, but perhaps most importantly, there was the matter of Ramus-Bey himself. The old man was exactly that, for all his power and knowledge. He was still a frail old man susceptible to all the foibles of such. He knew his body was weak and failing him, and this made him afraid. His powers had acted like a blanket of faith, but after that night in his chambers when he had been unable to repel the attack, he had started to doubt himself. Of course, he had said nothing directly, but Simeon knew. The irascibility of their initial encounters had returned, and when not irritable, the old man was openly hostile. He was equally bad-tempered with the adepts.

A Mage in such a mood was a liability: was he a deterrent or a loose cannon? Simeon wondered how could you guard a man who dismissed your advice?

They were nearing the end of the second period. It had been time enough for both men to settle to the new life, but things were still frosty between the warrior and the Mage.

"Security check. Everything OK last night. I'll make another check during the late morning. Today is your audience with the Chief Minister. I'll ride in your carriage with you, check it out first."

Simeon stood in the doorway, not wanting to venture into the chamber. It was cold enough, without the ice in the Mage's tone.

"I'm not senile, Simeon. I realise that I have the audience, though what that fool wants to talk to me about, I have no idea. I suppose I'll have to accommodate you, but I really don't see the necessity."

"The carriage is armoured, but once outside the boundary wall, there's no security back-up. Anywhere on the route..."

"Yes, yes, spare me the tedious details. You have your job to do." He busied himself at his desk, head down in papers all the while he spoke, not wishing to look at Simeon, which suited the warrior fine. If the old man didn't want to face reality, then he'd just have to do it for him.

"I do have my job to do. It's not one which I relish, believe me. I cannot protect you from all dangers, it's true, but I can handle most areas well enough."

Simeon's tone was barbed. They had not spoken of the last attack since the night it had happened, though it was obvious to Simeon that it had occupied the Mage's thoughts. Ramus turned to fix his bodyguard with a beady stare.

"And your implication being?"

"I have nothing to imply."

"Good..."

The Mage dismissed him by returning his attention to his work. Simeon lingered in the doorway, wondering if he should press home the issue. The moment had passed though. Simeon tried to put it out of his mind and immersed himself in his usual round. This was not without its own perils. Since the termination of the adept Tamlin, there had been several more pranks played on the bodyguard. Although none of them had been life threatening, they had nonetheless taken on a more spiteful tone, as though the adepts, if not blaming him openly for their fellow's demise, still felt that he was responsible. From simple thought forms, the pranks had now become more complex, more involved.

Only a short while before he had responded to an alarm on the east side of the Institute. Arriving on site, with his usual hand blaster replaced by a short-neck pulse-cannon, he had found that a cluster of the small, squirrel-like orange and yellow rodents that inhabited the smaller shrubs were gathered around a motion sensor. It wasn't the fact that there were so many of these normally retiring creatures gathered in one place that pulled him up short. It was the fact that they seemed to be making shadow puppets over the motion sensor in order to trigger it.

Believing his eyes to be deceiving him, he moved amongst them, attempting to scatter them with a kick. He realised that magic was at work when they failed to disperse, choosing instead to come together around his ankles. Blinking, he realised that the individual creatures were coalescing into one giant ball of fur which began encircling his ankles and threatened to trip him.

He thought about firing at them, but at such close

range, he was likely to take out his own feet as well as the fur ball. The absurdity of it was still striking him when he lost balance, pitching forward.

Suddenly, the situation was nowhere near funny. As he hit the ground, the impact jarred the cannon from his grasp. The ball of living fur grew, spreading up his legs and pinning his knees together.

He struck at the rippling mass, trying to find a hold that would enable him to disentangle himself. His muscles ached, lactic acid building quickly as he hyperventilated. His own body wouldn't give him the ammunition he needed to fight. Furthermore, the living fur that wrapped around him seemed to have no up or down, top or bottom. There was no head he could strike at...

The creature was not up to waist level yet, so there was still a chance. It seemed to grow faster the more he struggled, as though feeding off his movements. He stilled himself – not without effort, as every instinct told him to fight – and carefully felt for his belt. His blaster was not there – in using the cannon, he had left the other weapon to charge; the holster clip was still attached though, and it was this he intended to use. Unhooking it, he used the sharp metal clip as a weapon, driving it into the nearest piece of fur.

The apparition – for he was sure it was a magical construct – was solid and real enough to register pain. It made no noise but shivered and drew back, bleeding a viscous pale fluid over him.

Simeon had found its weakness. In making the thing animal-like, the wizard creating it had been forced to construct it like living flesh. Simeon knew enough about magic by now to realise that this was a low-level construct, the work of a minor adept, and not a master of the craft.

With a renewed assurance, he continued the attack, repeatedly driving the clip into the fur, making it shrink back. As it retreated down his legs and off his ankles, it split up once more into a cluster of rodents. Some ran. Others – those that had been the part of the whole injured by the clip – stumbled and fell. Then they faded away.

Breathing heavily, he stood and looked around. There were no sign of any rodents: either those produced by magic or those who had produced them.

Afternoon. Time for the Mage's audience with the Chief Minister. Time for Simeon and Ramus-Bey to lock horns again. At least, that was what it was beginning to feel like.

Simeon finished his routine inspection, then knocked at the door of the Mage's chambers. He entered on hearing his charge's grunted assent, and then accompanied him down to the carriage. An ornate vehicle, it resembled the kind of carriage that would once have been pulled by a Tallus team. Black, silver and grey livery, with an ornate hood design and large wooden-appearance wheels, it seemed like a relic. In fact, the carriage was a modern replica of an old design, with a particle beam driver and blaster-proof coating. Once the Mage was inside, there was little that could touch him.

Nonetheless, Simeon gave the vehicle a quick recce, ignoring the exaggerated sighs of his charge, before allowing them to leave the walled grounds of the Institute.

Simeon had not been out of the grounds much since his assignment, and all he could think of at every junction was how easy it would be to take out the Mage. A cannon of sufficient power could be mounted on a rooftop, and dismantled before the smoke had even cleared. It would have been more to their advantage to get the Chief Minister to come to them.

As it turned out, though, there was little threat either on the outward or return journey. In the Ministry building, Simeon was charged to leave the Chief Minister and the Mage to their conference. Waiting outside the ministerial chamber, as assured as he could be that his charge was safe, Simeon wondered idly if he could take this chance to try and catch up with Daliel in the military wing. Either as the counsel of friend and superior officer, or as an opportunity to psyche the possible enemy, it would help to set his mind at peace. All this was still running through his mind when he thought he caught a glimpse of Daliel. The squat, scarred man was difficult to mistake for anybody else. He began to move towards him, deep in conversation with a taller, blonde man in the charcoal robes of a junior minister. Who was Daliel talking to? Simeon didn't have the opportunity to investigate further as the doors behind him were flung open by the Mage, who stormed out. Simeon had been aware of raised voices for some time but it was only as the Mage exited that his words became clear:

"...will not be used as a mere bargaining tool! The pursuit of knowledge is a means in itself, and not the plaything of those with a desire for power without responsibility."

"You old fool – all power has responsibility. Mine is to the people who I serve, and yours..."

"You serve no-one but yourself. Until you become less selfish there is no common land on which we can meet to discuss this matter." He turned to Simeon. "I am leaving. Come with me or be left behind."

With which, the old man stalked down the corridor, the very air shimmering around him with his anger.

He didn't speak until they were in the carriage, and

only then at the prompting of Simeon.

"At least when there was a war they left us alone. Now we, who have devoted our lives to study that brings us closer to the Gods and to the ancient mysteries of the universe, have to become a part of their tawdry political plans."

"Is that why you resent me?" Simeon asked.

"No," the old man snapped. "There is more to this than you. I cannot tell you what he asked of me, only to say that it would be to break every oath that I hold sacred, to break every law of the universe by which I live. You? You are nothing more than an irritation."

There was little Simeon could say to this. He would only invite further contempt if he started an argument. However, the greater import of what Ramus-Bey said played on him. If Bethel's Chief Minister was asking him to do something he considered immoral, then was it not possible that... Before he had a chance to raise the matter, he was interrupted by something that he had not expected. A Mage with a conciliatory tone.

"I have, perhaps, been harsh on you of late Simeon. You are only fulfilling your duty, as any warrior should. You are a man of honour, I can see that, and you have had to work under less than auspicious circumstances. I should not vent my wrath on one who is only serving as ordered. I am also aware that many of the adepts use the practise of their skills as an excuse to bait you. There is no excuse for them to do so, and I shall endeavour to see that such juvenile behaviour desists."

"Thank you," Simeon said simply. The old man had given a lot of ground to him. Now was not the time to bring up any further matters. They could wait a day.

Or so Simeon thought.

Was it his imagination, or was there a lighter air about the Institute over the next few days? The Mage had delivered a reprimand and warning to the adepts, and seemed much happier in himself. Standing up to the Chief Minister had been a fillip to his confidence, and something of the man Simeon had started to know when he was first assigned was now returning.

The days, which had been monotonous and dull, relieved only by a low level of irritation, were now that much brighter. As he made his daily patrol and checked his surveillance tech, he noticed the changing of the blooms on the flora, and the changing habits of the fauna as the season began to turn. His relationship with the adepts was also much improved. He had no idea what the Mage had said to them regarding their treatment of him over the termination of Tamlin, only that they seemed to view him in a very different light... almost with respect.

All in all, life was looking good.

It was twilight. Beyond the walls of the Institute the city was alive. But within the grounds, with the sound deadened by the thick stone, life was still lived as it had been for hundreds of anums. The adepts, wizards and the Mage lived by the sun, the moons and changing of the seasons. The life of the magical academy was beginning to wind down for the night. Simeon had monitored the surveillance tech, and was calling in on Ramus-Bey before the old man slept. They had exchanged pleasant small talk and the guard was about to leave when the old man sat bolt upright in his bed.

"What is it?" Simeon asked, puzzled.

"Something... I'm not sure... it feels strong, but..."

Simeon had the portable surveillance monitor on his belt. He checked it: nothing was registering. Ramus-Bey shook his head. "It wouldn't. Not yet... it's a charm of some sort, but approaching power, not yet..."

"Another prank? I thought that things had changed," Simeon murmured, feeling a tinge of bitterness.

"If it is, I will come down heavily on whoever..."

"Wait – if you can feel this, then what about the others? The ones before..."

The old man shrugged apologetically.

There would be time to deal with this later, right now he had to get out on the grounds. He was ambivalent. If it was a stupid prank, he could hardly be bothered to expend the energy. Yet could he take the chance that it was that and nothing else?

It was no frame of mind in which to enter combat.

The signal registered on his portable as he reached the entrance hall. A massive surge, centred inside the main gate. It was as though something magical had just strode into the grounds.

As he opened the old heavy doors, he took in a magnificent sight. Three men high and two wide, it was a scaled beast with a beak for a face, and forearms the size of his trunk. It glittered and shimmered like it was made of flowing liquid metal, and moved with an eerie silence. Nothing that looked that heavy should be that quiet.

If it was a thought construct, then it was one of the most impressive he had ever seen. If it was organic, then that was something that made him go cold with fear.

This was no prank. This was that which he had feared for so long, and yet had grown tired of waiting for. Another magical attack.

Simeon didn't know how to tackle it. Conventional weapons were of little use, though if he could get close enough to try and overload its power... No, the blaster was nowhere near powerful enough.

The creature approached. The fight was going to be

far from pretty and far from noble. His first task was to deflect it from its course.

Simeon ran across its path, trying to drag its attention with him. The movement made it pause in its tracks, hooded eyes following him. He took the blaster and fired towards those eyes, hoping to make some impression at a supposed vulnerable spot if the creature were organic.

Nothing. It watched him impassively as the blaster fire hit.

OK – back-up plan, then... except that he hadn't had time to formulate one...

The creature turned towards the castle building. Thinking on his feet, Simeon realised that – organic or thought creature – what he needed to distract it was a lot of power.

The motion detectors were pulse powered: the cells within them had perpetual power, released in very small levels. Once a detector was manufactured, it could slow release for over a hundred anums.

Now that had to be a lot of power.

It would break the chain, maybe play into the hands of the enemy, but it was a chance he had to take. He was close to a detector. He scooped it up and ripped the cover from the back, tearing his nails on the catch. Fear meant that the blood which now slicked the detector was nothing more than a minor irritant.

The cell was wired to slow release. He was no expert mechanic, but he knew enough basic maintenance to know the one thing you shouldn't do. He smashed the small circuit board with a stone from the undergrowth, and directed the back of the unit towards the creature. Fumbling, he pulled at the two wires leading in and out of the cell.

Deregulated, the cell split under the strain of the power.

A beam of energy shot from the motion detector, directed only by the polycarbons that housed the instrument. Even they began to break down under the strain.

Simeon's fingers burned with a searing pain, forcing him to drop the detector. It was now harmless, all power released.

Simeon, too, was harmless. Hands useless, eyes blinded by the sudden flash of power, he had been thrown onto the ground by the burst

Like any magical construct, the creature lacked intelligence and was responsive to stimuli. In this case, it had been angered by the jolt of power. It was determined to search out and punish whatever had been responsible. Even if that something was laying prone, seemingly a threat no longer.

Simeon still could not see, but he could feel the forearms of the scaled creature as they picked him up, raising him above its head. It flung him down like a limp doll, and he hit the ground with a bone-jarring force. He heard, rather than felt, ribs crack. He was numb. He tried to turn and reach for his blaster, but his right arm failed to respond.

The creature picked him up again. It twisted him in its giant clawed hands, as though attempting to make a spiral of his spine.

Now he felt pain. It returned with a vengeance. He would have screamed if not for the fact that his voice had deserted him, his larynx seemingly forced into his brain, squeezed by the clawed grip.

He knew he would die. He had failed in his mission.

Then he felt the grip release. He fell, but was too numb to feel himself hit the ground.

Too numb to feel anything.

When Simeon regained consciousness he was in his bed. Warmth flowed through him, and he could feel his aching muscles drain of their hurt. He breathed in cautiously. His ribs felt fine.

Around his bed were four adepts, making passes over his prone form. These seemed to coincide with the subsidence of his pain. Ramus-Bey lurked in the background. His eyes met Simeon's.

"Feeling better?"

Simeon attempted to nod. He tried to speak but it came out as a meaningless husk.

"Don't try. It will take a short while for you to return to full health. Call it good practice for the young students," he added with a smile. "I suppose I'd better explain. I felt the surge of power as the thing materialised – and I was not alone. It was strong enough even to disturb the most junior of adepts. I saw the thing attack you, and knew you had little chance. It was a most remarkable charm that constructed it, I'll say that for whoever... anyway, even though that trick with the power cell was most ingenious, it only made the thing stronger. It did, however, distract it long enough for some of my senior tutors to counter the charm. Again, call it good practice."

Simeon was grateful: for that reason alone he did not ask why the Mage himself had taken no active part. That could wait. For now, he was glad to be alive. But there was more to come.

"I attempted to track the source of the charm. It vanished before I could find a true path, but I do know this, it came from outside these walls. I have accused you of attributing outside forces and motives to those things I have called pranks, or jokes. Perhaps you were right in some instances. Certainly, you were tonight..."

"So..." Simeon managed to croak.

Ramus-Bey paused for a moment.

"So the time has come for me to stop hiding from the truth."

# CHAPTER NINE

## Year Zero – Period Two

It took a few days for Simeon to regain full health and fitness. The charms worked by exaggerating the natural healing processes of the body but it was by no means an instant process. Ramus explained it to him thus: magic does not work miracles, rather it bends reality to the will of the practitioner. So, in the same way that a thought creature is the result of one man's imaginings made three dimensional by the bending of matter, then the rapid healing of injury is not achieved by the sudden creation of new bone and tissue, but by the acceleration of localised time around the wound.

Simeon thought that it made sense, but he really couldn't be bothered to think about it too deeply. For a start, he was still aching in every part of his body. The initial euphoria of being alive, and of not having several broken bones, passed into the dull throb of a regenerating frame. Any charm that had acted as an anaesthetic had long since worn itself out. So his movements were stiff and he remained for the most part in bed, passing time by watching teli-mage broadcasts.

While he did this, rising only when nature dictated, or to check the surveillance tech, the adepts and wizards rallied round. Once again, Simeon was aware that Ramus-Bey had spoken with them, but he had no idea as to the content of that speech.

Whatever the Mage had said, the academy was now a hive of activity. Nervous adepts patrolled the grounds – Simeon was as much aware of this from the alarms they inadvertently triggered as from their breathless reports to him. The tutor wizards were engaged in attempting to construct magical defences to repel any further attacks. Of this, Simeon had to listen to Ramus' despairing cries: "Have I taught them nothing? Their first real test outside of academic experiment, and their attempts to clear the stray thought forms... well, just don't watch the newscast tonight, that's all..."

The Mage had become a decisive, galvanised personality overnight. Now that he had acknowledged the threat was real, he was determined to assist Simeon in a task he now realised was larger than either of them could imagine.

Interestingly, he did not want Simeon to report the night's events to Daliel.

"We must not do this. In acknowledging that we struggled, we may inadvertently be giving succour to the enemy. If we deal with it as matter of course, not warranting any special attention, then we do not encourage a second attempt."

His choice of words was of particular note, for he had no notion of Simeon's unease about Daliel, or the source of previous attacks. Simeon would press him on this presently, but for now he felt compelled to check on the surveillance and defence in his enforced absence.

The Mage sighed. "Could I ever fault my apprentices and students for their effort? But the adepts are no warriors: if there was real danger, they would be as children. However, they are a presence and that may be enough. As for the magical defences... I know I have been harsh in my choice of words concerning those efforts, but in truth it is a thankless task. For a magical defence to work, it must be a counter-charm."

"And you can't counter a charm in advance, as you don't know what it is until it's actually on top of you?" Simeon cut in.

The Mage assented. "Exactly. This is why I feel we should keep word of this attack within the academy. The less anyone knows, the less they can realise the extent of our limitations."

When Simeon was left alone, he pondered on this. Mages had the power to reduce Inan to a pile of dust floating aimlessly in space. Yet they would find it difficult to defend themselves against any direct physical attack because of their age and frailty. Only, perhaps, if they had enough warning to cast a charm. To work great magic took time and effort. A magical attack demanded an instant response. It was that question of time that troubled him.

A warrior could stand alone against a physical assault. Success or failure depended on his powers. He could provide specific defence strategies that would limit attack opportunities, making it easier for him to defend the – comparative – surprise attack.

A Mage – a wizard, even – could not prepare any such contingencies.

So what was it, then, that made the Mages such a deterrent to further warfare? They had the power to destroy Inan, but not without time and protection. As an ultimate weapon, they were severely flawed.

Simeon considered this at length. If he had been able to work this out, then he could be sure that those in authority were also aware of this theory. The Mages became not so much an actual threat as one that was symbolic.

Which would make them a much less dangerous target for attack, with a greater symbolic significance for their elimination.

All in all, not the kind of realisation to give anyone pleasant dreams...

Simeon and Ramus-Bey did not speak of this. Neither did they speak of the suspicions that Simeon suspected they shared. Furthermore, they did not speak of the matter that had been gnawing at the warrior for some time. Why the Mage did not seem to take a direct role in any of the magical activities that went on outside Simeon's window. It was as though either man were afraid to open those particular doors. So they contented themselves with talk of routine.

Besides, Simeon had something else that had thrown his mind into turmoil. Something that he had been avoiding.

It was evening. The pink sun was almost down, the wan light of the pale moons casting a bone-white glow over the grounds. Inside his rooms Simeon had returned to bed after running an eye over the surveillance monitors. All was calm, which is what he had hoped for: it occurred to him that the optimum time for a follow-up attack would be while he was recovering. Whoever had sent the magical assailant must know of at least some of his injuries. To strike in the middle of this confusion would have been his choice.

Yet it hadn't happened. The anxiety he had been feeling was starting to abate. Give a day or two more and he would be well enough to face anything. Even now, the only real problem he faced was the stiffness in his abdomen, muscles complaining as he sat awkwardly on the bed.

So he was more relaxed than at any time in the last few days, and the least prepared for the shock he received on watching the newscast.

It was a piece on the recent trade delegation visit from Kyas. Although close to Bethel geographically, the smaller nation state had historically felt itself ostracised by the large continent and so had always allied itself to Varn. Now, for the first time in over five hundred anums, it was possible that the two nation states would start to trade. Although Kyas was smaller, it had commodities that Bethel wanted, and was in a stronger position than its size would suggest.

Which was not really the kind of thing that interested Simeon. But he couldn't be bothered to reach for the remote image changer by the side of his bed. It would have meant straining his lateral obliques – muscles he had only (too well) become aware of in the last few days. So he watched as the reporter's voice droned on, talking about a ceremony held at the newly established Kyan embassy in Belthan.

Who needed soporifics when you had newscasts? He felt his attention wander, until a brief flicker in the corner of the screen snapped him back to reality. It had been so fast that it had only registered on the edge of his consciousness, but it was enough to make him scrabble for the remote, wincing at the stiff ache in his side, and hit the rewind button.

The image flicked back, too far: he played it forward at half speed until he found the right spot, then hit it the loop function. The same few seconds replayed on the screen, over and over.

He studied it, not trusting the evidence of his own eyes.

It was her. For most of the loop she was out of shot, or was only partially visible behind the robes of the Kyan ambassador. But at the end, she was revealed as the ambassador bowed to the Chief Minister of Bethel.

Wanting to catch the optimum frame, he replayed it again and again until he was sure, then hit freeze.

She was in a ceremonial shift of purple and red, with a

lining of gold that showed on the scooped neck. Judging by the colours she had risen in the Kyan military. On Kyas, back on the farm, she had been in green and blue, the lowest level.

But it wasn't only her new ranking that interested him, he was looking at how the gold reflected on her skin, her long dark hair shining, her narrow face composed in a neutral expression. He knew that look, she was bored.

Ensign Jenna Eslo. Even bored, the sight of her excited a thrill within him: but one that was not without a bittersweet taste.

If she was here, why had she not tried to contact him? From her position in relation to the ambassador she was obviously attached to the embassy and not the trade delegation. There were strict protocols in formal society that told him this.

The part of him that wanted to give her credit told him that she did not know that he, too, was in the capital. *Ah yes*, his conscience replied, *but she knows you were repatriated to Bethel.* And she is here; in all likelihood since the embassy was established. What did she say to you? That if she were posted here she would find you? Has she?

He wanted to counter this by saying to himself that he was not sure that she had promised this: it could be that it was only what he had wanted her to say, what he had wanted to hear... but this was no argument, and in truth only reinforced the dread that she did not want to see him again.

If that was so, she would have to tell him to his face. When he was fully fit, when he had precautionary measures in place, then he would risk a few hours away from the academy. That was all it would take.

He resolved to handle the issue with speed.
Fate would stay his hand.

Ramus-Bey was a changed man in the time following
the attack. Where he had spent his time cloistered
away with his studies, now he became more outgoing.
Although he had always been the nominal head of the
Institute, his appearances to the adepts had been few
and far between, and he had been a remote figure. They
respected, rather than liked him and his irascible nature
had been something of which they steered well clear. It
was the wizards, ranking below him in prowess, who had
handled the majority of the instruction.

This had changed and instruction now became
something in which the newly revitalised Mage immersed
himself. The fact that the projects in which his students
and tutors were engaged had a more practical and
demanding purpose than at any other time only added to
his new-found delight.

He still spent some time on his studies, shut up in the
ice-cold atmosphere of his chambers, but he was more
inclined to take a break and walk in the grounds than at
any time before, marvelling in the flora and fauna like
one who was seeing them for the first time.

Which, Simeon supposed, he was. It was like the old
man had been wrapped in a bubble for a long time.
Now with the bubble burst he was able to take in his
surroundings more fully. "It appals me to say it, but there
is nothing like danger for sharpening the mind. Without
it, it is too easy to become complacent." Ramus said as
Simeon joined him on one of his walks.

"You're seriously telling me that you welcome these
attacks?"

"Welcome isn't the word I would use, but..." he searched for the expression, staring at the cerise-washed skies above. "We forget so easily that, for all our learning, we are not that far removed from the lowest of animals. I have spent my entire life searching for a truth that will bring me closer to the Gods, even to the point of using the knowledge I have learned to prolong that life, to purchase the necessary time to search further. I seek, like others before me, with me, and no doubt after me, to use my mind above my body. The mind is the thing that can set us free: that is what we have been taught. The mind, the will, is what shapes reality. The power to do that is to achieve godhead... or at least the closest that is possible.

"Yet, in that search, we so easily forget that we are animal. The mind and the body are linked, and are influenced by each other. They work in tandem. We try to sever that relationship, and then we wonder why we cannot feel the true importance of what we learn. We can know, but... the knowledge that my mortal shell is under threat brought first fear, then anger which I could not direct, and then the courage to fight back.

"Courage I learned from you."

Simeon didn't know what to say. There were many things running around his head, searching for expression. It was one of the least of them that found voice: "Why does a threat on your mortality mean so much? If you are searching... didn't you once say to me that you did not fear what lay beyond the end of life?"

Ramus-Bey smiled sadly. "Easy words to say when that isn't staring back at you. Perhaps it's part of mind and body being tied together that the thought of losing one part, regardless of your so-called beliefs, drives you into terror."

"Fear is nothing to be ashamed of," the warrior said

reflectively. "When I first entered training we had to scale walls, tunnel, fight in simulation exercises, learn how to use all kinds of blasters. But the thing that really made me break out in a cold sweat was as nothing compared to those. You want to know what it was?"

Ramus shrugged. "You'll tell me anyway."

"True enough... the thing that terrified me was the training for swamp warfare. Simulations where you had to use breathing apparatus, swim and wade in mud, crawling with insects. It was like being shut in a tomb while still alive. The water... that was bad enough. But swamp slugs, the way in which they attach themselves to your skin... I tell you, that was the real meaning of fear. It was such a small thing yet it went against all reason that I could not, for so long, conquer this terror."

"And how did you?"

Simeon shrugged. "I didn't. I still hate those things. But I forced myself to carry on. What else could I do? Especially as I was dispatched to the swamps of South Varn with the bridgehead force. That was where I was captured."

As they talked, the two men had circled the grounds and were now in the shade of the hanging trees that fringed the west wall. Beneath one of the trees a small ornamental pond housed a shoal of iridescent green and blue fish, which moved in ripples of colour beneath the clear surface.

Ramus-Bey stood on the edge of the pond, looking down.

"Strange you should find water so frightening. For myself, I had forgotten how wondrous it could be. It's many anums since I last stood like this and just watched... if this is the work of the Gods, then how can we ever aspire to it?"

"That sounds to me like you're doubting your life's work," Simeon commented.

Ramus looked up from the water. "Perhaps. I could not shape anything like Inan. No that would be so vast, so complex. I could make environments of a limited scale and a certain complexity, and they may have a span of some moment. But they would not be like this," he gestured around him, "and they would exhaust me. The Gods provide for a near eternity, their bounds. To venture even within hailing distance of such an achievement is more than one could hope. Yet all that happens is that one ends up as the political tool of men with base ambitions and limited imaginations."

"I agree," Simeon assented. "I have gained from you, too. My life was about being a warrior, about fighting for what I thought was right. What I was told was right. I accepted it and believed that my place in things had been ordained for me. I didn't think. I suppose I had imagination. I just had no call to use it. No encouragement... but you, and this place... it's different here. Thought is how you live. How could that not have an effect on me?"

"For the good?"

It was Simeon's turn to laugh. "That depends entirely on what you mean by good. Now there's something else that I thought I understood. I didn't have a clue..."

The Mage gestured to his bodyguard that they be seated. Now that the surface of their new understanding, and equally of their concerns, had been breached, it was time for them to talk earnestly.

While the Mage listened, Simeon outlined his theories concerning the sources of the attacks. Varn was an obvious starting point, simply because they were the old enemy. Other nation states could be discounted with the exception of Kyas. They, too, were an old enemy, where the others had been allies or neutral. There was, as a matter of course, an accepted flaw. Why should a former ally not decide to cause conflagration by such a spark? However, as a working theory, it was better to start with the known animosities.

Mages could destroy the planet. But destroying each other would be difficult: they were, within certain bounds, equally matched. To mount an attack powerful enough to be effective before it could be countered would require a level of application that could not be done at a distance. It would require a Mage to be smuggled into Bethel, close enough to strike with the required speed.

At this point, Simeon thought of the newscast on which he had seen Jenna: could one of the trade delegation, kept out of sight, be Wegnak the Mage? It would be difficult to achieve this.

"There is another possibility," Ramus mused, shifting uncomfortably. "There are those who, shall we say, do not follow the true path. Those who do not wish to conform to academic conventions and work their magical learnings from the outside. We do not talk of them, for it's unlikely that they should gain sufficient power to be a problem, but they do exist... perhaps one of them sees himself as a challenger."

Simeon agreed warily with this. He recalled his suspicions that the first major attack had been generated from within the bounds of the Institute. How, he wondered, could he raise this possibility? Furthermore, he had his own dark imaginings about his own nation state's governing body. Best, perhaps, to put this first to the Mage. Who was more open to this than Simeon had expected.

"It is not so far removed from something I had been thinking. You recall my disagreement with the Chief Minister, no doubt," Ramus-Bey said. "I shall not go into details, except to say that he wanted me to act in a way that would, at the very least, have been provocative. It occurs to me that if I fail to co-operate with him, in fact become something of a problem to him, then he is unable to remove me less he incurs the wrath of the people. Unless, perhaps, he were to make it seem as if I were removed by an enemy power, thus making me a martyr over which to wage war."

Simeon assented. "Daliel had reasons for placing me here. I have not the prior experience for this post. I would be – at least in the view of such a man – a minor obstacle. What if he has somehow made contact with a renegade wizard, and promised him your post if he helps to eliminate you?"

"It is an unpleasant thought, but not beyond the bounds of possibility."

Simeon looked up at the skies. They had been so long and so deep in conversation that the evening was beginning to draw in. The cloud cover that had made the skies cerise now blocked the moon's light. He shivered, noticing for the first time the chill of descending night.

"There is one other possibility – perhaps the most difficult against which to plan."

"That both a rival nation state such as Varn, and our own, are both attempting to terminate my life?"

"Then it had occurred to you?"

The Mage nodded. "Since that night when I was attacked in my chambers. It occurred to me that I could feel two power sources, and that it was their conflict that drove each back. Certainly, I had little to do with it."

This last confirmed Simeon's suspicions. It was time to be bold: "Why have you been holding back your magic? Surely this is the time to let it out? You'll be defending yourself, your colleagues, and your nation state. Is that wrong?"

The Mage bit his lip, emotion struggling to stay hidden on his face. "It's not that simple. I wish it were. There are a multitude of reasons that..."

He tailed off, seemingly distracted. Before Simeon had a chance to ask him what was amiss, the portable surveillance monitor he habitually carried began to sound an alarm. The touch-screen peeled layers of images to reveal men in battle-suits breaching the walls on all four sides.

"Military assault?" The Mage queried. Before Simeon could answer – it was all too obvious – Ramus continued: "Magical too. From close by. A sudden surge, and powerful. We must..."

"No time!" snapped the warrior, rising swiftly to his feet and plucking the old man from the turf as if he were weightless. Such was the healing power of the adepts' charms that this sudden exertion failed to reveal even any stiffness in his recently torn muscles.

Simeon drew his blaster and made for the castle at a brisk trot.

With both hands occupied, he was unable to track the number of warriors in the grounds, but initial impressions had been of a force eight strong. Not great odds. Even less so as a series of minor thought forms sprung up before him.

They were intended to slow him rather than cause any real harm. He side-stepped them easily, and as the wizards and adepts poured out of the castle building, dispersing to face the threats, their hastily concocted defence charms either dissipated the thought creatures, or conjured stronger forms to counter and battle them.

Blaster fire seared the air around them, cutting up the turf before them and forcing Simeon to skid to a halt, back-pedalling to avoid being blasted by the power beams.

In the midst of the encroaching chaos he somehow found a calm space in which to reason. As he moved towards cover, his mind raced in fractions of moments...

There was something odd... different... about this attack. The others had been purely magical, and aimed at eliminating the Mage. The use of physical means was not, in itself, unexpected: that was why he had been nominally assigned after all. But a physical attack would have to be subtle, by subterfuge. This was anything but: eight men scaling the walls in blue and green battle-suits, and firing noisy blasters was going to be noticed. How they intended to make their escape was an interesting – if academic – proposition.

Termination was not their aim: of this he was certain. There were easier, less ostentatious means. This was about taking the Mage, an abduction.

That meant that they were most likely under orders not to harm the old man. Another reason why the thought forms had been so innocuous.

Vortices of light and sound spiralled around the castle grounds as charm met charm, cancelling each other in clashes of manipulated matter. There was enough confusion and activity to keep the wizards and adepts more than busy.

This just left the eight warriors and Simeon, which seemed to him just as it had been planned.

But they were not to know that he had worked out their strategy. He could use that piece of knowledge against them. It was, in truth, all he had.

He scoped the darkening grounds as he made for the cover of a clump of hanging trees. He could see shapes moving towards him.

They were tracking his position. There was nowhere

he could hide. He was aware of the old man trembling, clutching at him. No time now to reassure him: besides, he wouldn't be fooled by any reassurance that was patently false.

All was against him, but he prepared to stand and fight.

# CHAPTER TEN

## Year Zero - Period Two

"This all feels so deliciously... wrong. It's quite, quite wonderful." The Mage Vixel smacked his lips with relish and grinned slyly.

Behind him, two warrior security operatives in brightly coloured ceremonial wear exchanged glances, then stared across at the bodyguard – dressed, as always, in a battle tunic – who stood across from them, facing his charge. He gave an almost imperceptible lift of the eyebrow. It was an acknowledgement to them, carefully delivered so that it would avoid the attention of the Mage.

Well, not quite...

"I know, I know," Vixel continued in mock regretful tones. "The old man's lost it. Never trust some doddering ancient in stupid robes. Lost in their own little world, don't know what it's like to be a warrior, and so on..." He turned to face them with a steely glare. It was all they could do not to flinch. There was an ice-cold quality there that belied his age and status.

"Have either of you grunts trained in the remote-view Intel programme?" He asked, his voice sharp, crisp and business-like.

"Sir, no sir," they replied as one.

"No, I suppose not," he mused, looking them up and down with the overt intention of insult. "Well, until you have, you can have no notion of what it is like to see an operation come together before your inner eye. There is no tech that can take you there quite like your own mind, gentlemen. If you could see... but no matter. This is an audacious mission, and it is frankly being realised with more than a little panache. Those fools have no idea what's hitting them."

"Uh, shouldn't you be..." his bodyguard began tentatively. He had been privy to the planning of this mission by default. It's hard to turn a deaf ear when you have to be by the Mage's side at all times. The other two warriors in the room had no idea of the part that Vixel was playing in the night's operation. If they had...

The Mage turned back to his bodyguard, face twisted into a sneer. "Cretin. Do I tell you how to prime your weapon? No," he answered without giving leave for reply, "so do not presume to tell me what I should be doing. The level of skill I have to deploy for this mission is next to nothing. I can do it without even consciously thinking. So *never*," his voice trembled with rage, "presume to talk to me in such a manner again."

The bodyguard stared straight ahead, taking the verbal lashing. Behind the Mage, the two warrior security operatives once more exchanged glances.

The Mage lapsed into an angry silence. These idiots had ruined his good mood. He would have to take solace from the confusion the mission was causing to that senile old fool Bey.

It was nothing compared to what more he had in store for him.


It had come to fruition following that fateful meeting between Vixel and his Chief Minister. The Mage had thought long and hard about his new relationship to Inan. Before the peace, he had been an academic, his burning sense of ambition and self occupied by the need to become the best at his craft, to attain levels of knowledge unrivalled by any other Mage in history.

Unfortunately for him he knew that he had the flaw of fallibility, the tempest of temptation within him. He was all too mortal, and did not have the spiritual depth of his rival in Praal. Not that he would have wanted to be that ascetic. He revelled too much in the pleasures of corporeality.

So Vixel was a bitter man, knowing that the thing for which he was striving was forever out of reach.

Then peace was declared. In the aftermath, a new kind of war: that of attrition on the nerves of the nation state governments. After such a lengthy war, it was an inevitability that peace would not be something to which there would be an easy adaptation. The transition would be fraught, and it would be a time of temptation for those who would seek to take advantage; who would seek to land a killing blow when the attention of the planet was distracted.

An ambitious man, one with intelligence and an equal level of cunning, could gain an advantage. Could make for themselves a name. More, could carve a permanent place in history.

Was Vixel not such a man? Did he not have the intelligence, the cunning, the drive to succeed?

So it had come to him, in the days following his meeting with the Chief Minister, a plan that would cement his place in history, whilst giving him great power and recognition in the now.

It was simple enough. The more he pondered the matter, the more it seemed to him that the attacks on the fool Bey were directed internally. Praal were above such things. He knew it was not his doing. The other Mages did not have sufficient power to achieve this from distance, and there was no indication from Intel that they had left their Institutes.

Vixel had always prided himself on his ability to step outside the circle. Most people could only think inside, where the circumference was closed and all were safely contained. Give them a situation, and they could only see it one way.

The Mage was not like this. He could look from the outside, escape the bounds of conventional thought and see the greater picture. He had insight.

His insight told him this: the only way that the current situation could be adequately explained was that Bethel had a rogue adept of great power and promise. It would be simple to persuade such an adept to go against his Mage if he was promised the post, and saved years of toil working his way through the ranks, hoping that he could outlive any rivals he may accrue on the way. In this, the military and the academy were not so far apart.

So assuming that there is a dark cabal within the Bethelian Ministry that has this aim, what do they hope to gain? They dispose of the fool Bey, crying that a rival nation state is to blame: undoubtedly they would pick Varn, as their old enemy. The rest of Inan is shocked at such an appalling act, and so joins Bethel in a planet-wide alliance. Varn is vanquished, and Bethel, by default, becomes the major nation state of the globe.

Who would suspect them? No-one who did not know about the rogue adept. To all intents and purposes, they would be a nation state stripped of their deterrent, open to attack and throwing themselves on the mercy of their former enemies and allies. By the time that they unveil their new Mage, seemingly from nowhere, the aim has been achieved.

It was a pretty plan. But what if Varn were to second-guess their old enemy? if they were to be blamed, then why should they not take advantage?

It was this audacious move with which he transfixed his Chief Minister. Attack the Mage, but not to terminate him: use magic to lay down a smokescreen, then take him. Spirit his body away to Varn where he can be kept until the Bethelian war machine, claiming his demise, is geared up for conflict. Then, at the last, produce him alive. Challenge Bethel to answer the charges that will be made against them, claim that the fool Bey was taken for his own protection by a concerned fellow Mage.

Varn becomes the saviour of Inan, preventing a plunge into total war. Vixel is the wisest of Mages, whose counsel and action prevented the destruction of the planet. His place in history is assured.

Meanwhile, Varn gets what it wants, and Vixel gets to play a few twisted games with the old man he has grown to despise over the anums.

It seemed, to the Mage, the best of all possible plans. He had put it before the Chief Minister, and from that moment he assumed a new role within the power structure of the nation state. Although Inan would never know the truth, Vixel became the first Mage to, in effect, lead his nation state. The full extent of co-ordination and planning was down to him.

Strategy. The deployment of military resources. Intel: the gathering and analysis of... all of these things were new to the Mage, but to a man of his training and intellect, used to the exertion of the will and the meditation upon the sublime, this was mere child's play.

In a very short time he was ready. He had marshalled the military and overseen their briefing. He had organised the deployment of Intel operatives in Bethel to determine the movements of Bey and his bodyguard. He also had counter-Intel operatives monitoring within the Bethel Ministry buildings. Before he left Varn, he had already briefed the Chief Minister on the double-dealings taking place within that institution, a division that would make their own plan that much easier to actuate.

It amazed the Mage that the Chief Minister seemed oblivious to the shift in power. If the man had been more intelligent, Vixel would have put it down to his giving the Mage enough slack with which to form a noose. As it was, he had to conclude that the man was a bigger fool than the target Bey.

No matter, the last stage of the plan was to move the military strike force and himself across to Bethel. Vixel had little doubt that he could control such a focused and ultimately diversionary magical attack from Varn, but he wanted to be a part of the action. What was the phrase he had heard the grunts use? 'On the ground.' Yes, he wanted that visceral thrill.

So, while to all intents and purposes the Mage went on a meditation retreat in the bowels of the Varn Institute, in truth he and his bodyguard had sneaked from the castle cellars, through the sewer system, until they surfaced in the Ministry building. It was less than dignified, but necessary. The watching world must believe him still in Varn. By the watching world, of course, he was thinking of the Intel of other nation states. Even their best surveillance tech could not penetrate the inner sanctum of an academy.

Disguised as a minor bureaucrat in a delegation dealing with the sanitary engineering in the recently established embassy in the heart of Belthan (a nice touch, he felt: a sanitary engineer who had engineered his own escape through the sewers... if only the world could see the awesome symmetry of his genius), he had travelled by conventional means to the capital of Bethel, and once installed in the embassy had resumed his true role.

It had taken only a day to set in stone the final arrangements. Only a few hours before, he had led the final briefing and despatched the military detachment. They had left the embassy in a variety of disguises, singly or in pairs. Beneath these workaday raiments had been their battle suits. Their rendezvous times had been synchronised. Deep within the basement of the embassy the Mage had sat, remote viewing the progress of the strike force. He had penetrated the walls of the Bethel Institute, and observed the long discussion between the cretinous bodyguard and the senile Mage.

They were groping towards what was happening around them, but the painful slowness with which they reasoned made Vixel wince. He would be putting them out of their misery. It was a kindness, in truth.

He watched as the strike force attained optimum positioning. It was time to begin the magical diversion.

Really, it had been too simple. He had hardly exerted himself. Which was why he was able to divert his attention to haranguing the extra guard he had been allotted, in case the raid backfired and the embassy came under attack.

It was a remote possibility for even the ultra-cautious Chief Minister to consider. To the Mage, it was ludicrous.

As he returned to directing his phantom diversion, to observing the progress of the strike force, it would only be fair to say that his mood bordered on something that could be called... well, nothing less than smug.


The warriors in the strike force had been specially chosen. As any transmissions via communication devices could have been monitored by Intel or surveillance tech, the Mage had insisted that only those warriors who had, at some point in their military careers, been through remote-thought Intel training could be considered eligible. His reason was clear. If they had a modicum of training, they would be able to synchronise their attack to his psychically delivered trigger signal.

Each of the strike force wore heavy work uniforms from different trades. They had appeared to be Bethelian workers who had been employed to work on the embassy building. As it was still partly under construction, and there was a steady stream of such workers throughout the day, it was easy for them to move unobserved. The heavy work clothes hid their weaponry well.

On leaving the embassy grounds, they had made their way to the designated points around the Institute by a variety of circuitous routes. To attempt to follow them would have left baffled any warrior security whose suspicions had been aroused.

Once in position, they awaited the signal. Until that moment, they remained in disguise. The streets of the capital were still busy, so it was easy for them to blend in with those at the end of their working day.

When the command came, each warrior knew that speed would be of the essence. They had to enter swiftly, hit hard, obtain the objective, and get out in a matter of moments. They could not allow the Bethel warrior security time enough to respond. Tracking by surveillance tech was not a problem: the Mage had assured them of this. Once they had their objective, he would switch his diversionary charms. His focus would be on blocking the energy flow of the tech, disrupting it to prevent tracking.

All they had to do was get in and get out.

When the signal came, it was a wash of images and sounds that flooded into the minds of each of the assigned warriors. They saw Simeon and Ramus-Bey by the pond, talking. They saw the ectoplasmic wisps that preceded the birth of the thought forms that would occupy any magical defences that had been set up, and they saw the location of each warrior as clearly as if they had been standing next to their fellows. Finally, deep in the mix, they heard one echoed word...

*Go.*

They divested themselves of their workers uniforms, revealing the camouflaged battle suits beneath. Working in pairs, they boosted themselves over the walls before anyone passing by had a chance to even register what was going on. In moments they were there and then gone. Their Intel training on low level magic gave them the ability to cast a weak charm that, whilst not making them invisible, confused the air around where they stood, leaving anyone who did catch sight of them unsure as to what, exactly, they had just witnessed. The discarded uniforms were all that remained to mark their passing.

Once over the wall, they were – ironically – in more secure territory. Just as the walls kept out the sounds of the city beyond, so too did they keep in the sounds of conflict.

Just as he found it simple to construct the thought creatures that now impeded Simeon as he attempted to marshal Ramus-Bey to safety, so too did Vixel find it a simple task to keep the trained minds of the strike force tuned in to images from around the grounds. Thus they could see each other's progress as they made their way, unerringly, to the Bethelian Mage, and could see the adepts and wizards doing battle with the thought creatures.

They had been briefed that the bodyguard known as Simeon 7 was a man of little combat experience, who had been picked by his own side to act as a stooge. His lack of ability would betray him, and make him easy to take out. So none of the warrior strike force were expecting what was about to happen.

As they converged and approached the Bethelian Mage, a team of three separated from the main body, and fanned out, laying down a criss-cross of blaster fire to prevent the bodyguard reaching the relative sanctuary of the castle. All the warriors were confident they could flush him out if he did attain cover, but to do so would necessitate time that they could not spare.

The covering fire achieved its aim. Simeon had to turn away from the castle and head for cover.

Inside their minds, the strike force could see the layout of the castle grounds. They knew where there was adequate cover for the man Simeon 7 to hide his charge and make a stand.

In truth, he had little in the way of choice. There was nowhere else except for this copse that offered anywhere near the same degree of cover. So even as he headed for the foliage, the strike force were anticipating his move.

He loosed some fire at them. It was nothing more than they had expected. It was easy to deflect.

Once ensconced in cover, they expected him to make a stand. He would naturally assume they were out to eliminate the Mage, and so would be prepared to give his life to preserve the other. But the bodyguard had other ideas. From the relative safety of the copse he laid down fire and sought to divide the strike force, tearing up the turf between them, and forcing them to split up and go wide.

Could it be that they had underestimated his intelligence?

The grounds of the castle were now almost in darkness. The moons overhead were obscured by a bank of cloud, and little ambient light from the city penetrated the gloom. Deep within the copse, the bodyguard kept the Mage close to him, and it was hard for the approaching warriors to see the two men, even with the aid of night vision tech.

This confusion was deliberate. It became clear to them that the bodyguard had realised that their aim was to capture rather than kill the Mage, and that they could not take him out and risk hitting Ramus-Bey. While he, on the other hand, having driven them apart, could concentrate his fire on specific targets with no such concerns.

Their only hope for a swift resolution would be to circle the copse as best as possible, closing as a clutched fist on the target within. But in order to do this they would have to eschew blaster fire. The copse was small, but not so small as to make it easy to contain their target. There was room enough for manoeuvre, and so they could not risk hitting the Mage, nor each other.

Meanwhile, the bodyguard was able to place a few shots from relative safety. One or two to judge his target distances, then a third with deliberate aim. Obviously, without night vision aids and a blaster with only limited power, he had to be cautious. But his aim was good: within a few shots, two of the eight man party were hit. One was dead, the other incapacitated, rolling in the undergrowth squealing from the open wound that had once been his face.

As they penetrated the copse, the strike force of six found that things were not as simple as they would have hoped. To Simeon, it had seemed nothing more than a clump of hanging trees, offering scant cover. But hanging trees were an unknown species in Varn, and their very alienness caused problems for the enemy. The thick, twisted roots that Simeon stepped so nimbly over caught at their feet. The branches covered in heavy leaves dripping down like static water almost to the turf, obscured their path. The limpid limbs were awkward to shift, made noises that gave them away. Conversely, Simeon, used to their weight, moved easily amongst them, dragging the Mage in his wake.

Within the obscured dark of the copse, it was difficult for the strike force to know which of the shapes and sounds were the enemy, and which were themselves. A question partly answered when a brilliant energy blast took out another of their number.

Five left standing. They had to obtain the objective and clear the wounded and dead. Fast.

So tight were they now that Simeon could no longer risk blaster fire for fear of giving away his position. Five to one: the odds favoured only one side.

And yet, despite this, the five members of the strike force had a creeping sense of unease about their position.

Despite the odds Simeon chose to attack. He had little option but to try and take them out one by one; yet in so doing he would, of necessity, give away his own position. It was a no-win situation.

He circled one of the Varn warriors, who stood silently, balanced on the balls of his feet, poised to respond to the slightest sound. Simeon did not give him that chance. Close enough to make out the darkened shape of the warrior, yet not close enough for the man to feel his presence, Simeon stooped and snatched at the sparse grasses that grew in the shade of the hanging trees. He scooped a handful of small stones, and deftly threw them to the left of the Varn warrior.

The warrior followed the direction of the sound as

the stones hit branch and tree. When he looked away, Simeon hit him from behind, taking him down with a blow to the small of his back that paralysed him with pain, allowing the bodyguard just enough time to land a second, disabling blow before the screaming nerve endings in the Varn warrior's spine calmed and allowed him to react.

What Simeon could not know was that the remote magical link with Vixel also tied the strike force together. When their man went down, they knew exactly where to find the bodyguard.

Before Simeon was on his feet, the remaining four men converged. It was swift and brutal. Blows rained on him, crippling limbs. The breath was driven from him by a savage kick beneath the ribs, and darkness fell with a combat boot to the temple.

The strike force would happily have extracted reparation for their fellows by killing him, but were stayed by a command that sounded in their minds.

*Leave him.*

They did not question the voice. There was much to be done, and quickly.

Locating the Mage was easy. They found him cowering beneath a hanging tree, a frightened old man; terrified beyond the capacity for any kind of rational thought.

A slight figure, he acquiesced from fear when one of the strike force hoisted him onto his shoulder as though he was nothing.

The downed warrior was briskly revived. Still dazed, he assisted in the recovery of the two wounded, and one dead.

Carrying their burdens, the remaining strike force members made their way through the thought creatures and the whirling vortices of charm-clash until they hit the appointed spot. They were just within the boundaries of the Institute. Looking around, one of the warriors took an explosive charge from his battle suit and laid it at the base of the wall. It seemed, at first glance, to be a measure of desperation.

But perhaps not. As it exploded, the detonation disrupting the recording sensors on the surveillance equipment still operating, a holoship appeared within the grounds, unmasking itself. It was unpiloted, guided remotely by another part of the Varn Mage's magical intellect. The strike force, using the cover of noise, smoke and debris left in the wake of the detonation, embarked with their precious cargo, and the holoship masked itself again before lifting them over the wall, regardless of the gaping hole left by the explosive charge.

Eyewitness and surveillance Intel would elicit only this: that there was an explosion at the wall; that the enemy were standing on one side before the disruption, and on neither side when it had cleared.

All would be confusion. Which was just as Vixel had planned.

With the strike force free, he lowered the magical attack as swiftly as he had brought it into play. The counter-charms of the Bethel wizards and adepts, now having nothing to fight, dissipated; leaving many confused and exhausted.

An uncanny silence descended over the grounds of the Institute. As if requested by the Gods. The clouds obscuring the moons of Inan now parted, the pale light of the twin orbs illuminating the carnage below.

The wildlife had gone to ground, that which survived the battle. The bloodied remains of much of the fauna now littered the grounds. Explosive magical energies had taken chunks from the castle building itself: the interior was visible through gaping holes, while the area around the large double doors was now littered with broken stone. The grounds were scored by the marks of battle, turf and soil ripped up and scorched. Foliage lay in smoking ruins.

And in the middle of it all, unconscious and alone, lay Simeon 7.

# CHAPTER ELEVEN

## Year Zero – Period Two

It did not take Simeon long to regain consciousness. He was aware first of the pain, rising from a throb to a scream. It seemed to run the length of his body in a continuous loop, as though using him for a running track. Opening his eyes required a strong nerve. Even the pale light of the moons made his head explode in a myriad of colours. But after the sixth attempt, things began to settle into shapes that he was eventually able to distinguish.

It was when his brain began to register once more his sense of smell that the true import of the situation hit him. The air was thick with the scent of charred flesh, warm blood, stone dust, and the sweet smell of burnt wood and grass.

He slowly stood. He hardly recognised the grounds around him. In the distance he could make out wizards and adepts moving slowly amongst the wreckage.

Where was Ramus-Bey?

He looked around hurriedly, but it made his head spin.

He cautiously began to move across to where the majority of the academy magicians were clustered. They seemed to be moving just as slowly as he, which gave him some obscure comfort.

Najwin, a junior adept – noticeable because he was so tall and gangly – detached from the main body and drifted towards the warrior. He, too, seemed stunned by what had occurred.

"What..." croaked Simeon as the young adept came within hearing.

"Something... everything," the adept replied, his voice

seeming to come from a thousand light anums away.

Simeon heard no more. The effort of staying upright was too much. Blackness crept in around him before he had the chance to do anything else.

When he awoke again, he was in a cell. A small, stone room in the lowest depths of the military buildings. It was equipped with a bed, toilet and a surveillance transmitter.

Mindful of what had happened before, Simeon pulled himself up and swung his legs so that he was seated on the edge of the bed. His cuts and abrasions had been dressed, and he was wearing a black shift. It was cold in the stone depths. He felt nauseous. His muscles were stiff, and one leg felt like it wouldn't move too quickly under any circumstances. His mouth felt like a sewer, and his head throbbed. But, all things considered, he'd felt worse.

The question was: how long had he been unconscious this time? Long enough to be brought here, to be cleaned up, but beyond that?

He looked up at the transmitter.

"Well, I'm conscious. Let's get on with it..."

He knew why he was here. Ramus-Bey was either dead or missing. He was the bodyguard, and he was still here. There had to be an investigation. Although he was less than pleased at being treated in such a manner when he had fought against overwhelming odds. It was as though he were a part of the plot, rather than one of the victims. An innocent bystander.

No. Perhaps not. What if he was considered to be in league with whoever had mounted the attack? Whether it was internal, or directed by another nation state, the fact that he was alive could be considered a sign of collusion. His duty was to lay down his life for his Mage. Although why he had been left alive after being struck down...

Trying to think so much, so soon after regaining consciousness, was making him feel even more nauseous than before.

He could hear footsteps in the corridor. Two sets. They stopped before his door, and the lock mechanism whirred. Two warriors in black formals stood before him.

"Questioning," one of them said. His voice was hostile.

Simeon tried to stand. He still felt slow, cumbersome. It wasn't good enough for the warriors, who jerked him to his feet. They half walked, half dragged him from the cell and down the corridor.

Simeon swallowed hard, preventing the vomit that the sudden movement had stirred. He had a sinking feeling in his stomach that had little to do with his physical state. The attitude of these two suggested that he had already been tried in his absence, and found wanting.

If that was the case, nothing he could say would make any difference.

They flung him into an elevator. This time he couldn't stop the vomit. They looked at him as though he were less than dirt. He wanted to ask them why they were acting like this, but from their expressions and the way they carried themselves, he knew that the first words he uttered would be no more than a signal for them to beat him.

Best to stay quiet, see where this was going.

Two levels, then they hauled him out as the doors opened. Dragged him along a corridor lit with muted lighting and soft wall hangings. Three doors along, they stopped and knocked. A voice murmured from beyond, and the doors were opened.

Simeon was thrown into the room. He fell face first onto a rug. At least, he considered with some bitterness, this was a better class of floor to be thrown on...

"Well, well... I think you've got a lot of explaining to do," growled a familiar voice.

Daliel had led the investigation himself. As Simeon's superior officer, it was his place. Which, of course, suited him just fine, there was a lot to understand about what had occurred.

Repeated study of the surveillance tech Simeon had installed told them nothing. There were some images of the strike force as they gained access and hunted down their prey. All that really told the investigators was these were well-trained men. The disruption caused by the explosion left a hole in the evidence. They appeared to vanish without trace.

The only conclusion was that something magical had occurred.

Daliel alone knew that the attack did not come from within. In truth, no-one had been more surprised than him when the alarm had been sounded. His adept had not been ordered to act, and certainly he had not deployed any of the warrior security who he knew to be personally answerable to him. In truth, even the deputy minister with whom he colluded did not know of their existence. They were Daliel's own fail-safe plan.

This meant that the attack must have come from another source.

Like any true son of Bethel, Daliel thought first of Varn. Intel reports had stated that their Mage and Chief Minister had been meeting with a greater frequency than usual. This had been followed by the Mage's meditational retreat. Although there was no way of following him into the depths of the Institute, there had been no indications of his leaving the grounds.

Daliel was not so sure. He checked Intel reports on the Varn embassy in Belthan. Although there was still a large amount of construction work going on, the embassy staff had elected to stay. Which was unusual. Other nation state embassies had temporary offices during this time of adjustment.

The heavy-set and grim-faced security chief shut himself away with surveillance recordings from the day of the attack, taken from a number of imagers surrounding the Varn embassy building. Some were in public, some were not...

It took several viewings and the use of a cross-indexing and a bit-matching programme, but eventually he had identified eight men who appeared to leave the embassy although there was no trace of their entry. Six of them had been picked up by imagers near the Institute walls just before the time of the initial attack. Two had evaded initial detection. The imagers were blurred and distorted by simple magic, but when enhanced gave enough detail to suggest that these men, stripped of their work clothes, were the strike force that had attacked and taken the Mage.

Given the indication of magical activity, Daliel wondered further if it could be that Vixel was involved. He ordered up the Intel reports of arrivals from Varn within the last period, particularly those who were affiliated to the embassy staff.

One old man, hidden away in a delegation, seemingly a minor bureaucrat. It was impossible to tell, even with a bit-match programme on the separate holovid images. Impossible because a low-level masking charm had been used. Either an error on the part of the Mage, or a piece of hubris. In masking, he had given himself away. Had he just assumed that no-one would check?

Daliel pieced together the plot for himself. He knew that Simeon had no part in this, but the greater populace demanded a scapegoat. Daliel needed one too. There would be a public enquiry, if not a trial. In this, previous magical attacks may come into public domain, leading to questions about why nothing had been done earlier, why there had been no precautionary measures taken. Which may, in turn, lead to the discovery that these attacks had not originated from a foreign nation state.

Daliel had to avoid this. The best way to do it would be to simply give the public what they wanted: a scapegoat. To merely brand Simeon an incompetent would not be enough. To completely defer public attention, to cover every last track, it would be necessary to create a figure of public hate.

Who better than the bodyguard who had let the nation state's greatest treasure and greatest defence be taken? Better yet if it could be suggested that he was somehow in league with the enemy.

The taking of the Mage – and he had to assume that was what it was, as no body had been recovered – had a purpose that he could not yet define. It was still possible that it could be turned to his advantage, in the same way that his initial plan had revolved around the blame of Varn. But that was for the future.

For now, his carefully laid plans had been shattered. It was a time to limit the damage.

And the best way to do that was to question Simeon himself, turn him inside out so that the fool would condemn himself with his own words. He had kept him sedated for several days, isolated from the outside world.

Simeon would have no idea how long he had been kept in the cell; nor what the outside world may be thinking of him. He would be confused. He would expect his old friend to go easy on him...

All of this passed through his mind as he waited for the guards to bring Simeon to him. Passed through and out as he heard the sharp rap at the doors. As he bade them enter.

"Well well... I think you've got a lot of explaining to do," he growled as Simeon landed at his feet.

Two men sat in a room, on either side of a desk. One was Daliel, the other the deputy minister with blonde hair and an expensive taste in wines. They had been sitting in the room for some time. In silence, each absorbed with their own thoughts.

Finally, the Deputy Minister spoke.

"The talk is that there will be a show trial. The man is condemned from his own mouth. A certain grace will be shown to the idea of a defence, but there is little doubt that the man is a traitor through and through. There is even evidence of his having colluded with the enemy during his tenure on a prison farm. A nice touch."

"I thought so," Daliel murmured.

"You will, of course, not name her?"

"Of course. Once she is known, then she has a chance to explain the truth. If she is blackened anonymously, she will stay in the background for fear of stigma."

"You appear to have thought of everything."

"I hope so." Daliel rose and went to the side table where a decanter and two glasses were laid. He poured drinks, then brought them back to the desk. It did not escape the minister's notice.

"I did not..."

"Understand this," Daliel said softly, but with an undertone of threat that cut across the minister's protest, "the balance of our relationship has changed. As a junior minister, destined for greatness, you were the one with the ability to lead the campaign. You had the contacts, the profile. I had the ability to carry out the real work, to soil my hands.

"But I have all that I need to go my own way. I can change this trial. I can direct it any way that I wish. If I choose to reveal that there were previous attacks, and that they were not directed from outside, I can bring forth evidence to place you firmly in the middle."

The minister smiled indulgently. "But surely you implicate yourself if you implicate me. Even if you believe you have covered your tracks..."

"I have. Of course, you could always attempt to drag me in if the matter came to trial, but really... the word of an obviously guilty man, seeking to lessen his punishment by blackening others? Who would give that credence?"

The minister pondered this for a moment. "Do not think for one moment that your threat has in any way caused me fear. Nonetheless, I applaud your playing of the system. You leave me little option other than to concede that the balance has shifted in your favour." He raised his glass. "I salute you. I will, of course, regain the upper hand if at all possible."

Daliel raised his own glass. "Naturally. I would expect nothing less. As long as we understand each other."

The two men drank in silence for a while.

"Very well," the minister finally said. "We have made our own keep secure. But what now? What of Varn's plans for Ramus-Bey?"

"I think that they matter little," Daliel said at length.

"Whatever they choose to do, they have created a vacuum. It is, I think, time that we groom our man. He has a breach into which to step. Once he is there, then the fate of Bey is immaterial."

# Year Zero – Period Three

The young adept Najwin had been uncomfortable for some time. It had seemed to him that Simeon was to bear the brunt of the blame for the disappearance of Ramus-Bey. In truth, the adepts at the Institute had grown attached to the bodyguard. He had come through the testing time after the termination of Tamlin, and in their eyes had proved himself to be a true warrior on the night that Ramus-Bey was taken. This was something that all at the Institute had sought to impress upon the warrior security who had conducted the investigation.

If any others had noted the hostility of the warriors, they had not remarked upon it. But Najwin had known it. He could feel it in every movement and glance, dripping from every syllable they uttered. And he knew that Daliel was leading the investigation. It was obvious that it would have only one conclusion.

Simeon 7 was dead, even though he still drew breath.

This was not what the adept had wanted. This was not right. And there were, he was beginning to discover, many things of greater import than the acquisition of power.

So if no-one else was prepared to do something to aid Simeon, then he would.

Timing was everything, the trial would begin in a few days. It was all over the holovid broadcasts. Simeon was to be beamed live across the globe, while the nation states waited for Varn to come out and confirm that they had mounted the raid. So far, they had neither denied nor confirmed their part in the affair. They had stayed aloof, confident that Bethel would not attack them while deprived of their ultimate deterrent.

Najwin had to act quickly. There was one thing that he could give Simeon, one thing that would enable him to make his escape at the right time. But it was something that he could only teach, perfecting it would be down to the bodyguard, and he would need some small amount of time in which to practice.

So it was that the lanky young adept found himself walking out of the gates of the Institute and into the cold city morning. He had spent sleepless nights trying to decide the best time of day to go; trying to work out when he would be least missed. Eventually, he realised that he must risk all to chance. He may be missed at any time, or not at all.

Fortune, he hoped, would favour those who showed courage.

Courage was something that Najwin needed badly. He felt as though the weight of Inan was upon his shoulders. It had seemed so simple to begin with, so easy. Magic had always interested him, and it was something to which he took instantly. The casting of charms, the power of the will, and the understanding of how these things worked was something for which he had to spare little thought. While others had to sweat to make even the simplest charm work, he had been able to spin spells from a very early age. It was obvious that he was gifted, and that his future lay in the Institute.

Yet it was also at this early stage that he realised that to be too precocious would be to invite spite. Tutors would mark him down; fellow students would sneer. So he began to downplay his talent, to pretend that he had to try hard.

It made him fit in better, but it also did something inside. A part of him had grown bitter and resentful. It was not his fault that he found magic easy. Why should he have to pretend it was hard, when nothing more than an accident of fate had made it otherwise? When he looked at the Mage, it made him even more resentful. In his time at the Institute, he could not recall the Mage ever casting a charm of his own. He would teach the theory of magic, and instruct on how to prepare for a charm. But actually demonstrate? Never, to his knowledge, had this happened.

He had begun to wonder if Ramus-Bey were not, in fact, some kind of charlatan. The thought that a fraud was proclaimed Mage, while he had to pretend that magic was hard so as to avoid being picked on... it became too much.

So Najwin was a perfect target for Daliel. How the scarred man had known of his skill he had never asked. He had only heard the warrior offer him the moons and the stars.

The problem was that it had seemed so simple in theory, but the further he was dragged in, the more complex it became. These were people with real feelings, real pain. Termination was real. His thought creature had caused the death of Tamlin. In the aftermath, he had blamed Simeon: if the bodyguard had acted more swiftly, the young adept would have lived.

He knew he had been lying to himself over this. If not Tamlin, then Simeon and if not him, then some other poor soul who had been in the wrong place at the wrong moment.

There was only one man responsible: himself. He could

not turn back from wherever this road would lead him. He was in too deep for that. Daliel would not allow him. He was scared of the warrior, there was no doubt about that.

But he could not allow Simeon to be terminated. One death on his conscience was more than enough.

A simple masking charm allowed him to leave the Institute and make his way through the centre of the city unnoticed. He would not show on Intel surveillance, and none of his fellow adepts had seen him leave. If any missed him, he would think of some excuse later.

He arrived at the military building. He had been here once before, in company with Daliel. He had used a masking charm then, for a similar reason. Taking a deep breath to calm his nerves, he walked into the building, unobserved by man and tech.

He knew that Simeon was here, but he did not know where. If he had the time, he could explore at leisure, eavesdrop until he gained a clue. But time was at a premium.

He waited until the main entrance security were changing shift, and then went to the reception tech terminal. He had a good working knowledge of tech, and so was able to access the floor plans and records for the building. He worked swiftly, and although he could not be seen, anyone who came to use the terminal while he was standing here would bump into him, or see that the terminal was accessing classifieds.

He called up the information he required. Now he needed to make sure that his steps could not be traced. Magic could only work so far on tech like this without leaving traces, but it was enough. A disruption charm shorted the terminal and wiped the records. It would be put down to an energy surge, a wiring fault.

Najwin moved down the levels of the building, hopping between elevators, making sure that nothing anomalous would show on surveillance tech, such as an empty elevator moving by itself. It took longer than he would have liked, but finally he was standing in the corridor where Simeon's cell was housed.

He waited until a guard brought food, then followed him in. He waited until the guard left, then made a pass at the surveillance imager in the cell. Within the databank for that imager, on the central frame, the same few bits of information looped on themselves in a perpetual motion. The imager would not register as defective, yet neither would it record what was happening in the room.

Now it was safe to drop the unmasking charm.

Simeon started back in shock as the adept appeared before him.

"What..." he looked up at the imager. "Surely..."

"It's safe. We won't be seen. Do you know what's happening?"

"I assume I'm going to be held responsible for all that has happened. There has been a certain edge to my interrogations," he said, unable to keep the irony from his voice.

"Who has interrogated you?" Najwin asked.

"A man named Daliel. He was my immediate superior, so he has the authority... but I suspect he has a lot more than that."

"To say the least," Najwin interjected. "Listen, and don't speak. I fear you are to be terminated, at least to further the plans of one man, if not an entire nation state. Not that they are the same..." He caught the question in Simeon's measured gaze, and shrugged. "I have something to confess to you. It leaves me in a light that... well, I'm not proud of and now I'm scared. So listen..."

Najwin outlined all that he knew of Daliel's plot, and did not flinch from his own part. When he had finished, Simeon was perplexed.

"So why here? Why now?"

"Because I have to draw a line somewhere. I shall never be the Mage I wanted to be as I have another's life on my conscience. It's too late for me – I shall go back to the Institute until you are safe away, and then leave. Magic is all that I am good at, but I am not good enough for it. All I can hope to do is less harm. If you pay attention and you practice what I am about to show you, then you may have a chance."

"I have never been a man of magic. How can I..."

Najwin shook his head. "No, no – we can all do something. This is a very small charm. It is localised, and cannot be sustained long. But long enough for your needs. Now watch..."

He taught Simeon the simple masking charm. Made him go through it until it started to work.

They were still working on it when they heard the approaching footsteps of the guard, returning to collect Simeon's untouched meal.

"I must release the imager and mask myself again," Najwin muttered urgently. "Practice this as often as you can. It may cause a slight disturbance on surveillance, but you'll have to hope that it doesn't get noted. It's not much, but it's all I can offer."

Swiftly, he made a series of passes, fading in a watery blur before Simeon's eyes.

The door of the cell opened. The guard looked down at the untouched meal and sniffed. "I should have eaten that, if I were you. Make the most of all you can get, traitorous scum. Your trial begins in two days. It's just been announced. Three days, and you'll be as dust." The guard emphasised his point by spitting on the floor at Simeon's feet before collecting the untouched food and leaving.

As the cell door closed, the room felt empty. Simeon knew that Najwin had gone. He could not excuse what the adept had done in the past, but he had tried to make amends. Simeon could also see that the experience would scar the young man for life... if he had any kind of life expectancy at all, should Daliel get wind of what he had done. But it wasn't the passing of the adept that made the cell feel empty, now he knew when he was to be tried. He was truly alone with his fate.

The only thing that stood between Simeon 7 and death was not justice; it was his ability to master one small piece of magic. It wasn't very much at all, yet the thought made him feel better. It was, he thought as he practiced the passes, fitting that his fate was now, quite literally, in his hands.

# CHAPTER TWELVE

## Year Zero – Period Three

When his trial came it was much as he had expected. Those who watched it on the Inan-wide broadcasts were surprised at how detached the accused seemed from the proceedings. The newsvids and newsheets speculated at some length on his mental state. Was he psychotic, catatonic, or simply pumped full of suppressants to ensure that he was of no danger during his trial? A few renegade theorists speculated that he was sedated so that he would not give away any details about the nation state conspiracy that had set him up as a figurehead to appease pubic anger. If he had not been deprived of any access to the media during his time of internment, Simeon would have found this last idea of some bitter irony. The conspiracists, who were the cretin fringe of any society, were closer to the truth than they knew.

The truth was a little more prosaic than anything that the endless speculating could imagine. Simeon knew that he would be painted blacker than the uniform he was alleged to have disgraced. He knew that the trial was nothing more than a show, and he knew that he would be found guilty and sentenced to death. On the most basic of levels, he had been denied access to his defence counsel and had no knowledge of the man who stood up in the trial room to present his defence. A defence that seemed to consist, in essence, of little more than a simple 'he did it, he was wrong, he throws himself on the clemency of the court'. Whether his counsel was in league with Daliel and whoever he served, or whether the man felt that Simeon truly was guilty and had been told he was too mad to consort with, the defendant neither knew nor cared.

Bizarrely, there was another reason for his silence and seeming catatonic state. As inappropriate as it may have seemed in the circumstances, Simeon was actually terrified of the cameras as he sat in the trial room, under armed guard. The thought that he was being watched by millions across the planet made him acutely aware of every move, every breath. He was not a man who had ever pushed himself forward in a crowd and now, faced with the knowledge that he was under intense scrutiny, he felt appallingly self-conscious. Which, he considered at night as he was led back to the comforting obscurity of a cell where only a guard watching a surveillance imager could see him, was an odd priority of concern for someone staring his own demise in the face.

Except that he was not. He knew he would be found guilty and sentenced to death. He knew, too, that he could use the charm he had been perfecting to walk out of the building when the time came. He was formulating a plan for the aftermath of such an eventuality. He just had to wait for the right moment.

So he bided his time. The trial would be over soon enough.

In the event, it took four days to confirm what he had known from the beginning. The court put on a good show for the waiting world. The decoration in the trial room was sparse, with just a pair of ceremonial hangings depicting the Bethelian figures of justice and parity to cover the cold stone walls. Dark wood benches housed the jury, soberly dressed in robes of black and slate grey.

The counsel for the prosecution and the defence reported their evidence to a judge, who directed the jurors where necessary on obscure points of law. Not that there was much to obscure in this case. The sombre black and purple plush of the robes worn by counsel and judge contrasted with the dynamic holovid images used to demonstrate the case against the defendant. Grainy, pictures of the night in question were presented to show the attack, and to highlight the way in which – after some deft manipulation – Simeon appeared to lead the Mage to a point where he was meekly handed over to the enemy. There were allusions to the fact that the strike force had appeared to originate from Varn, but given that there had been no response from that nation state as to culpability at this point, the emphasis was rather on the treachery of the defendant.

Were these manipulated images down to Daliel and just a few co-conspirators, or was the whole of the Bethel Ministry involved? Simeon spent most of his time in the trial room wondering about this as his name was blackened beyond the darkest judicial hue.

He had a simple aim: get out, get the Mage, and see what crawled from the woodwork. He had no time for intrigues, even though he had been entrapped in one. He would only be able to work out what had been going on, to deal with it in some way, once he had flushed everyone out into the open.

And so he sat through the farce that was his trial, feeling the eyes of the planet upon him, and withdrawing into himself until he could effect an escape. He did not know what the outside world would make of him, and could only surmise that they would loathe him as the lowest form of life. He couldn't feel aggrieved. If he had been sitting at home, watching the teli-mage broadcasts, he may have felt the same way. The truth would emerge eventually, or he would be terminated in the attempt.

At the end, he sat impassive as ever while the jury

proclaimed him guilty, after a deliberation that was so short that they did not even leave the trial room. He was made to stand while ignominy was heaped upon him, and he was described as the vilest and lowest creature in the history of his land. It was an invective that would have withered the hardiest of warriors, hitting at the heart of what they had been trained in, and believed in... and yet it washed over him. Commentators around the globe believed him either arrogant beyond imagining, or a man with a broken mind.

Neither was true. Simeon hardly heard the scathing indictment, having closed his mind to the judge's words. Despite knowing his own innocence, despite his plans to clear his name and regain the day, he also knew that to listen and absorb these words would anger him, and cause him deep sorrow and depression. The only way to cope was to shut them from his mind.

So Simeon never registered the sentence bestowed upon him, and it was only afterwards, when he was returned to his cell, that he discovered how long he had been granted before termination. A guard repeated the sentence to him upon request.

There would be three days, during which time a public platform would be made, and broadcast space across the globe cleared. On this third day, he would be executed in the centre of Bethel at the peak of the day. His execution was to be transmitted live to every nation state on the planet.

It would also signal the last moment of the ultimatum delivered to Varn: show your hand, and declare innocence or guilt. If not, then face the wrath of the rest of Inan, as the so-called alliance formed post-treaty would act as one and take retaliation.

When Simeon was alone in his cell, he pondered on

this new turn of events.

Now, it would seem, there was more onus on him than ever to put things right. Not only must he clear his name and rescue Ramus-Bey, he must act to prevent another war. Varn may be guilty, but the beginning of another conflict would signal an internal revolution in the Bethel Ministry from the faction that included Daliel. These two actions combined could prove to be more incendiary than any other nation state would realise.

Yet, he realised that the thing foremost in his mind was the old man. He had let down Ramus-Bey, and he wanted to atone for that.

But could one man alone do this?

A smile crossed his face. It would have confused the guard watching the surveillance imager, but it made perfect sense to Simeon.

For he was not alone.

He wanted it to be like this.

The market square in the centre of the city of Belthan would be cleared for the event. The stalls and units where traders plied their wares – from the most basic and unrefined grains to the smallest of holovid receivers and communicators – would have been swept from the old flagstones, which were covered with the hieroglyphs of age. The buildings surrounding the square – both those of ancient stone and those of steel and glass – would have been cleared for the day, and warrior security installed to keep order within the crowds below and to ensure that nothing would go wrong with the termination.

Crowds would have been gathering from early – perhaps even from the night before – and the square would be packed solid. A mass of sweating, excited people, seeking revenge and the satiation of their bloodlust. Amongst those who lived in the capital, or had travelled from outlying towns and other parts of the continent – perhaps even from other nation states – in order to witness this historic and vengeful event, there would be holovid crews from around the planet, with newscasters of differing styles, all presenting their take on events.

Simeon, taken from his cell, comes into the scene almost at the last. Hysteria has been mounting, and now the crowds must have their sacrifice. He is to be taken to a platform, led like an animal through the hissing, spitting masses, to be raised above them and ceremonially terminated by a blade of tempered steel with a burnished golden hilt, kept for such a purpose since the day of the seventeenth Chief Minister, over three hundred anums previous.

He is laid on the slab, stretched out, with a guard standing by to ensure that he does not move at the last. The executioner, selected from the warrior security by a random registration generator to ensure no stigma attaches to the post, raises the blade. As he waits for the signal to bring it down, Simeon makes a few simple passes, and is rendered invisible.

From his record, and from his ranking, there is no way he should know even such a simple piece of magic. Confusion reigns, and in the chaos he is able to make his way through the crowd unseen.

He would have liked it to be that way. It would have appealed to his sense of drama, his sense of righteous indignation, which had grown as he waited for the day of termination. It would have seemed fitting.

It was also completely idiotic, and if he was going

to make this work he had to cover as many angles as possible.

Much as it would be pleasing to walk away from the scene of intended termination, there were too many factors dictating against it. Firstly, he would have to get through the crowd without being jostled or hit by anything that may be thrown. One well-aimed missile could ruin his plans before they began.

He could be secured to the slab, or his hands bound as he was led to his execution. That would really ruin his chances.

Even if he did manage to render himself invisible before the sword fell, the confused crowd could be as much of a hindrance as an aid, rather than allow him to lose himself, they could impede his progress. Furthermore, he knew that although he would be invisible to the people in the square, he would still register on any security imagers as a disruption of space. He could still be traced, albeit with great difficulty. If he were to be delayed, then this would give his enemies time.

No – no matter how much it appealed to his sense of drama he must make his break before they came to lead him out to his demise. But he must time it well, too early and they would have the manpower to track him. The optimum time would be when the crowds were assembled, and the last preparations were being made.

It seems to be a ritual of every society throughout time that the condemned man has a last meal. A chance, perhaps, for the doomed to sample the delights of the material world in its most primal form – the need to feed – and so gain a greater insight into what they are about to lose. Or maybe it was a chance for those about to perform the execution to show some mercy to those about to leave this mortal veil. A remnant from the days of sacrifice to the Gods.

Simeon pondered on this, and concluded that – fascinating though it may be at any other time – it was of no importance whatsoever to him right now. All that mattered was that he was to be given a last meal of his choosing. To be delivered on the morning of his termination. By one guard.

There would never be a better time.

As he waited for the guard to arrive with his meal, he dressed in the drab black uniform he had been given. It was a battlesuit, stripped of all insignia as a sign of his complete degradation. He didn't care. It was a damn sight more practical than the shirt he had been forced to wear up to this point, and would serve him well for his escape. Once dressed, he sat on his bunk going over the passes in his mind. He would have only one chance to get this right. How he wished that he had also been shown the charm with which Najwin had looped the surveillance imagers. It would have bought him some more time.

He heard the guard approach and flexed his wrists, hoping that it would look to the imagers as though he were nothing more than a little stiff, a little anxious on his final day.

The guard unlocked and entered the cell. He carried a tray on which there was a wine glass with a yellow and magenta liquid. Beside it lay a plate with delicately seasoned roots and vegetables in a wine sauce, artfully arranged around a steak of rare Tallus.

Simeon, who had been on a diet of slops during his time in the cell, felt his stomach rumble. He was so hungry that for a fraction of a moment he almost considered forgoing his plan in order to eat first.

It would have been an incredibly stupid idea, but at

least the thought served a purpose. The expression on his face as the tray was wafted before him completely fooled the guard, and deceived those who watched the surveillance imager.

As the guard placed the tray on the floor, and made ready to pass another in a long succession of sarcastic comments, Simeon made a few simple passes. They were small movements of the hands, which he attempted to mask from the imager by hunching over as he sat on his bunk. He could not totally hide it, but could make it so that it would take several viewings of the security disks to work out what had happened.

As he made the passes, he focused on them, and what they would mean. They were a ritualisation of his own desire to bring about the change. The combination honed a part of his mind that was now unlocked. The power to change a small part of the world was now his. "What the..." the guard exclaimed, steeping back and into the tray of food as he turned, only to find that the subject of his latest, wittily sculpted insult had seemingly disappeared from the room.

For a moment the guard stood, dumbfounded, eyes searching. There was nowhere that the prisoner could be hiding and yet... the guard tried the door to the cell. It was locked, just as he knew it was.

Bewildered, he opened the door and rushed out, determined to raise the alarm. He tugged the emergency cord that ran the length of this level. Simeon slipped out, and made his way swiftly away from the panicking guard. He knew that he would show on imagers as a disruption of the air when the images were viewed closely. But if he moved quickly, to a casual viewer the disruption would barely register.

He had noted where he was in the building when he

had been taken to interrogation, and then again to his trial each day. It was easy to negotiate the corridors in the middle of such an alarm. Guards were rushing from one point to another, following procedures that probably had no bearing on a situation like this – he knew what warrior security could be like for trained procedure as much as anyone – and all he had to do was to literally avoid bumping into any of them.

Simeon made his way up to ground level, and through to the reception of the building, tracing in reverse Najwin's route a short while before. It was made simple by the confusion. Attention was focused on the lower levels, and the higher he went, the easier progress became.

He took several deep breaths as he left the building, savouring the cold autumn air after being in an air-conditioned cellar for so long. Briskly he began to move away from the building, avoiding the square to which it was adjacent. To cut across on any other day would have taken him a quick route to his destination. But today, filled as it was with people awaiting his termination, and warrior security who were probably hearing about his apparent escape at this very moment, it seemed like a bad idea.

Besides which, with only a few hours to go until the scheduled time of termination, the streets around the square were deserted, and it was simple for him to move quickly through them, snaking down alleyways and side streets until he had completed a semi-circle, and had come up at the rear wall of a castle he knew only too well.

The gaping hole blasted by the strike force was still there. Through the gap Simeon could see that the lawns and pockets of foliage had been cut back and some adepts were in the process of replanting. There was little sign of the wildlife that had once roamed free, and the place seemed strangely lonely without it.

Simeon stepped through the gap and into the grounds, still keeping the charm in operation. Near to him, the adepts looked up, sensing a magical intrusion.

It was the moment of truth. Simeon needed help and he believed he would get it from the academy. Not a single wizard or adept had been called at his trial, and he believed this was because their evidence would not uphold the view of him presented to the world.

He stood within the bounds of the academy, looking around. He could see that some reconstruction was taking place, the wizards using their magic to remake and remodel the debris into its original form. Like the adepts, they could sense a magical intrusion. Walking towards the group of adepts, he let the charm drop and waited for their reaction.

"Simeon!" Almost as one, the adepts exclaimed their surprise, then rushed towards him. He was embraced, clapped on the shoulder, and subjected to a barrage of joyful celebration.

The wizards joined the adepts. Despite their own apparent joy, they were more circumspect. Before he had a chance to answer any of the questions flung at him – or, indeed, to pose any of his own – he was whisked into the Institute. Once there, the wizards established magical defences around the grounds.

"A precaution," muttered Avathon, who had been considered the natural successor to Ramus-Bey, but seemed less than pleased with his status as head-by-default of the Institute. He seemed ill at ease with having to lead. "These have been testing times. We have been given no help in repairing damage. We have viewed your so-called trial, but had been denied the chance to speak in your favour. Ramus is... I don't know. I can feel he still lives. Now you, who knew no magic before, rejoin us with a charm surrounding you."

Simeon quickly told the assembled academy what had happened to him since his incarceration, and some of the conclusions he had drawn. When he had finished, he could see from the expressions around him that some questions had been answered.

"Najwin is a fool, but at least he has reached that point where the ultimate choice between good and evil must be made," mused Avathon. "I have been unable to follow him for the last few days. Yet I sense that he has not joined the Gods. I suspect he knows that his only path to redemption lay with renunciation of that which tempted him. He has cut himself off from the path. It is to be regretted. Yet he has taught you well, and enabled you to rejoin us."

"I can forgive him much for this," Simeon affirmed. "He was not a bad man, just a stupid one. As was I. I have allowed myself to be a tool. That cannot happen again. I need your help to put this right."

"You will have all that we can offer, of course," exclaimed Avathon, a view endorsed by the murmured agreement of the assembled academy. "You have proved yourself a stronger man than those who make themselves your betters. But the strongest are those who know when they are in need of help, and are not afraid to ask for it."

Instinctively, Simeon reached out and grasped the wizard's arm. "You have no notion of how much I wanted to hear that," he smiled. "Now, before we go any further, you said that you knew that Ramus was alive..."

The wizard assented. "Everyone who practices magic leaves behind them a trail. I suppose the best way to describe it to you is that they leave a trail of disruption, of ripples, like that left by a pebble in a pool... no, better still, like the tracks of a large animal through a forest. It is possible to follow these, as I have with both Ramus and with Najwin."

"So you know where Ramus is, I mean exactly?"

"Oh certainly, dear boy. Give me a map and I could point him out to you."

"And yet no-one has approached you from the Ministry?"

Avathon shrugged. "Given what you, yourself, have told us, is that any surprise?"

"Perhaps not," Simeon said softly. "I was just hoping that I was wrong about our governing body."

"You may be, not everyone is aware of the possibilities of magic. Given the way we have been treated in the past few days, we have been understandably cautious of showing our hand."

"So, our order of the day is simple. Locate Ramus, then retrieve him. He is, I assume, in Varn?"

"With Vixel, I should imagine. I can follow him, but cannot communicate with him due to magical shielding. Only in an Institute, with a Mage, would there be that degree of strength. Vixel must have been near when the attack occurred, as the degree of magic used was incredibly strong, and he would have had to swamp Ramus' own defences before they could be brought into being."

Simeon had his own views on that matter, but allowed the wizard to continue.

"There is little we can do to aid you in a physical sense, I am afraid. We have no resources when it comes to weapons, and no physical transport. We can provide you with a holoship. It will be slow, but it will aid you in escaping detection by our forces as you leave Bethel, and also in escaping detection in Varn. Other than that, we can, though, track your progress and try to add a long-distance magical attack to your physical assault when the time comes. The problem is that we are far away, so our powers are reduced."

Simeon nodded slowly, but his thoughts were racing. The men of the academy were willing enough, but were on the wrong end of an uneven equation.

There was, however, one other he could draw on for help. If she would... certainly, it would even the matter up more than a little if she did.

He had considered it in the abstract, but now that he thought of actually approaching her, he felt a nervous flutter in his stomach.

"Gentlemen, I thank you for believing in me and for offering help. Right now, the greatest thing you can do is to keep me secured here until nightfall. I must rest and re-equip. Only in the dark can I get that which I need."

"A holoship could get you out of here right now," one of the adepts piped up.

Simeon allowed himself a grim smile. "True, my friend. But I can get myself a holoship and pilot who owe me and that would leave you more options for back-up. I just need to wait a short while longer. We've had to wait days as it is. A few more moments cannot hurt."

"Can you be sure of his co-operation?" The same adept urged.

"*She* was always singular," Simeon grinned, "but I think I can sway her. However, if I am to do so, then I must rest."

He allowed an adept to lead him to his chambers. Stripped only of the surveillance equipment, it still housed his blaster and charger. It would not be much, but it would be something. More than he had needed when escaping, for sure. His own battlesuits were still stored in the room. He would change after resting. If he was going into battle, then he would go as a true warrior of Bethel, no matter what the show trial had made him out to be.

And yet, as he laid his head down, his last waking thought was this: what in the name of the Gods was he going to say to Jenna when he saw her again?

# CHAPTER THIRTEEN

## Year Zero – Period Three

It was a very different Belthan to which Simeon awoke after a few hours rest. The adepts and wizards had divided their time between the tasks they had embarked on when he arrived, those preparations they must make for long-distance charm casting when he reached Varn and keeping an eye on the state of the nation through the newscasts.

While he showered, prepared his battlesuit and blaster, a succession of breathless young adepts filled in the details of the day for him. The crowds in the square, cheated of their heart's desire to see a traitor put to death and their nation state honour appeased, had resorted to the most basic form of protest imaginable. They had rioted, and for some time the warrior security forces had fought to contain them without striking out. With the eyes of Inan upon them, it would have been a disaster had the riot been suppressed with force. Minus a Mage, Bethel was already in a position of weakness – regardless of the way in which this could be flipped into a strength using the treaty alliances. A populace in turmoil would be a clear sign to potential enemies, asking for a resumption of hostilities and the breaking of that treaty.

The warrior security had trod the line with infinite care. There had been few casualties, and now the square had been cleared. Outside the walls of the Institute, an uneasy peace now settled over the capital.

But this had taken time, and had taken attention away from the seemingly impossible escape of the prisoner.

The staff and students of the academy may, to some

extent, have shut themselves away from the world in order to pursue their studies, but they were not complete innocents. Their limited contact told them that it was only a matter of time before they would receive a visit from the military. There was no way that such an escape could have been effected without the use of magic. Who else could have helped Simeon but a member of the Institute? Particularly as they had been overlooked at the trial.

With this in mind, the staff and students knew that they had to shield Simeon until he departed, and then successfully cover his tracks. From the information they had shared between them, they had all assumed that Daliel would lead any investigation, as he had before, and would therefore lead any raid or interrogation party.

So it was essential to get Simeon moving as soon as was possible after he awoke refreshed. In the meantime it was essential that he rest. While adepts mounted guard, with low level magic to alert them to the presence of any warrior security, and at the same time to effect a delay that would not arouse suspicion, so the wizards prepared for his departure.

A plan was formed that was simple yet flexible. It needed to be, for it was not long before Daliel and a small troop of warriors came calling.

Simeon was still resting. Nothing short of an explosion beneath his bed could have stirred him. The problem was to hide him from prying warrior security eyes. The defences and early warning established by the adepts gave them time to prepare for the approach of Daliel and his men. As he advanced through the gates, complaining of the thought forms that – seemingly accidentally – slowed his progress, he was greeted by a smiling Avathon.

"We are honoured to be granted a visit from our

protector," he said, keeping all trace of irony from his voice as he watched Daliel survey the shattered grounds.

"Enough. You know why we are here," Daliel answered without ceremony.

Avathon was a picture of wide-eyed innocence. In truth, some of the adepts thought he was overplaying, but... "Why, to see how we are progressing in our repairs."

Daliel stared at the wizard. Was he really that stupid, or was he acting? He held Avathon's gaze for some time, but the wizard maintained his facade. Eventually, the security chief decided that the man was an unworldly idiot.

"The traitor Simeon 7 has escaped. We are looking for him."

"And you think he is here?"

"I think he might be," Daliel replied. The wide-eyed innocent act was being a little over-played now: if the wizard *was* that much of a fool, he should be flustered, worried. He was too calm.

Without further ceremony, Daliel directed his men into the castle. He would engage no more with the wizard.

Avathon allowed them to pass, although one gesture could have stayed them. There had been time enough.

The troop spread out and searched the castle. They were thorough, and would have brooked no interference from the adepts.

Daliel directed the operation and saved Simeon's chamber for himself. If the man would be anywhere, it would be resting up in here. He had his blaster at the ready, yet could not shake the feeling that his men had been allowed too free a hand.

He advanced slowly, scanning the rooms.

They were empty.

Calling his men together, he advanced on the wizard, who had remained outside the castle.

"It appears that you are safe, and the traitor is not here."

"That is a relief. Though, of course, he would have had to have entered without our knowledge."

There was a long silence, then: "I shall detail a cordon around the castle. Just to make sure."

Avathon met Daliel's eye. "That would give us some peace of mind."

The security chief left, a feeling of great irritation within him. He knew that the wizard was lying in some way, but could only hope to smoke him out with patience.

Avathon waited for the troop to exit the gates, then allowed himself a smile. Turning, he strode into the castle and called for the adepts.

"Where is he?"

With a pass of their hands, they revealed a sleeping Simeon, strung on skeins of energy that both kept him aloft, and also invisible. They had carried him between them for the duration of the search.

Avathon nodded to himself. "Put him back. We shall say nothing of this. He has enough to concern him when he awakes."

And so he slept on, unaware, while preparations for nightfall continued. When he awoke, Simeon was suited and armed, and the wizards outlined to him the extent of the charms they could use to assist him from such a range. As far as was possible, they agreed that Vixel would, in all likelihood, keep the Mage at the Varn Institute, and so it was decided that it was for this building that Simeon would head in the holoship.

It was dark. Outside the walls, peace now held an uneasy sway.

It was time.

"May the Gods go with you," Avathon said softly, clapping Simeon on the shoulder. "We shall do all that we can."

"Thank you – thank you all," Simeon replied, returning the gesture, then directing himself to the assembled wizards. "I don't have to stress the importance of this to Inan, but yet more important is that we do the right thing by Ramus-Bey. He needs us, and we must not fail him."

"You shall not, I know this," Avathon said.

Simeon smiled. "I hope I can live up to your expectations. But what shall you do when the military return?"

"Evade the issue. What else? You will not be here, and there is no sign of your having passed through. As long as we present a facade of complete ignorance, then all will be well."

Simeon laughed. "It will be appropriate," he chuckled, thinking of the man he had once called friend, and whose convoluted plans now tangled him in knots.

Without further delay, Simeon left, taking care and good wishes from those gathered in the hall of the Institute. As he walked out of the door, he made the passes taught him by Najwin, and before their eyes faded from view.

He did not look back.


Now that the streets were clear he was able to make swift progress. In virtually no time, he had made the distance between the Institute and the embassy of Kyas.

Like all the new embassy buildings that had been established in every nation state capital, this was still undergoing construction in parts. Because of this, security from the Kyan military was not, perhaps, as strong as it may otherwise have been. It had crossed Simeon's mind that there may be extra guards awaiting his arrival, if Ensign Jenna Eslo had been truthful with her superiors about her past.

Ah, who was he kidding? She had acted up to this point as though she had never met him. Why should that change, now?

The embassy building was a new construction that had been built around the shell of a much older stone castle. Like many embassies around the planet – and indeed, those others contained within this capital – this was no accident. To use a building made during wartime, and then to rebuild around that, and to make it better, was an obviously symbolic act, and something that was intended to ritualise the meaning of the peace.

In practical terms, it was a crock. Admittedly, it gave the crafts and guildsmen who worked on them a fixed term of employment. However, it made work and living conditions difficult for embassy staff. Unfinished sections could not easily be secured, heating and lighting circuits were prone to malfunction; water supplies could suddenly cease while essential works were carried out.

Added to this, the location of the embassies did not help. All were gathered within a few streets of each other, in the hearts of the capitals. Again, this togetherness had been partly symbolic. But for those who worked in the buildings, it meant that they were close to people to whom they were still adjusting to as allies not enemies.

This was of some considerable help to Simeon. It meant that he had to cross only a few streets and squares. It meant that he was able to gain access to the embassy building with ease, as security measures were stretched, leaving gaping holes through which he could have walked even if visible to the naked eye. It meant that he was able to wander the corridors of the embassy with impunity, in search of Jenna.

Of course, it didn't tell him where she was. So while he was able to save time in reaching the embassy, once inside he felt that the time saved was trickling through his fingers.

Ensign Jenna Eslo had not had a good day. Admittedly, there were those who had it far worse, but that was the problem. One of those in line for a really bad day was someone she had spent no little time trying to forget. She'd been doing quite well, too, and then he'd got himself mixed up in a treasonous plot, and now had somehow escaped death by devious means.

There was a part of her that had never wanted to forget him. And yet, the manner in which she had become involved with him could spell nothing but trouble for her if it ever emerged. If she had continued the relationship, then there would have been no way that she could have kept it quiet. Furthermore, there was the question of commitment. There were things that he had said to her, things that she was not sure she could reciprocate. Not because of her feelings for him, but because of things within her that she had not wanted to examine too closely. So she had decided to treat the end of hostilities as a chance for her to make a clean break with both Simeon and her past. From now on she would concentrate on her career, and bury the other stuff... the things that she did not want to have to face.

Her posting to Belthan had not been the greatest of starts. Any other nation state would have been preferable. Having said that, the chances of Simeon being posted to the capital – even staying in the military after cessation of hostilities – was remote.

Up until the trial, she had no notion that he was within walking distance of where she now lived and worked. Then the taking of the Mage had occurred, and it was not enough that the whole of the planet was now on a war footing; Jenna now had to contend with the knowledge that the man who had turned her personal world upside down was responsible for turning the rest of the world likewise.

How could she forget the cretin when he was on the teli-mage broadcasts all the time? It was no wonder she couldn't sleep. She'd tried, but each time the blissful oblivion had crept up on her, some memory had intruded and jolted her violently awake.

So now she stood at the window, looking out on the courtyard of the castle keep. The old stone walls were still visible, though in places new walkways were encased in glass, giving access to new levels.

She had the strangest feeling, shivering slightly even though it was a mild night. Below her, a routine guard patrol swapped banter as the two men crossed on their circuit. She recognised one of them as the warrior who was always staring at her, and had invited her to join him on his evening off. She had declined. Another warrior was the last thing she needed. Why didn't diplomatic attachés ask her to go out with them?

She could feel something supranormal in the air. The only people in the embassy with those kinds of skills would be other Ensigns, like herself. Yet neither of the other two were in the building. One was on leave, the other had an engagement in the city. Besides which, she knew how their magic felt. This was something else entirely.

She felt it fade as suddenly as it had appeared, replaced by a feeling of a different kind altogether. A more familiar feeling, of being watched, and by eyes that knew her well.

"I'll say this for you, you know how to make a entrance," she said as she turned to face Simeon 7.

"You knew it was me?"

She shrugged. "Who else would have this sense of drama," she remarked with a certain dryness.

"Aren't you going to ask me why I'm here?" He questioned.

"You'll tell me. First, I'd like to know how you got past the security. Strikes me that we need to do a lot more checks, and somebody's definitely slacking. Unless, of course, you've got some help?"

He laughed shortly. "Let's just say that there are some who believe that I'm not the traitor I'm made out to be."

"They're in the minority, then."

He paused. "And you?" He asked quietly, not sure if he wanted to know the answer.

She shook her head. "Whatever else, you're not that. Maybe I could see you being used as someone's proxy, manipulated before you had a chance to catch on to what was happening."

"You know, that's not far from the truth,' he shrugged. "I could put it right, but I'd need some help."

He let it hang, trying to read her reaction. "So you escape termination, break into a nation state embassy, and want to coerce a member of a delegation from another nation state to assist you in... what, exactly?" She asked, trying to keep her tone as level as her face, but still feeling it rise. "Why do you think I would help, exactly?"

"I'll tell you why." Simeon spoke softly, evenly. Inside he was torn. Part of him wanted to hear her say she would do it because of how she felt about him. Part of him didn't want to deal with that until he had at least tried to save the Mage. There were such things as priorities. Part of him still didn't know what to say to her.

So he told her the whole story, from the beginning. Aware all the while that time was ticking away, time that he should be using to get on the trail of Ramus-Bey. Yet his best chance of getting to Varn undetected lay with Jenna. She listened carefully. It sounded ridiculous. Plot and counter plot. Old friends who would double deal for a sniff of power. Old friends that she had known, too, making it all the harder to grasp what he was saying. Yet, Daliel had always seemed to have the air of a man who would always look out for himself above others.

Ultimately, she felt that she had to believe him, no matter how absurd it seemed. The Simeon she had known would have been incapable of dreaming up such a convoluted and complex series of conspiracies. He was a straightforward man.

"Okay," she assented, "I believe you. Don't ask me to explain why, but I think you're being honest with me. Though I don't really understand why you're here," she added.

"I need a holoship to get me into Varn undetected. The only way that the guys at the Institute can really help is if they can focus on one set of charms."

"So, you came for no other reason?" She questioned, aware as she spoke that she wasn't sure what answer she wanted to hear.

"Maybe you're the only person I trust too," he said, drawing near to her. She could feel the warmth of his body, his breath on her skin. Feelings ran through her that had nothing to do with the question in hand. From the look in his eyes, she could see that this was also true of him.

Piloting a holoship into Varn, carrying a convicted Bethel traitor, whilst being an attaché to the diplomatic staff of Kyas. How many international laws would she be breaking if she did that? Where would she end up?

That was what she should have been thinking. She knew that, but the only thing she could think of was this: why don't you touch me, you idiot?

He did. Almost as though he could read her mind. She didn't need to tell him that she agreed with his plan. The way that she melted into him told him all that he needed to know.

It was only later, when he was pacing the deck of the holoship, that doubts crept into her mind.

But by then it was too late.

In his cell, within the dank basement of the Institute in Ilvarn, Ramus-Bey awoke to yet another day of mind-numbing tedium. Truthfully, he still felt an idiot at having frozen like a frightened animal during the attack on his own Institute. He felt foolish, old and useless at the way in which he had allowed himself to be taken. He felt impotent at the way in which he had allowed himself to be detained here, in these demeaning surroundings. He felt ridiculously feeble-minded that he could not work out why he was being kept alive and captive. Most of all, he felt a sense of dread and tedium – a strange cocktail, it must be stated – at the prospect of another day of being baited by Vixel.

Honestly, it amazed him that the arrogant bastard hadn't been killed in a fit of pique by one of his own students. Obsessed by his own greatness, and more than keen to impress this very greatness upon anyone within earshot, it seemed that the sole purpose of his abduction was so that Vixel could amuse himself day after day by impressing upon Ramus-Bey the sheer genius that he – Vixel – had shown in masterminding and executing this entire scheme.

Which was all very well, but there seemed to be no other point that Ramus-Bey could see. Which, frankly, made the whole thing childish.

Something he would gladly have pointed out if not for the fact that the Varn Mage may have been tempted to use more than his tongue for punishment. There were some things that this may reveal... things that, for reasons of his own, Ramus would rather not have brought to light.

So he kept his own counsel. Vixel would know he was awake and send his bodyguard to collect him, even though there was no surveillance tech. For which Ramus was grateful: even though he knew he was magically observed, to have an imager on him at all times would somehow have seemed more intrusive.

Today, however, was to be a little different. When the bodyguard appeared, he did not have the slop that passed for breakfast with him. In reply to the Mage's questioning glance, he informed Ramus-Bey that this morning Vixel wanted him to eat with him.

Already, this was a welcome break in an already tedious routine. A break further enhanced by his being led to an outdoor terrace where, in the sun, Vixel sat beneath a shade, a table spread out before him with fruits and sweetmeats. He beckoned the Bethelian Mage to join him.

Ramus was glad to do this, albeit with a certain sense of foreboding. Something which Vixel was quick to pick up on: "My dear, sweet man, you think I am doing this for the purpose of the fall – when it comes – being the greater?" Then, when Ramus-Bey said nothing: "I can't blame you for this, I suppose. No, my dear old fool, I have decided that to taunt you would serve no great purpose. It is time you were told the truth. I would have hoped that you could have worked it out, but in truth I don't feel that this is very likely..." He paused, giving Ramus-Bey a questioning look. "No, thought not."

It was designed to be insulting, and achieved its aim with ease. Leaving it to sink in, Vixel gestured to Ramus that he should eat.

"Assuming – as I'm sure you do – that I am simple with age, then pray enlighten me as to my purpose in being brought here. As far as I can see, to terminate me would have been a simpler option." Ramus said.

"Ah, but not as much fun," Vixel said. "Besides which, to do so would be to set a course of war with no turning back. Whereas to take you, and then at the last to reveal that you are still living, well...

"Things have been rather fun since we bought you here. Your bodyguard has been tried and convicted for collusion. Rather ironic, considering how hard he fought to save you. I can only hope that my own guard would be so efficient, should a similar situation occur.

"However, that is neither here nor there. I can see, much as you try to hide it, that the news of his conviction has upset you. But fear not, my dear old fool! He must have some friends, as his escape has been made, effected by magic. He came close to ruining our plans."

"Speaking of which," Ramus interrupted, keeping his voice as level as possible, not wishing to betray his relief at Simeon's escape, "I still do not understand why I should be alive, other than as a foil for your base humour and egotism of course."

"Ah, I shall allow you that. Why not, when you so signally fail to grasp the greater import? It's simple. If you are terminated, then war is inevitable. Even now, Bethel is demanding retribution, pleading with the other nation states to join them, bereft as they are of the great weapon – that's you – that shall give them parity with other nation states, meaning us, of course.

"Well, they look so forlorn now, don't they? But they will not when we reveal that you are alive, and also reveal the counter plot that we foiled and so, effectively, saved your life."

He announced this with a flourish, expecting Ramus-Bey to express shock and outrage. He was a little deflated when this did not happen.

"Ah, I see that the notion of a plot from within Bethel itself had not escaped you or your bodyguard. That's... interesting, I think. After all, why did not the military respond with greater speed and alacrity to our little operation? Why are certain sections of the Ministry not driving themselves frantic over the loss of their Mage, while other sections are?"

Ramus-Bey, buoyed by the disappointment of Vixel over his reaction, decided to open up a little. "It would be true to say that myself and Simeon knew that we had been attacked from two sides. One we assumed to be Varn, as it was nothing more than you would expect from such sewer scrapings. But the other seemed too close to home. It did not take much to work out that at least one section of my own government intended to terminate me, and replace me with a rogue wizard. One, I might add, who showed some exceptional powers. Whoever he may be, he would have been a match for you.

"We knew there was an internal threat. But we were ready for it. What we did not expect was such an all-out and blatant attack from the old enemy."

"No, I didn't think you would. That was the genius of

my plan, after all. Force the hand of those in your own government who would have sought to place blame. See what they would do."

"And is it proving to your satisfaction?" Ramus-Bey questioned.

Vixel allowed himself a small, smug smile. "I should say. The outrage we're seeing is genuine, and those who would have subverted from within are running around like headless chickens wondering how they can take advantage. Of course, they cannot... only we can." His smile switched to full beam. It was disconcertingly humourless, and made Ramus-Bey feel distinctly uneasy.

"So how, then, do you propose to take such an advantage?" he asked.

Vixel sighed theatrically. "Today you shall be paraded at a meeting of the Varn Ministry. This will be broadcast across Inan. Not only will we show that you are alive and well, and well-cared for, but we shall also reveal to the waiting world the extent of the conspiracy that we have uncovered within your own nation state. Yes, we snatched you – but it was for the greater good of Inan. Ooh – what's that I hear? Could it be the grinding of tables turning?" He added, laughing at his own joke.

"Why do you think I would co-operate with you in betraying my own nation state?"

Vixel's smile did not waver. "Because it would clear the name of your bodyguard. I feel, from what I know, that you would be hard pushed to put a nation state that has betrayed you above a friend who would have laid down his life for you. I think that you – unlike a more sensible person such as myself – are easily swayed in that way. The blame placed on the bodyguard by your nation state's own rogue elements is an unexpected bonus, I will admit. But never let it be said that I am less than adaptable:

every situation can be turned to one's own advantage if one has the wit. Which, of course, I do."

His grin remained fixed. Ramus-Bey could feel himself start to sweat under such scrutiny.

Dammit, by the Gods, the bastard was right.

# CHAPTER FOURTEEN

## Year Zero – Period Three

She'd asked him if he had a plan.

He told her he had.

Sort of.

As far as Simeon could see, there was only one way to get down from where the holoship had landed, and that was the hard way.

"We'll take the south stairwell," Simeon said softly.

"Any reason?"

He shrugged. "It's as good as any. We just need to stay alert, take nothing for granted."

"Okay, but you can see the motion sensors can't you?"

"That's part of the plan," he smiled.

"So you do really have one and you weren't just giving me a line?"

He shrugged. "Let's just do it..."

She grimaced. "You're... impossible. If we'd taken a chance and landed in the grounds of the Institute, then..."

"... then we would have been detected easily by the lowest adept. They're alert to magic, the military aren't. I should know. So are we going then?"

Jenna pulled the invisibility charm in tight to them, so that it covered a small area that barely extended beyond the tips of their fingers. Simeon went in front of her and began to descend the stairs. He set a rapid pace, and within a matter of steps they had set off the motion and weight detectors. An alarm sounded in the distant recesses of the building and the lights on the stairwell were killed, plunging it into darkness. The imaging tech set in the walls would, he knew, have switched over to night vision as soon as this happened, but still it would not betray them. If anything, the slight eddying of air that an invisibility charm caused would be less detectable.

He could feel Jenna close up behind, bumping clumsily into him as he slowed a little.

The fact that they had killed the lights told him that whoever was on duty had been suitably thrown by the motion and weight detectors registering on what – via the imager – would seem to be an empty stairwell. They would hope that a lack of light would throw whoever or whatever was on the stairs into confusion, buying vital moments to recce and regroup for the warrior security.

Basic training. Basic manoeuvres. Basic mistakes.

Simeon had his night vision headset on his battlesuit belt. It was designed to accompany the surveillance Intel equipment he had left at the Institute, but could still function as infra-red when not in sync.

The stairs came into focus. He could see the lines of the motion detector beams. He knew that beneath the stairs they crossed would be the corresponding weight detector pads.

More importantly, he could see the damn stairs. It'd be a shame to come this far and fall down like a cretin.

"Stick close," he muttered to Jenna.

Picking his way carefully, he continued to lead her down.


In the secure tech centre it was an ordinary morning, and the two warriors on duty were idly chatting, barely paying attention to the monitors in front of them. They were more concerned with Team Security's chances of winning the silver pennant in the warrior games challenge. They were itching to revenge themselves on

Team Ministry Sec, who had defeated them three periods back, in the Peace Treaty Celebration Games. These days, now that the peace looked like it might actually stick, there was little to be vigilant about. Strange how the habits of many anums can suddenly break down and die.

Even the threats of Bethel were considered empty posturing: outside of a few high level ministry operatives and their opposite numbers in the military, most Varn warriors believed that the Mage Abduction Scandal (as it was already dubbed by newsheets and newscasters) was a piece of double-play by Bethel to stir up war. As a result, they found it hard to step up from level zero to level two security.

So neither man was paying much attention until the alarms started sounding. Jolted out of their complacency, they scrabbled at the controls and faders of their monitor equipment, trying to make sense of readings and images that flatly contradicted each other.

"There's jack out there," one of them shouted over the noise.

"Must be something," returned his companion. "Must be..."

"Bastard piece of shit is malfunctioning is all," the first one yelled. "There's nothing up there. Look at it, for the Gods' sakes!"

"My friend, I can see that, and so can you. But the machine says there's something there. So we need to respond, cover our own damn asses, right?"

A nod of agreement was all he needed. He hit the call button, and deployed a troop of warriors, flipping on a headset as he did so in order to report to his superior, and the duty troop commander.

In a matter of moments they were deployed.

Even in peace, these were well-trained men. From leisure to attention in less than five, they waited, armed and with Intel/surveillance headsets to cover communication and vision.

It didn't take a lot of skill to read the confusion on the troop commander's face, and when he told them that they were to cover a breach in the south stairwell corridor leading from the keep, it was no great shock to hear that their enemy was of unknown number, size and origin. The motion and weight sensors had caught movement, but were inconclusive.

Keep a clear head. Keep eyes and ears open. Keep those trigger fingers frosty. No way did they want to screw up and blast one of their own.

They moved out, taking the stairwells to the fourth level at the double. From here they spread out so that they sealed off the whole south wall of the building. Staff were ushered from offices and meeting rooms. As military operatives, all staff were armed. They also knew their place. A suspected assault on the castle was a specialist training operation. In such a situation they complied with orders and deferred to the duty team.

It was smooth. By the time that Simeon and Jenna had picked their way halfway down the stairwell, both the tower corridor and the whole side of the building had been effectively evac'ed and sealed, with only the duty team waiting for them.

"It's too quiet. They've got something planned," Jenna whispered.

"Of course they have," Simeon snapped back. "Each building like this has a duty team of some kind. I don't know how Varn organise their warrior security, but I'll take a gamble that it's not that different from how we mobilise."

"Well, duh! That wasn't exactly what I meant."

"Look, I don't know exactly what they have planned but what I do know is that we should assume that whatever their strategy, they will have cleared and sealed at least one part of the castle. Which is good."

"Good? What definition of good are you using?"

"The one that says we have only a duty team to fight through, and not a seemingly infinite number of people blocking our way."

"Point taken. We'll have to move fast when we reach the bottom of the stairs, or..."

"They'll be able to pinpoint us from the minute disruption on the imagers. I know. I have every intention of moving fast, believe me. This is what we're going to do..."

There were a dozen men in a duty troop. Three were positioned in cover around the foot of the stairwell. From their respective positions, each had a clear shot at the mouth of the well. Orders were to fire on sight.

"Sir, how can we fire on sight if nothing is registering on the imagers?"

"The motion and weight detectors have placed whatever is in the well three-quarters of the way down. When it crosses the last beam, then you will be ordered to keep up a barrage of fire. Fire low, high, and middle. Dammit, whatever it is, it can't get round that kind of barrage."

There were, however, contingency plans for if it should. Nine men were left. They were placed at corridor junctions, and each was fed Intel from the tech centre.

As both normal, light and infrared showed no results, and the motion and weight detectors had yielded too little information, and that of seemingly contradictory data, electro-magnetic field detectors had been brought into use. These were trained on each corridor, and were up and running with rapidity. In theory, they should show any disturbances, and could be used to pinpoint fire.

All it needed was for whatever was on the stairs to hit that last motion detector beam, and playtime would begin.

Simeon could see the beams criss-crossing the last three stairs. The first line tactic was obvious. Wait for them to cross those beams, and then set up a barrage of fire. As soon as they hit the few unprotected stairs between the beam they were about to cross and the beams at the foot of the well, then they were in a no-man's land where Varn trigger fingers would be flexing.

Simeon's tactic was to make that flex turn into a nervous twitch.

When he had guided Jenna past the last weighted stair, he stayed her with a touch. She could see the bottom of the well – although, with no night vision headset of her own, she had no idea of the detector layout – and tried to breathe shallowly, quietly. She knew that Simeon would be barely able to whisper any instructions.

They did not move. She could almost hear her nerves singing with the tension.

"Wait," he breathed.

She trusted him. She had to.

"I don't get it. It's passed the ninth motion beam, and it seems to have stopped."

"Are you sure about that?"

"The bastard thing's invisible and doesn't register except on the motion/weight scale. Even that's weird, like it's not got a constant mass or something..."

The minute fluctuations of two people moving slightly out of sync had confused the tech, making its readings incomprehensible to anyone who didn't actually know that there were two people trying to move as one. To the warriors trying to make sense of the scale, it seemed to be some strange, invisible behemoth.

Which was why one of the two duty warriors on tech watch posited the following:

"Look, are we doing the right thing here? This doesn't look like a military assault to me. It looks like magic. So shouldn't we be pressing for..."

"Hey," his companion replied, "we're pressing for nothing. We're just doing this by the book. Whatever that is up there, it's got a duty team on its ass."

"Yeah, but..."

"Yeah, but nothing!"


The three warriors positioned at the foot of the stairwell were sweating. They knew that the objective was past the last motion detector before the final clutch of beams. Once it hit them, they could hit it.

But there was nothing.

What was happening? Was it waiting for them? Had it managed to bypass the beams and bypass them? None of them had felt anything go by but if it were invisible, maybe they wouldn't be able to feel it pass.

Had it just dissipated and vanished, as mysteriously

as it had arrived? Hey, that would suit them (who wants to try and fight something you can't see?), but it was unlikely.

"Sir, nothing happening this end. Request new orders."

"Fire a warning blast, see if you can flush it out."

Synchronising their firing, the three warriors put blasts into the mouth of the stairwell at high, low and medium heights. The bricks of the stairwell were lit up by the bright energy of their fire. Chunks of stone powdered.

Smoke and dust filled the air after the final volley.

The three warriors waited in silence.


In the stairwell, Simeon stood his ground. He had been expecting something like this, and so was able to keep control as the first volley of blasts hit. If anything, he felt a satisfaction warm through him. This was what he wanted: their nerve had cracked, and they could no longer restrain their fire.

They were rattled. Good.

Behind him, Jenna wasn't so prepared. When the first volley hit, and the cloud of stone dust hit the back of her throat, it was all she could do to stop her stifled scream of shock turning into a coughing fit. Simeon shielded her from the worst excesses of the blast, but she could still feel the heat as the stone was pulverised by the energy beam.

Simeon had been sure of himself: he had stayed back this far after casting an eye over the angles at the foot of the stairwell. Blasters were wonderful weapons, but he'd never seen an energy beam yet that could fire round corners.

In the silence that followed, he turned and breathed in Jenna's ear: "Stay."

Leaving her standing on one stair, he moved carefully down two, so that he was within one step of the first of the three beams. It was low enough for him to stretch over it, and take a look around the corner of the stairwell. He hoped that she would be able to extend her invisibility charm so far, but to be safe he made a few passes and cast his own as he looked round, cancelling it as soon as he drew back. Hopefully, it would have been so brief that she wouldn't have registered the change in magical energy.

She was looking at him a little strangely as he turned to face her, but he wasn't sure if it was the magic, or merely because she couldn't work out his tactics. He wasn't going to give her the chance to clarify these thoughts. Time was of the essence.

"There are motion detectors on the last three steps. They don't know if we're here or not. Follow me, jump when I do, and try to land on your feet. Don't worry about the charm – we want them to see us. But be ready to do it again, yes?"

She realised what he was planning. He squeezed her hand, and then turned back towards the foot of the stairwell, drawing his blaster. Jenna did likewise.

He got to the fourth step, then hurled himself forward, lifting his feet up with a bend of the knees as he did. Jenna took a deep breath, then followed suit.

It all happened so quickly. One moment they were looking at an empty stairwell, the next they were under attack.

A man and a woman. He was in dark battledress, a Bethel warrior easily discernible even as he flew through the air. She was in a short battle tunic, camo style, with the colours of Kyas. Both of them had blasters.

There was confusion both amongst the front line warriors and back in the tech room. They had been dealing with a shapeless, invisible mass; now they had two flesh and blood warriors.

Even as they hit the ground – he smoothly, she stumbling slightly but still keeping her feet – they began firing.

The first shots went wild, as they blasted in an arc, trying to locate their targets. It took only a moment for each of them to lock on to one of the covered positions. A shot from the woman ripped through the battlesuit of the Varn warrior, scoring into his shoulder. The pain made him black out.

One down.

The male warrior's shooting was less exact – or less lucky – but he took out a chunk of ceiling that caused a blinding cloud of dust, the debris falling on the concealed position and forcing his target to retreat.

Two out of the game.

But the third had not been fired on. He judged that the male warrior was the one to take out first. He drew a bead on him as the man whirled to locate him. Their eyes locked over the sights of his blaster. And then the man in black did something with his hands, and disappeared from view.

The Varn warrior cursed. His training kicked in, and he whirled to take aim at the woman. She was staring open-mouthed, and was an equally open target. He was about to squeeze off a blast at her when he felt his weapon being knocked upwards. He fired a shot that blew a hole in the ceiling, and felt a fist crash into his jaw. It drove him backwards, the blaster tilting up so that it spiralled back over his head. He tried to keep balance, lashed out at air hoping to take out his opponent by accident, and felt a blow to his ribs that impacted like a heavy combat boot. He gasped out his breath, and before he had a chance to draw air back into his aching lungs another boot caught him in the chest. Sharp, burning pain seared his upper body, paralysing him. A fourth blow caught him under the chin and the world went black.

Simeon appeared once more in front of Jenna, who was still slack jawed. He had been so keen to keep his own little trick as a surprise that he hadn't figured on her reacting like this.

"Jen – do it!" he yelled, shaking her.

Snapping out of her trance, she cast the charm, enveloping them both, though, on reflection, she realised that this was hardly necessary.

Simeon took her by the arm and pulled her down a corridor.

"Okay, so I should have told you," he babbled, "but we can argue later. Now we've got to get out of here. We stick as close together under your charm as we can."

As he spoke, he pulled her down the corridor, keeping his voice as low as possible under the clamour of the alarms triggered by the blaster damage.

"We try and pick past them... only fire if we have to... try not to give ourselves away."

"What the..."

In the tech centre, the two warriors on duty could not quite believe what they were seeing. Two men down and one thrown back. The mysterious presence revealed as two people. Appearing and disappearing.

"This is magic. This is nothing to do with us. They have people for this, right?" One of the warriors asked, punching in a security code.

The warrior was correct. In every military hierarchy across Inan there were warriors who were assigned to deal with anything that used magic to achieve military ends. In this case, the warrior in question was reviewing the holovid recordings of the appearance of the two rogue warriors over and over again, enhancing the image.

The woman he didn't know. She had a Kyan Ensign's battle uniform, but that was all he could say.

The man, on the other hand... that was a face that anyone with even a passing interest in current affairs would recognise. He was the man the whole of Bethel was searching for; the man who had been proclaimed a traitor in league with Varn. The man who had just taken out two warriors of the nation state he was supposed to be in sympathy with.

The Chief Minister would have to know about this. There had been rumours around the Ministry and military buildings about what had really been going on. Unless this particular warrior missed his guess, the rumours were true.

Simeon didn't know the layout of the building, but he knew enough about this kind of old construction to figure that if he kept going in one direction and downwards, then he would come to ground level and a way out onto the streets of Ilvarn. It was simple. It was also something that he could not have pulled off without the invisibility charm.

Simeon and Jenna moved at speed through the corridors. The blaster that each of them carried had only a limited charge. They had used some of that in their first assault. A second assault could drain their weapons totally. Negotiating a duty team that couldn't see them was a relatively easy task. It was only when they hit the ground level and the exit that they realised that they had would have trouble.

The Chief Minister had been informed. A detachment of warrior security had been sent to the Institute, and Vixel had been informed. Given that he was using magic along with warrior skills, it was obvious that Simeon 7 would know where the Mage was being held. If he had been given magical assistance, then it was a given that he had been able to track Ramus-Bey to the Institute.

In truth, it was seen as nothing more than a safeguard. There was no way that the two intruders should be able to escape the building.

Simeon cursed. There were over a dozen warriors clustered around the outside of the building. The area inside the exit had been left clear. The building was deserted at this point: the streets outside, beyond the gathered warriors, had been cleared. Like many fortresses across Inan there had been adaptations over the years, subject to the whims of fashion and practicality. Now they were faced with a strengthened glass wall. It gave anyone who wished a great view of the outside. Conversely, it gave those outside an equally great view in: this didn't matter while they used the invisibility charm. It did, though, mean that if they wanted to get out, they'd have to announce themselves by breaking through the doors and fighting through the cordon. Invisibility could only take them so far. By the very act of getting through this barrier, they would have to betray their position.

"Go to the right, get ready to fire, and run like hell," Simeon said before making the passes that brought his own charm into being. She moved off, and lost sight of him as he passed from her area of charm.

Jenna waited.

Simeon appeared out of nowhere with a shimmer. He fired three times into the middle of the doors. The blaster fire shattered the glass doors and wall, the beam defracting in the shards. It would harm no-one from this range, but would serve a certain purpose.

He vanished before the blaster fire reached him, and had already dived across the floor as the beams flew over his prone body. The remainder of the doors and wall vanished beneath a hail of blaster fire.

Jenna took off at a run into the gap. She had no idea what she was doing, driven only by blind panic. She could see where the warriors were aiming, and so knew where to avoid.

Behind her, Simeon was acting as a distraction by reappearing, firing a few well-aimed shots at the warriors beyond, then vanishing before they could successfully direct their fire.

His shooting had made a gap in the ranks; Jenna took her chance and charged through, unnoticed.

Now she could see that Simeon was trapped, and could not evade the continuous fire indefinitely. She fired from the rear, causing confusion in the warrior ranks.

Some turned to return fire, pulled up short as they realised they had no direction in which to aim. Others kept firing at the building.

It was enough. Simeon, invisible, was able to pick his way through the gaps in the ranks. His only problem now was how to find Jenna. He yelled at her to move out and took off to his right, heading for a side street. He kept running until he was out of view of the warriors, who were still firing at empty air in each direction, then briefly cancelled his charm, giving her a chance to locate him. He would be picked up on surveillance imagers, but hopefully only for a fraction of a second.

Jenna suddenly appeared in front of Simeon, running into him. He held her as she hit against him, realising that he would now be in her charm field and so safe from surveillance.

"Why...why am I doing this?" she breathed at him. "I hate you! Gods, I'm scared."

"Because we have no choice. Because it's the right thing. Because we can't stop now..."

"We might have to."

He frowned, looking over her shoulder to where the random firing was still occurring. "We'd better keep moving, they'll catch on we're not there before too long." He started to move off, taking her arm. Then it struck him. "Why might we have to stop?"

"Do you know where the Varn Institute is from here?"

# CHAPTER FIFTEEN

## Year Zero – Period Three

A feeling of exhilaration swept over Simeon as he and Jenna searched the streets. The invisibility charm allowed them to move freely, and they were able to catch the wave of disbelief that swept through the people of Ilvarn and revel in it. Ordinary citizens were emerging from the buildings, murmuring discontent at the events. From the tenor of the snatched conversations they heard, they were able to determine that the people of the capital were as ignorant of the presence of the Bethel Mage in their midst as was the rest of the globe. Rather, many of them launched into ill-considered diatribes against their own government and military, questioning both competency and parentage.

This was most instructive. It told Simeon that the people of Varn were about as ready for war as anyone else on the planet. It told him that the reasons behind the fighting at the military building were either being suppressed, or had not been released to the public.

Either way, it gave them some time. A hostile and mobilised populace would make their task that much harder. Assuming, that was, they could find the Institute.

Another advantage of an invisibility charm was the ability to move amongst the people and listen in on their conversations. Strangers would not be able to elicit information with direct questions, but invisible strangers could glean useful information from scraps of half-heard chatter.

It was a roundabout way of doing things, but given the

lack of options, and the small size of the capital, it was fairly simple for Jenna to lead the two of them to within sight of the Institute.

Now the sense of exhilaration passed, and the reality of the situation hit home. Simeon realised that he had been on a high because the initial break-out had been much more simple than he had feared. It gave him a sense of confidence in his abilities that was, perhaps, far from warranted.

Breaking through a defence force that could not see you, that was taken by surprise and did not know where to direct their fire was one thing....

This was another.

"Oh..." Jenna mouthed simply. A syllable that said more than any curse.

The walls of the Institute were manned by battalions of warrior security, with a fair sprinkling of troops. The latter were distinguishable from those who served in the capital by the scars they bore and the battered condition of weapons that were no longer deployed for war, but had been kept as favoured tools.

On the one wall that they could see, a head-count elicited thirty-four warriors forming a security cordon. Could it be assumed that there would be a roughly equal number on the other walls?

So, about seventy-to-one, then.

Simeon had to hand it to Varn, that was a quick and efficient deployment. His confidence sank even more. Jenna noticed his discomfort.

"Sim, we've come this far. We can't stop now. Look, we're invisible, we can find a way past them, just like we did back there," she gestured in what she assumed to be the direction from which they had originated. "All we have to do is think it through. I could get us over there with a holoship, and..."

Simeon stayed her with a gesture. "Not that easy, Jen. This is the Institute. You think that they won't be able to see through our simple charms? You think they won't be able to see a holoship? Even the lowest adepts have more power than we do."

As soon as he said it, he realised what the answer must be. He could only hope that Avathon was as good as his word.


Vixel was less than happy when he heard what had happened. In fact, the words incandescent rage would not even suffice. His bodyguard had delivered the news to him, something he was less than happy to be doing.

"You people are morons!" the Mage shouted. "Two people, one of them the escapee from Bethel, manage to penetrate our capital and break through the supposed cream of our warrior forces? Are you people even worth my time?" The bodyguard wisely said nothing, allowing his charge to calm down. Finally, Vixel spoke again.

"Very well. Gather the wizards and adepts. I shall address them." He held up his hand as the bodyguard made to speak. "Don't tell me that your fellows are massed outside and can deal with this. In the first place, I know they are there. In the second, I would not even trust them with the care of a dog!" His voice rose again, and he caught himself. "Go. Do it. Then bring Bey to me."

Vixel calmed himself while his bodyguard rushed to complete his tasks. He knew the wizards and adepts would be waiting, but first he must deal with his rival Mage. It did not improve his temper when Ramus-Bey was brought to him with a sly grin painting his wizened features.

"So," the Varn Mage began, keeping his tone even, "you have either been told, or have guessed."

"It isn't difficult. Varnians running about like headless chickens, a whiff of magic in the air. There is an attempt afoot to rescue me. Surely you must have expected this?"

Vixel was taken aback. "No. Of course not. Did you not listen to anything I said to you?"

"I had faith in the goodness of one man," Ramus replied.

Vixel sighed. "Anyone else, and I wouldn't credit such a statement. But from you... very well, you old fool, you were right. Somehow your idiot bodyguard has escaped his own people, reached Ilvarn and is most likely on his way here. It says little for our conventional forces that they have so far failed to halt him. However, I feel this is a good opportunity to demonstrate to the Chief Minister that the time has come to put magic over conventional weapons. Where the might of the warriors have failed, a few adepts shall triumph. We shall have sport with this man before we kill him."

Ramus-Bey's eyes blazed. "You shall do no such thing! I shall..."

"You shall do nothing!" Vixel barked. "If you seek to use your powers, then I shall counter them with mine. And," he added with a mocking grin, "we really don't want that, do we?"

The old man was returned to his cell and Vixel went to counsel his wizards and adepts.

"This fool Simeon 7 believes that we have Ramus-Bey here. Such a charge is ludicrous, and as fine an example of delusion as I have ever heard. He will stop at nothing to attain the inner sanctum of the Institute. He must not pass."

He continued to outline his strategy.

Like the rest of the population of Varn, those at the Institute had no knowledge that Ramus-Bey was in their midst.

As Vixel briefed his wizards and adepts so, on another continent, a similar conference was taking place. Avathon and his senior staff wizards had been monitoring the progress of Simeon and Jenna. They had seen, as if through Simeon's eyes, the situation around the Varn Institute. They had felt his sinking confidence, and had echoed it with their own empathic despair.

They knew it was time for them to act. Their powers would be greatly reduced at this distance, but if they could strike first they could pre-empt the Varn magic.

Avathon delivered a rallying call to his people. It was simple in essence: their magic would form a bridgehead, allowing Simeon and Jenna to strike with a more physical means.

Vixel believed solely in magic. He was an arrogant Mage.

Avathon believed in the realm of the magical *and* that of the physical co-existing. He was of a more humble mien.

Although neither was aware of the other's stance, their actions would be about more than the fight for one man.

Simeon's plan was simple. It was a reasonable working assumption that only the bodyguard for the Varn Mage, or anyone who was in charge of day-to-day security and surveillance at the Institute, would know the regular security checks and routines. Any warrior security drafted in without prior briefing would be at a disadvantage. Certainly, for the purposes of this mission he would assume that the warrior security stationed around the walls of the Institute would not have a similar knowledge. They would have no idea who was, or was not, a regular caller at the Institute. Routine deliveries, the everyday: these would be unknown to them, and they would, hopefully, be too distracted to stop and check.

First thing to do was to take a delivery vehicle. The first one to hand would do. All the better if it was a laundry vehicle, as then they would be spared the second task, which would be to find some Varnian clothes with which to blend in.

Of course, they weren't that lucky. They found a deserted grocery vehicle, left by its driver for some unknown reason in a side street. That was luck enough to begin with, Simeon supposed. It would be simple to by-pass the ignition codes and start the electron-drive that powered the vehicle. In such functional vehicles as these, codes were simple, as was the circuitry that powered them. If he didn't get it one way, then he could another.

That was the theory. As Simeon sweated over the codes, he wondered if it had been such a great idea. The doors of the vehicle had been left unlocked, which suggested that the owner did not plan to be long absent. Also there was every chance that the vehicle had an alarm, and a wrongly entered code – or an attempt to by-pass the system – would court disaster.

"Hurry up," Jenna murmured as she watched yet another passer-by crossing the end of the street. Each time someone came into view her heart leapt into her throat. She knew that the vehicle's driver would not know they were there until he tried to enter the vehicle, and so would be easy to overpower. But if there was even a chance that he or she could, in their surprise, raise an alarm...

Her tension was getting to Simeon. He abandoned any attempt to crack the coding, and went straight for the heart of the matter.

Getting the cover from the tech unit under the steering column should have been easy, but under her gaze he was fumbling. Beneath were the strands of fibre-optic that linked the drive to the entry-code pad. Pull the wrong one, and any alarm fitted would blare out. Pull the wrong one and the entire system could die, leaving them without the transport necessary for his plan to succeed.

Jenna grabbed his arm as he was about to separate the fibre-optic strands. He cursed to himself as he only just managed to control the muscle twitch that would have rendered the strands asunder all too soon.

He followed her gaze. Another passer-by: this one turned down the side street, paused, then entered a dwelling at the top of the road.

"Don't do that again," he muttered through gritted teeth. "Let me concentrate... just a second more."

He held his breath as he snapped the fibre-optic, waiting for the deafening blare of an alarm that did not sound. Instead, the engine purred into life.

He breathed out and wiped his brow. "Now stay here and don't let anyone else come along and steal this bastard... even its rightful owner," he whispered before slipping out to complete the next stage of his plan.

So Jenna stayed watch, to ensure that the driver did not return and take their transport. It would be simple to disable him.

It took Simeon longer to procure clothes for them than it had to crack the ignition code. Any other time, and the use of an invisibility charm to revisit childhood days of stealing washing as a prank would have had a certain sentimental allure. Now, it was just another nerve-wracking inconvenience.

On his return they dressed quickly in the brightly coloured Varnian clothes. Loose and flowing, they were able to put them on over their own, tighter, clothes, and were thus spared the problem of concealment. The last thing they would want to give them away were discarded uniforms.

It was not until they were within sight of the Institute that Jenna voiced her qualms, spurred to speech by the sight of the cordon of warriors.

"Are you sure this will work?" she asked.

"If you want the truth, I think it may be one of the worst ideas I've ever had. But it's the only one I can come up with right now. How's your Varnian dialect?"

"Poor. What about you?"

"Not bad. One good thing about being captured on a raid, you get to learn the native tongue."

They approached the gates of the Institute. One of the warriors ringing the perimeter detached himself and approached them.

Simeon stuck his head out of the vehicle window.

"What's this crap about, then?"

"Classified, citizen, can't tell you that. Can only tell you to turn back. No-one is allowed through."

"You're joking with me, right?" Simeon asked affably. "You got any idea how much shit I'm gonna be in if I don't deliver? Those weird guys in there start to moan 'cause they don't get their goodies – and I don't just mean the victuals, right?" He added in an undertone, nudging the warrior and indicating Jenna. "Like a little sweetmeat for the eyes right?"

The warrior eyed Jenna and grinned salaciously. "I get your meaning."

"C'mon, friend, I'm delivering wines, meats and dried fruits. Do I look like a danger to you? Ask the main man in there, he knows I'm due," he added. It was a massive risk but Simeon could only assume, based on his own experiences, that the bodyguard would be too preoccupied to be bothered.

The warrior screwed up his face. Thinking clearly didn't come easy.

"Okay... but only because she's so sweet," he added, winking at Jenna. She simpered, feeling like she wanted to throw up.

They passed through into the grounds, the warrior now behind them and explaining to another warrior, who had arrived late on the scene. Simeon accelerated towards the castle as much as he dare without drawing attention, hoping to put as much ground as possible between the vehicle and the cordon. It wasn't going to be long before the guard's ardour broke and he would remember that he was supposed to be on the lookout for a male and female stranger.

The vehicle shuddered as the rear end was ripped apart by blaster fire. The pulse of energy knocked out the vehicle's drive. Simeon yelled at Jenna to follow, and jumped from the vehicle before it had stopped moving. They were off like a Tallus at the gambling meets, searching for cover before the first shots reached them.

In the Varn Institute, the wizards and adepts prepared to flex their magic. Conventional forces had already fallen down because of their stupidity. It was time for the real power to take over and squash this bug of a problem.

On another continent, Avathon knew it was time. His people could feel the pounding adrenaline and fear of Simeon 7, could see the conventional forces flounder in his wake. It had not been a good plan, but it had bought just enough time to get them in. If Avathon was in the Varn Institute, he knew that he would choose this as the time to start a magical attack. Therefore, it was time begin the counter attack.


"Sim, what..." Jenna was unable to complete the question, already short of breath as she followed Simeon on his winding path through the fortress.

Around them, bizarre things were occurring. Thought creatures were forming and then dissipating in whorls of light shot through with black. Energy fields flickered and died before springing up again to meet counter-fields that crackled with hissing, spitting opposition. The ground beneath them moved as it was churned up by the rumbling forces of magical warfare. The turf beneath their feet became a moving carpet of wildlife, fleeing in blind panic and finding new threat with each direction.

But if their progress had been slowed, at least they were within the circle formed by the magical attack and counter-attack. Inadvertently, this had done little more than form a barrier that prevented the warrior forces from following the intruders.

"It's Avathon and the others I knew they were as good as their word," Simeon yelled. "You precious jewel," he screamed at the air, knowing that the wizard would feel the meaning.

They were within sight of the main doors of the keep. Imposing, thick wooden constructions that would require more than blaster fire to penetrate them. Thought creatures guarded them and, as they drew near, the amorphous creatures drifted from the doors, forming into huge scaled beasts with sharp talons and razor teeth in horned beaks.

There was no way that the energy from a blaster could overload them, even presuming that they would be able to get close enough without being ripped to shreds.

*If ever I needed you, Avathon, its now,* Simeon screamed mentally.

The wizard and his team did not let him down. Smaller thought creatures, of similar type, formed behind Simeon and Jenna, and moved to engage the Varn defences. These Bethelian magic forms were weaker because of the distance from which they were cast, but they were not designed to defeat their foe. They were there to create a distraction and allow time for Simeon and Jenna to slip through.

Simeon could not believe their luck as the castle doors began to swing open. However, as he saw the opponent waiting for him within, he figured that it was just what he should have expected. It was his opposite number, the bodyguard of Vixel.

"So you're the one who's causing all the trouble," the bodyguard said. His voice was soft and low, yet seemed to cut through the noise around them. "Wouldn't think it to look at you, but you've been resourceful so far. Pity it has to end." He looked Simeon up and down. "I believe in fair combat. I have weaponry, you have nothing. Will you come hand-to-hand?"

It crossed Simeon's mind that the bodyguard – armed as he was with a blaster and mini-cannon strapped across his shoulders – had not seen Simeon's own weapon. For one moment, he considered it... but duplicity was not his style, and when all was said and done the bodyguard was approaching him as a fellow warrior, regardless of allegiance.

Simeon assented, and gestured for Jenna to stay back. He unholstered his blaster and put it on the floor as the bodyguard did likewise. He waited while Simeon divested himself of the Varn garments he had stolen, until he was down to his battlesuit.

The two men stood opposite each other, a few lengths apart. They nodded to each other – a courtesy – and then crouched, circling and waiting for the first move.

For Jenna, it was a bizarre moment. In the midst of the chaos, the two men exuded an aura of complete calm. They were completely within the moment, focused on their imminent combat. The crackling, charged energy of the magical atmosphere did not penetrate their consciousness. Neither did the baying of the warriors beyond the wall of charms, desperate to gain access.

Whatever happened next, Jenna reasoned that it had better happen soon. The long-distance magic of the Bethel Institute was starting to wane, and the Varn magic was beginning to win by sheer strength.

Oblivious, the two warriors circled each other.

Simeon feinted, drawing a retort from his opponent. It opened up the left side of the warrior's body. A swift kick, high on the ribs, scored first blood as the heavy combat boot ripped at muscle and tendon. The bodyguard grunted, twisted away to lessen the impact. Simeon followed up, but was too slow. The bodyguard countered with a roundhouse punch that caught Simeon on the side of the head, stunning him. His balance wavered, and his opponent followed the advantage by driving Simeon to the ground, bringing his weight down on Simeon's chest.

Lights exploded before Simeon's eyes as he felt his lungs constrict. Through them he could see his opponent lift his hands above his head, doubled as a club.

The bodyguard sat high on Simeon's body, leaving his legs free. As the man leaned back to gain the optimum swing so Simeon, with what little energy he had left, brought his knees up sharply. They caught the bodyguard on the small of the back. It was enough to break his momentum and unbalance him.

Simeon scrambled to his feet fractionally ahead of his opponent. He took a wild kick, unable to balance and aim at the same time as air still raced into his aching lungs. The kick was either a good or a lucky one. It caught the bodyguard on the right temple. His eyes rolled up into his head, and he folded like a card player with a bad hand.

Simeon had proved himself, finally, in combat, yet was still too dazed to appreciate it. He tried to shake his head to clear it, but only succeeded in making everything spin.

Jenna was at his side to stop him falling. Anxiously she looked over her shoulder as the Varn magic began to gain ascendancy. Then she looked at Simeon. She promised herself that she'd never compare him to one of her pets again. But if they didn't move, she'd never have the chance to put that promise into action.

"Sim, come on," she urged, leading him further into the keep. He followed, regaining himself with every step by force of will. Now they were here, what was next? Where, in the name of the Gods, was Ramus-Bey? How would they find him?

They stumbled through the vast, echoing stone of the vestibule, and through a set of double doors of lesser thickness and height than those to the outside. What they saw stopped them dead. Before them were the wizards and adepts of the Varn Institute, each absorbed in their own internal worlds. Their hands moved in complex patterns, pirouettes of design that effected charms. Each was looking inwards yet watching the world outside, winning the battle against the Bethelian wizards.

"Wrong room," Jenna muttered, backing up and pulling the still dazed Simeon with her. Or rather, she would have backed up if some unknown force had not rooted her to the spot. She stared ahead at the wizard responsible. He smiled grimly, as was about to make a pass that she could only assume would deal with them permanently when he froze, staring behind her.

Vixel had entered. It was as though he had materialised from nowhere, though in truth he had probably just walked in without her hearing him. She found herself released from the magical bonds. Simeon, too, as she felt him slump against her.

"You've done very well, I will grant you that," Vixel said. "Perhaps it says more about our own forces than it does you. Just for that, I cannot have you terminated just yet. Oh no, that must be in public view. To prove our point."

"That we cannot be subjected to unwarranted attack," affirmed the wizard who had come close to snuffing them out, with some triumph in his voice.

"Unwarranted? I came to get Ramus-Bey back!" Simeon shouted.

"We don't have him, you of all people should know that," the wizard snapped in reply. "It was your people that sought to throw blame upon us and stir up war again!"

"You cretin! You think I would do all this for no reason

other than to throw blame on you?" Simeon hissed, wincing at the pain that was starting to throb through him. He realised that there were some positive points to being hit so hard that you were numbed. Nonetheless, he attempted to focus. "My government seeks to blame me for their own ends. What your government wants is none of my concern. I just want to put things right."

"But he is not here," the wizard insisted. "We are only defending ourselves from attack."

"If he is not here, then why has our own magic traced him here?" Simeon insisted.

"Because..."

"Because I am here!" Ramus-Bey said.

Vixel turned, furious at the way things were going. His best-laid plans were coming apart and mostly because this old fool wouldn't do as he was told.

"What are you doing? I told you..."

"I should always do what you wish?" Ramus-Bey answered mildly. "It would seem churlish not to come and meet those who would seek to save me."

The Bethel Mage strode past Vixel, and laid hands on Simeon. The exhausted, injured man would have expected a surge of light within him. Instead he got a feeble pulse. It was, for him, a confirmation of something he had feared. Which made what happened next less than re-assuring.

"You did not know I was here?" Ramus asked of the assembled Varn wizards and adepts. Their astonished expressions gave him answer. "You will not object, then, to my leaving with this man and this woman?"

"You will do no such thing..." Vixel began, but was cut short by the uproar from his staff. In the confusion, they had let their magic cease, and the warrior hordes could be heard approaching. A few passes from one wizard, and once more these men were held at bay, if for a different reason.

"We shall do nothing more to help you, Vixel," this wizard said. "I believe I speak for all when I say that this is not why we study. We do not wish to sink to this level. We are appalled at our Mage doing likewise. We are ashamed to realise what we have become entangled in."

"You utter imbeciles! You do not understand..." Vixel turned to Ramus-Bey, Simeon and Jenna. "I shall not permit you to leave. I have the power!"

"You forget, it seems, that I too am a Mage," Bey interrupted. "Do you really want to match your power against mine? Especially when I find your 'impenetrable' cell so easy to negotiate"

Vixel laughed. "You old fool. You really want me to say what I think of your abilities?"

Ramus-Bey fixed him with an ice-cold stare, perfected over many years of card play during the long winter evenings at the Institute.

"Do you really want to put it to the test?"

He held Vixel's stare. He believed he knew the nature of people well enough to judge that the Varn Mage was an arrogant man whose arrogance was built on cowardice. Would he take a risk on an uncertainty?

"Very well, do as you must," Vixel spat. "It does not matter if I do not use magic, or if none of these fools do. You shall never get back to Bethel without being stopped by the military. I shall be surprised if you get as far as the gates before you are wiped from the face of Inan."

Vixel turned his back on them and stalked out of the hall. The wizards and adepts seemed at a loss, not knowing what to do now that their Mage had shown himself to be unworthy. For them, this was deeper than the immediate future of one Mage. It was their whole calling that was being brought into question.

They were not the only ones who were unsure of their next move. Ramus-Bey, Simeon and Jenna stood apart from the Institute staff, feeling safe in their presence, but as yet unsure which path to take when the time came to take their leave.

# CHAPTER SIXTEEN

## Year Zero – Period Three

There was a phrase that rose into Simeon's mind. Something he had read long ago in one of his story pamphlets. It went something like: "it was the best of all possible times, yet paradoxically the very worst, if such a thing be possible in itself." A wordy phrase, perhaps understandable as he had heard that the writers of such pamphlets were paid by the word, but one that he could pare down easily. He had wanted to write such pamphlets at one time. A simple enough ambition, scuppered by his inability to think with any originality. So he had become a warrior, like his father before him, and look where that had got him.

It was strange how such seemingly unconnected thoughts went through his head as he stood in the hall of the Varn Institute. Yet they did, in their own way, make sense. In the first instance, it was both the best and worst of times as he had found Ramus-Bey, and the old man was alive and well. Yet, he had located him deep in the heart of enemy territory, and was now surrounded by more Varnian warriors than he would care to consider, kept at bay only by the good auspices of wizards who objected to their own nation state's actions. Simeon's lack of originality when it came to ideas had manifested itself all too well with his arrival in Varn and his entry to the Institute. Neither had been achieved with much subtlety.

Let's face it, he thought, if I had any ideas about getting out of here, then I wouldn't be standing around thinking about how I'm standing around thinking...

Time for some kind of action. He turned to the wizard who had led the revolt against Vixel.

"Sir, I am honoured by your action, and in your debt. Your decision to opt out of this fight has been of great assistance to us, and yet..."

"You are stranded," the wizard finished with a wry grin. "You realise that we cannot help you, of course. We may not wish to assist he who was our Mage," Simeon couldn't help but exchange a glance with Ramus-Bey at this indication that things would radically change in Varn, "but at the same time we do not wish, in all conscience, to assist those who are against our nation state."

"I understand this," Simeon replied, choosing his words with care, "yet you must surely be able to see that we are in a position that is considerably less than of our own making. We did not wish to be in the middle of a foreign nation state, making a kind of war with its forces. We are only here because of the actions of others. I would not ask you to act against your own nation state, merely to consider the difficulties of our position. We seek to gain exit without conflict. Surely..."

He let the question remain unspoken. The Varn wizard's brow puckered in a frown as he considered this. Finally, after what seemed like an age, he spoke.

"You are correct. I... we..." he added, gesturing to the wizards and adepts who had been waiting in silence for his decision "...cannot in all conscience go against you for what you have done. I would only hope that, if we had a Mage worthy of such, we would also have a warrior with the fortitude and courage to do as you have. But such fine words are of no assistance to you. No – action of some kind is called for, even if it be the action of non-action."

Simeon and Jenna exchanged a puzzled look. It

sounded good so far, but neither of them understood what constituted 'the action of non-action'. They were about to be enlightened.

The wizard continued: "At present, we are still keeping a magical barrier around the Institute, which prevents our warriors from gaining access. We must remove this. But," he raised a hand to forestall any protest, "at the same time this does not mean that we will raise any magical barriers to impede your exit, nor will we use our magic to follow you. That shall be entirely down to the military, and more physical means."

"You need say no more. We are indebted to you for your even-handed actions. If we fail to make it out of Ilvarn, then we shall know it is not by your hand. We could not ask for more." Simeon said.

Then the two men exchanged formal bows. An old, courtly gesture from another time, it was something rarely considered in this new age and yet, as she watched them, Jenna could not help but consider that this was an entirely appropriate gesture.

"Now go, and may the Gods assist the just," the wizard said after a moment's silence.

The first stage of the escape plan – although to dignify it with such a term was questionable – was simple enough. Knowing that no magic would stand in their way, a simple invisibility charm enabled Simeon, Jenna and Ramus-Bey to evade and pass through the Varnian warrior ranks that were now released from their own charm. Not that avoiding them was easy. It was a force large in numbers, fired up by the fury and humiliation of being bested by two people, and intent on bringing matters to a swift conclusion.

A large party entered the Institute, to be met by a body

of wizards and adepts who were silent on all matters of question. It was only a matter of time before Vixel descended from his attitude of high dudgeon. When this happened, then there was no guarantee that they could continue to use the charm. With the courage of not having to look Bey in the eye, he may opt to use his powers.

So it was essential to get past this group of warriors. Out into the grounds, and the extent of their problem became apparent. The longer it had taken the Varn military to gain access, the more men they had poured into the operation, in hopes of breaking through. There were parties of warriors searching the grounds, and a cordon flung around the gates which, Simeon could only assume, would stretch beyond sight and around the walls of the Institute.

Instructing them to move quickly, stay together and follow his lead Simeon led them through the maze of warriors, and when they reached the gates he stayed them with a gesture before moving into his own invisibility field, recce'ing the forward position.

A vehicle was approaching, carrying representatives from the Ministry, presumably to speak to Vixel, and this gave the fugitives an unexpected break. Simeon considered that his planning may be poor, but so far his luck was holding.

He returned to where Jenna and Ramus were waiting. Whispering, he directed them to follow and wait for the guard to part in order to allow the vehicle access.

They hurried to the gates, barely reaching them in time to take advantage of the temporary parting of the cordon. Moving so close to the vehicle as it passed that they could hear the heated voices of the Ministry officials within, they were past the cordon before it had time to regroup.

Now they were out of the immediate danger zone. But, in truth, the danger was only just beginning.

Once outside things changed. As soon as it was known that they could have used magic to escape, there was every chance they could be tracked. Simeon had every faith in the intentions of the Institute, but no faith in either the disgraced Mage or the resolution of any adept when threatened. The attitude of the Varn Institute staff had made their cowed acquiescence to established order clear: they had momentarily stood up for their principles. But how long could Simeon rely on that being sustained?

It was time to make a switch. They must now use disguise and physical means to escape from Ilvarn.

For Jenna, this was simplified by the fact that she still wore the Varnian raiments they had taken to help gain access to the Institute. But Simeon had divested himself of these in order to fight with Vixel's bodyguard. Bey still wore the clothes in which he had been taken.

The first task was to get some appropriate disguises. Jenna, as the one who was already disguised, was despatched to steal some suitable attire.

While she was gone the two men conversed in hushed tones.

"I appreciate your actions, but I fail to see how you plan to get us out of here," Bey said.

Simeon grinned mirthlessly. "That makes two of us. We could get Jenna to cast a holoship and fly us home under the surveillance tech. It may take some time, but..."

"But they must now know that's how you got here," Bey finished.

"Right. I didn't think that one through. Conventional tech wouldn't see us, but all they'd have to do is launch their own holoship fleet, and then those bastards can track and engage."

"Correct. So what are we to do?"

Simeon looked the old man up and down. "You're the Mage. You can destroy us with a raise of the eyebrows, right? That's what you said once. So, in theory, one wink and we won't be here, we'll be back in Belthan." He paused, waiting for a response that didn't come. Eventually: "So is there something that you want to tell me?"

"Such as?"

"Such as you've lost the ability to cast charms and you've been hiding it? I felt hardly any power off of you when you touched me in the castle."

Ramus-Bey grimaced. "I wish I could say to you that it was as simple as knowing or not knowing, but it isn't. I have, for some time, been in turmoil over this. The problem is that it becomes a contentious matter to resolve. While I was studying, I refrained from practice above a certain level because I did not believe that the wielding of such force was becoming with the spiritual path that was the true purpose of such learning. Yet this was not without cost. Without practice, I had no way to test the power that I was supposedly accumulating. How strong was it? How could I control it? Was there, in fact, anything there? I had no way of knowing without flexing that power. What if I could not control it?"

Suddenly, Simeon could see what had happened. Bey was unwilling to attempt to use his power for fear that he would either be unable to reign in that which he released, or that he would find nothing there, and his studies would have been for nothing.

"This is not the time for us to take risks," Simeon said decisively. "We shall use physical means. Magic would be too easily tracked."

It was obvious to both men that he was saying this to appease Ramus-Bey, but both could acknowledge that this was a necessity if they were to move. To become embroiled in a great philosophic debate at this moment would be at best pointless, at worst an open invitation to be captured.

The sooner Jenna returned, the better.

While the two men talked, Jenna ventured into the heart of Ilvarn. She could feel her stomach turn over with a mix of excitement and fear with each step. She couldn't help feeling that the Gods had been smiling upon them, as by rights they should not have been able to escape the castle with such ease. Even if she could snatch some clothes for the two men, it seemed to her that without a plan of some kind, they were doomed to capture.

The streets of Ilvarn were awash in colour, teeming with people who were either trying to make their way into the cordoned off area around the Institute to see what was going on, or trying to go about their everyday business regardless of what was occurring. While this made it easy for Jenna to hide herself in the crowds, it also decreased the chances of being able to steal without being seen. Jenna wandered in the alien crowds, jostled by those who moved around her. She needed to be swift, but was hindered by having no knowledge of the locale. She needed to steal clothes for two men. One set to fit a tall, muscular man, the other to fit a wizened old man.

It was then, watching the crowds move about her, that inspiration struck. She noticed that many of the older women wore veiled headdresses to shield them against the sun that beat down. If she could take old women's clothes for the Mage, then who would suspect two

Varnians taking their aged female relative for a stroll?

It wasn't the greatest plan ever hatched, but it would have to do. With a renewed enthusiasm, she went about her task.

As she did, keeping an eye out for any opportunity, she pondered their situation. A holoship was out of the question. It would be too slow, given that word of their escape would soon spread – perhaps already had – and would escalate the war footing between Varn and Bethel. Moreover, just as Simeon and Bay had reasoned, she knew that the *Peta* would be easily tracked by other holoships.

By foot and by vehicle. That was the only way. But as yet she hadn't managed to work it out beyond that. She hoped to the Gods that Simeon had made better progress.

It was then that the opportunity presented itself, so suddenly that she almost missed it.

A clothing store. A delivery vehicle with the rear doors left open, the driver occupied in transferring stock from the rear to the store. A jostling crowd against which he had to push. With the heaving throng moving against him it was an almost impossible task, particularly when a small, furry pet on a leash tangled itself around his legs, causing him to tread on the tail and solicit a yelp. Add an outraged owner trying to hit him, and the stuff of domestic comedy becomes written on the streets.

Back home, she would have stopped and laughed along with the others, maybe joined those who tried to intervene as the situation turned rapidly into a melee, but here she was in a foreign land, and she had work to do.

Nervously glancing around her, she rummaged on the racks in the back of the vehicle, where clothes were hanging, bagged and ready for delivery. She found the old woman's costume easily enough, hanging near the doors. To find male clothing, she had to risk stepping up into the vehicle itself. How she would deal with discovery she had no idea. She preferred not to think of it. She cast a glance around as she stepped in, hoping she had not been spotted.

Inside, the vehicle smelt of chemical dyes and cleaning agents. It was dark, and the metal had absorbed the heat of the day, making it a sweat box. The women's clothes she clutched were clammy in her hand. With her heart racing and sweat pouring into her eyes, she raced through the clothes, searching for something that seemed to be the right size. After what seemed an age, she found something and snatched it from the rack, balling it up with the women's clothing as small as she could.

Taking a careful look out of the back of the vehicle, she could see that while it seemed an age to her, it was actually no time at all. The furore outside had still not resolved itself and she was able to leave the vehicle and slip away without being noticed.

"This is really too much! I fail to see how disguising myself as a woman will do any good whatsoever," Bey complained as he pulled on the headdress and secured the veil so that only his eyes were showing.

"Save it!" Simeon said shortly. "First thing we need to do is steal ourselves a vehicle and head out of Ilvarn."

"They'll be expecting us to do that," Jenna said

"Look, we need to get out of Ilvarn fast, and Ramus is an old man who can't walk that far or that fast. I figure we have more options if we can get into the mountains. There are more places to hide."

His tone would brook no argument, and in truth, she could think of nothing better in the short term. So, the three of them suitably disguised cast off the charm and became visible once more. They headed up the alleyway.

"Take his arm like he's your mother," Simeon whispered, "and leave any talking to me."

The streets were no longer the bustling thoroughfares that Jenna had experienced a short while before. The crowds were thinning out as the day slid into evening and there were armed warriors patrolling the streets. Bey leaned into Jenna, as though he were frail, and Simeon stayed one pace ahead of them, as he had noticed was the norm.

He still had only the vaguest notion of where they were in the capital, but figured that as soon as he could steal a vehicle, he had a strong enough grasp of the local dialect to use road directions to get them out. He had a notion to try and take a battlecruiser, if he could work out how to break into a base. Either that or go for the long haul and the coast, maybe steal a boat and try to reach neutral territory.

The easiest thing would be to head for the Bethel embassy. But there were too many factors militating against this. It would be closely watched by the Varn military and there was the strong possibility that their presence would not be desired by certain elements within their own ministry.

Come to that, reaching home would only be half the battle. How would they be greeted? What exactly was the attitude of the Chief Minister to them right now?

One thing at a time. Get out of Ilvarn.

Simeon was careful to take them on a route that avoided the possibility of accidentally doubling back. Despite the disguise, he did not look like a native of Varn, and Ramus was hardly a typical old woman. Already, they had attracted some curious second glances from passers by. Luckily, they had not yet been challenged, but he had no wish to ride his luck too far.

They found a domestic vehicle after too long wandering around. Bey's pace had slowed, and the old man was obviously becoming exhausted. Tighter security had made it harder to find open vehicles. On those few occasions when he had come close, Simeon had been dissuaded at the last by the appearance of warrior patrols in the streets.

It was a small vehicle, but just large enough for the three of them. The power levels were low, but enough to get them out of the city if he was careful. He jumped the ignition code and drew away slowly, hoping that the owner would not grace them with their presence.

"I hope you can read these signs as well as you assume," Ramus-Bey muttered from the back of the vehicle. "For if we have to get out and make a run for it, then I fear you will have to leave me behind."

"After coming all this way to get you? Not a chance," Simeon replied. "Anyway, I came top of the course when we did basic Varnian dialects in training."

But what the old had man said did give him cause for concern. To come this far and have to give up Bey would make a mockery of their efforts. Yet, unless he could come up with a plan – any plan – that extended beyond getting out into the mountains, they would like as kill the Mage from exhaustion as be able to carry him back to Bethel.

Simeon did everything he could to make them as inconspicuous as possible. He took an indirect route onto the highway leading out of the city, keeping his speed low and being particularly attentive to the etiquette of the road. He wanted nothing to occur that could attract the attentions of the warrior patrols.

Finally, after a nerve-jangling trip around the outer edges of Ilvarn, he headed for the turn-off that would take them up into the mountains. Along the way, he had taken note of the number of checkpoints and the way in which they operated.

There were three main highways that led to the mountain roads. Each of these had a checkpoint at the turn-off. Each checkpoint was manned by a warrior, who would stop and search vehicles working on a pattern of every fourth vehicle. He had driven past his chosen turn-off at the beginning of their trip and had verified their practices by taking a ring-road detour to double and triple check. He was aware that it was using what little power he had in the vehicle, but what use would power be if they blundered into capture?

The fact that their system was so rigidly applied suggested to him that the checkpoint warriors had no idea what they were looking for. As long as they could remain inconspicuous, they would be safe.

As they approached the turn-off, he counted vehicles. There was one being checked, and three cars between theirs and the warrior patrol. It was an irony that the back-up caused by the checkpoint enabled him to allow another vehicle to slip into a gap he created, and thus replace them as the next to be pulled over.

"Jen, talk to me like we're having an argument," he said as the vehicle in front was pulled over. "No way will they want a domestic dispute on top of this."

It worked. They were waved through by a warrior who gave Simeon a look universally recognised as sympathy.

Once on the mountain road Simeon was able to, if not relax, then at least be a little less tense. There was a turn-off within a few poles for the city's civilian air terminal, and most of the traffic was headed there.

Within a short while, they were the only vehicle in sight on the highway. Simeon checked the power, which was running into the 'pulse alert' zone on the indicator dial.

"Time to bail," the warrior said softly, turning the vehicle onto the shoulder of the highway. It was fortunate that there was little lighting or surveillance tech on such isolated stretches. With luck, the vehicle would not be found for hours.

With the help of Simeon and Jenna, Ramus-Bey was able to negotiate the treacherously rocky terrain that began almost as soon as they were away from the road. Such were the steep crops of rock and the sparse vegetation that they were hidden from the highway within moments.

"I'm sorry... I fear that I am already almost done for," the Mage panted as Simeon set a strong pace.

"Don't worry, we won't go much further," Simeon replied. "I just want to find us some shelter for the night, somewhere we can rest."

"And what then?" Jenna questioned.

Simeon sucked in his breath. "That, Jen, is one of the things we've got to decide while we're resting."

Hopefully, he added to himself, while we're trying to work it out circumstance will overtake us, Gods alone know they have so far.

# CHAPTER SEVENTEEN

## Year Zero – Period Three

They found a small cave. Barely more than a recess in the rock. It tapered from an opening taller than Simeon to a point where it was necessary to scramble on their hands and knees to go further. Even then, the cave was barely the length of two men, and scarcely wider. Scant consolation that being pressed so close together preserved the warmth of their bodies, they dare not build a fire for fear of being seen. Already, in the distance, they could hear the low-level buzzing of reconnaissance craft, sent to scout the land around Ilvarn for any sign of them.

Ramus-Bey fell into an immediate and deep sleep. Jenna and Simeon stayed awake for some time, trying to formulate a plan. The only thing they could agree on was that they were both to be found wanting when it came to imaginative strategies.

"Your problem," Jenna yawned, "is that you're re-active, not pro-active. Ask you to do something and you sit there with your brain ticking so loudly I can hear it. But pitch you into a situation, and you come up with something."

"Your faith in me is touching," he muttered with more than a hint of sarcasm.

She touched his arm. "No, you don't get it do you? I can't even re-act. I don't know how. I don't have that warrior instinct that you do. Look, you've got us this far. I hate to tell you this, but I think it's up to you from here on."

They sat in silence. He didn't know what to say to

her. Simeon wasn't going to lie, yet at the same time he did not wish to take away her hope.

Eventually, she fell asleep, her gentle breathing contrasting with the rasp that emanated from the sleeping Mage. Simeon disentangled himself from her and crawled out of the mouth of the cave. The night sky was clear, and the chill winds that crawled through the mountains prickled at his skin. He was tired, but he could not sleep.

He looked over the terrain leading back to the highway. It would be surprising if their vehicle had not been discovered by now. If he was in command of the search, he would have spread it out beyond the city. They were safe for the moment though. The terrain was rough and rocky, with little to leave a trail for any tracker. But, given a little time, there would be something that anyone with experience of the terrain could pick up on. From there, finding them would be simple, and what did they have to defend themselves? Blasters with drained energy cells and an exhausted Mage who doubted his own powers.

He sighed. It didn't look good.

Up in the sky, distant stars battled for attention with the flickering lights of airships. There were many of them: far more than you would expect for a simple reconnaissance. Furthermore, they were in all sectors of the sky, rather than concentrated over Ilvarn. There was nothing stately about their intent. It took him some while before the import of their presence struggled through the fogged tiredness that was clouding his mind. When it did strike him, it was as though he had plunged into an icy pool.

The direction. The size.

There was more than one fleet up there. More than one nation state.

It looked like the peace was over.

# Belthan

Deep in the bowels of the Ministry building, Daliel waited for his pet minister to come to him.

On another level, in a chamber overlooking the busy streets of the capital, twelve men were gathered around a table. At the head stood the Chief Minister. The table was oval, made of a hardwood lacquered and varnished over generations to a blackened sheen. Legend had it that this was the very table over which the war had first been declared, half a millennium before. Certainly, it was the same table over which the formula for the peace had been studied and discussed.

Now it was the table over which war was, once again, to be declared, but not willingly.

Eleven men sat around the table, uneasy, none wishing to be the one who would break the silence and drive the Chief Minister to an even more apoplectic state.

"Well? Will no one tell me the truth?" The minister thundered, emphasising 'truth' with a slamming of his fist on the table.

Another queasy pause, broken eventually by the most junior minister present. He was tall and blonde, and as he spoke his mind drifted to the man waiting for him in another part of the building.

"Minister, it would be a reasonable assumption to work from that all we know could be false. Should I say, all we think we know..."

"Cretin! Ramus-Bey is gone. Simeon 7 is gone. We know this. Gods alive, man, we saw it with our own eyes!"

"That isn't what I meant, Minister. Those facts are evident. But from this we have extrapolated much that is little more than supposition. We do not know for certain that the Mage is in Varn, neither do we know for sure that that is where the man Simeon 7 has headed. We do not know that Varn was behind the attack on the Institute, neither have we been able to confirm or deny the existence of a plot within certain elements of our own ministry and military networks to make it seem as though Varn were behind these actions. In truth, we know very little for certain. And on this basis we are prepared to plunge Inan into another war?"

While he spoke, the minister sitting directly opposite, another junior, shook his head with increasing vehemence. As the last syllables hung heavy in the room, he rose to his feet.

"We are defenceless without the Mage. The parity between nation states is based on the presence of such a threat in each of those very states. We must act, before we are overrun. All other nation states recognise the significance of what has occurred, and have made tacit agreements to either stand down or to back us. After all, if Varn can strike at Bethel in such a manner, what is to prevent them doing the same to Kyas, or to Turith?"

The Chief Minister listened to the man, then gestured him to be seated.

"Gentlemen, there is truth in both arguments. Truth and sense. But while we thrash around in a puddle of muddy speculation, time passes. With each passing moment the danger to our nation state increases. Already we have been without our ultimate defence for too long. Our vulnerability increases with the day. Varn, for her own reasons, says nothing to either confirm or deny the accusations. This stalemate cannot be allowed to continue. The people clamour for action. They are right. Only action will tip the hand of the enemy.

"Ready the air fleet. We mount the attack as soon as possible. You have all the orders you need, gentlemen. Now leave me to consider all our fates."

The Chief Minister turned his back on the men at the table. He looked down on the streets below. Exchanging looks between them, realising that a decisive moment had been reached, the eleven ministers and junior ministers rose from the table and headed for their respective offices. From there, they had set procedures for such times. Procedures they thought they had seen an end of a short time before.

For one junior minister, there was a greater and more pressing concern. One that awaited him in his office.

# Ilvarn

The Chief Minister and Vixel were alone in the minister's chambers. Sumptuous hangings in richly dyed, thick fabrics covered the walls. They served more than a decorative purpose. Through them, little sound could bleed in or out of the chamber, and right now the Chief Minister valued the privacy this bought.

"You just let them go... you... just...let...them...go!" His fury mounting to a scream with every drawn out word, the Minister stalked the floor, pausing to turn and yell in Vixel's face. "What were you thinking man? You could have stopped them with ease."

Vixel, despite the humiliation and anger he felt at being talked to in such a manner – similar to one he would frequently use with his adepts – remained on the surface a picture of calm and composure. Only the glittering points of his eyes revealed any indication of his true feelings. When he spoke, his tone was as calm and wryly detached as ever.

"Of course I could have stopped them. Of course I could have locked horns with a fellow Mage. Of course I could have risked a magical battle in which neither would give ground, escalating the use of power until we succeeded only in reducing Inan to ashes. Of course I could have done that... but somehow, I didn't think that it would have been advisable."

"Don't try and be funny with me," the Minister hissed, coming up so close that the Mage could feel flecks of spittle hit him in the face. "You told me that he was a senile old fool."

Calmly, Vixel took out a kerchief and dabbed at his face. "And so he is. But that does not mean that I was willing to risk one last throw of the die so early in the proceedings. The military should have been able to deal with them. Their failure is the greater."

"What about your academy? Where were they when this was happening?" Again, the sarcastic hiss, the spittle in the face.

Vixel dabbed at his face once more. "We had what, in the interest of economy, I shall call a doctrinal dispute. I shall deal with them as appropriate. I should think that we have greater matters of import. With the fool Bey at large, and Bethel threatening war, I would have thought it politic to track him down and eliminate him as soon as possible."

The Minister was visibly shaken. "Kill him? But the idea was to show him off to the world, to reveal the plot within Bethel, to make ourselves the saviours of peace on Inan. This..."

"Is the only option left to us," Vixel interrupted. "The plan was based on Bey being useless. I think we can no longer take that chance. Besides, his presence here is known, and if not known then widely assumed and taken as fact. Circumstances have changed, can you not see that?"

The Minister turned away, mind racing. Such a course of action...

"You are right, of course... It... I..." he stammered, "yes... I must launch our air fleet and order a blanket ground search. But what it means..."

"It means nothing until it has taken its course. The only meaning will become clear after the event. The tide has flowed from us, and we must follow in its wake," Vixel murmured. Then, louder, "and one more thing, Minister."

"What?" the Minister replied with a distracted tone.

"If you ever spit in my face again, I shall destroy you. Remember who I am."

The Minister paused, but said nothing, only now was he beginning to realise the ramifications of dealing with such a man as Vixel.

# Belthan

Daliel sat, impassive, and listened with care to all that the junior minister had to say. How he felt that their plans had come to naught. How he felt that the best thing to do would be to cut their losses and run. How the coming of war would cover their tracks. With their adept now gone, and Bey in enemy hands, there was nowhere left for them to go.

"Gods alone know that I do not want war. The purpose

was to achieve our aim by bypassing such an event. But now that it is an inevitability, then we should use this to our advantage, shouldn't we?"

He gave Daliel a questioning, almost pleading look. The squat, scarred warrior sat impassive, saying nothing. After a pause he stood up and walked slowly to the wine decanter, pouring himself a glass of the two-tone liquid, drinking it down in one draught. All with little sign of urgency. Finally, he turned to the junior minister. When he spoke, it was in slow, measured tones, underscored with an edge of menace. His words were carefully chosen and enunciated, as though he were reining in his anger.

"Do you take me for a cretin? Are you deceived by the way that I look? War is now inevitable, but rather than mask our duplicity it will expose it. When Varn strike back, they will do so with more than conventional weapons. They will use the media to reveal how their plot ran parallel with one from within Bethel. An investigation will follow. Perhaps, if I can control this, then I can effect a solution that will be of some use to us. But even if I can do this, while Simeon and Bey remain alive, along with that harlot who is helping them, then there is danger to us.

"Do you think that they will keep silent if they are saved by our forces, or somehow manage to escape the Varn military? Of course they won't. Perhaps, if we are lucky, Varn will want to terminate them. Perhaps, though, we cannot afford to take that chance."

The junior minister gaped, slack-jawed. In his attempts to find a solution that would salvage their lives, if not their careers, he had taken care to make sure that no blame would come to be focused on them.

What Daliel was suggesting would render all this as dust in the wind. For the junior minister knew what such action would entail.

"You can't ask that of me. I would be found out, questions asked! It would lead directly to us."

The truth of his position hit him hard. If he did not act as Daliel wished, then there was a strong chance that his duplicity would be uncovered. If he did act as the Intel chief commanded, then his actions could not be more obviously signalled if he invited the newscast media into his office while he signed the order.

Daliel, seeing the way in which he had crushed the junior minister, smiled inwardly. He put his arm around the blonde man's shoulders, and guided him to his desk.

"Did you really think that we could let them live? Did you really think I would be fool enough to leave my back exposed, and not have contingencies? Yes, the order will come from you. But you will have been acting in good faith from information received. Our Intel tells us that Varn seeks to eliminate the Mage – whether it does or not is unimportant – and so the Chief Minister orders you to direct our forces to effect a termination on sight, hoping to blame it on Varn. You need not worry, you see, a memo will be planted in the system, copies 'accidentally' mailed to select other ministry personnel. There will be evidence enough to prove that you were only acting under the orders of a higher counsel. It is that counsel who will be held responsible. Of course he will deny it, but this whole affair has been badly handled from the public's point of view. Someone will have to pay, and why not a figurehead?"

Throughout this discourse, the junior minister's visage had been brightening as the import of Daliel's scheming was revealed to him. The Intel commander had found a way to apportion blame that was little short of genius. With one move, he had prevented their duplicity being revealed; eliminated a threat and cleared the way for them to continue their forging ahead towards power.

"Daliel, how could I have doubted you?" The junior minister whispered, his voice reduced to a husk by the emotions running within him.

"All too easily it would seem," purred the Intel commander. "If I am truly to protect myself, then I have to protect you as well. But mark this well. As easily as I have done this, so could I also reverse the process and destroy you. It would be nothing personal, believe me. We can be very useful to each other, and you have a nature that I understand. But you are still young, and have much to learn. I think the nature of our relationship must change. You have believed yourself to be the better man because of your standing. Standing is not everything. I am the better man. Never forget this." These last words he whispered close to the minister's ear. With a satisfied smirk, he stood back and clapped the younger man on the shoulder.

"Now," he said in a more cheerful tone, "to business. I have a command memo to plant. By evening it will be safe for you to send the order to the air fleet. Who, by my timepiece, should be well under way by now. And by morning? Ah, my friend, by morning all our problems shall lay in the past."

Daliel left the room. The junior minister sat alone and silent, pondering his fate. Like an echo from the other side of Inan he too was beginning to see the ramifications of facing away from the Gods and dancing with the devils that lay beneath.

The sun had barely had time to rise beyond the horizon before they were awoken by the sounds of battle in the skies. Jenna and Ramus-Bey had huddled together in their sleep, in search of warmth. Simeon lay just a little apart, having slumped at the mouth of the cave while trying to maintain a watch. The noises from above jolted him awake. He was instantly aware of the cramps and stiffness caused by the cold and his awkward position. He could hear Jenna and Ramus at the rear of him, coming round. He should check that they were okay, but his attention was immediately commanded by the activity above them.

Like some ritual dance, the battle began to unfold. With stately grace the large battlecruisers broke formation, moved through the pink skies of morning and assumed new and dreadful shapes. Around them, dancing pirouettes in the air, smaller attack craft spun webs of pulse fire, breaking through defences and peppering the hulls of the larger ships with the bright and incandescent colours of destruction.

Formations shifted patterns in the air as some craft were slowed by attack, while others surged forward, the larger pulse cannons of the battlecruisers coming into play as each sought to eliminate their enemy. Streamers of smoke from damaged and falling craft festooned the battle arena like garlands of death as the dance continued.

Simeon looked around to see that Jenna and the Mage were also watching. But it was nothing that they had said or done that attracted his attention. He looked beyond them to the rising and falling ground leading back towards the highway.

Trackers. Not far behind them, warriors, armed with blasters and a cannon.

Their aim was obviously not to capture.

Jenna cursed. "They're not going to ask us politely to go back to Ilvarn with them are they?"

"We've got to move," Simeon stated bluntly. He looked at the Mage. "Are you up to this?"

Ramus shrugged, and smiled weakly. "I'll have to be."

They began to move, keeping low to the ground. Simeon tried to pick a way through the sparse foliage and rock cover that the uneven terrain provided. His aim was to keep them out of sight. If he could see the trackers and warriors moving towards them, then chances were that they would be just as visible.

Their progress was quicker than on the previous day. The night's rest had been good for the old man, he was able to move at a swifter pace and with greater ease. But as Simeon kept up an uneasy glance over his shoulder to see the trackers and warriors slowly gaining ground, he realised that this was not enough. They had a large force on their tail, heavily armed and they themselves had nothing.

"They're gaining. It's only a matter of time," he gasped between breaths as they scaled a small incline. He looked to the Mage. "If there was ever a time to take a chance..."

Ramus-Bey held his eye. The old man's face was haggard with effort, drained of blood. He seemed to be on the edge of exhaustion already. But still he could not bring himself to cross that mental line. He declined with a barely perceptible shake of the head.

"The risks are too great," he whispered, voice shaking with exertion.

"Then we may as well stop and face them, face the inevitable," Simeon said. It was a last desperate throw of the dice, designed to force the hand of the Mage.

At that moment, the very ground around them roared and bucked, throwing soil and rock into the air. The solid rock beneath them became a treacherous, living and moving thing, seemingly intent on throwing them into the gaping maw that had suddenly opened before them. The air sang with heat, ears were painfully hammered by sudden pressure change rendering all as silence for the briefest of moments.

To Simeon it seemed as though he was struggling through air as thick as a Varnian swamp, making his movements slow, clogging his lungs, slowing his brain.

As his hearing returned, the roar became overpowering, then faded briefly before swelling up once more. He struggled to his feet and looked up. Above him attack craft of the Bethel air fleet swooped down on the warriors and trackers who had been in pursuit, blasting into them with pulse cannon fire. The screams of the wounded and dying were lost in the overwhelming sound of the attack, making them seem like puppets on a distant stage.

One of the Bethel ships detached from formation and turned back, heading straight towards them. Simeon watched, unable to move, unable to believe that this miracle had happened, that they were about to be rescued.

Then it struck him that the craft was moving too fast to be preparing for a landing. Rather, it seemed like it was homing in for an attack.

Simeon yelled, a wordless cry of warning, as he turned and tried to locate Jenna and Ramus. The old man had been hurt in the first explosion and Jenna was leaning over him. It looked like his leg had been cut, but how badly it was impossible to tell. With an awful, time-slowed clarity, Simeon saw the both of them look up.

The warrior threw himself across the gap between them, catching Jenna around the waist and bundling her down onto the Mage. His momentum carried them, tangled into a ball, away from where they had been a fraction of a moment before. They rolled over on the jagged rock, catching on gorse-like bushes, tearing at clothing and skin. Each turn was another painful, jarring blow. The Bethel attack craft carved a path through the rock with pulse cannon fire, throwing earth over them. If they had stayed where they had been before Simeon's leap, the pulse fire would have ripped them to shreds.

As the craft completed its flight path and span out to be met by an approaching Varn craft, Simeon pulled the Mage to his feet. Ramus-Bey was moaning softly to himself, his ageing bones sorely treated by events. At any other time, Simeon would have sought to protect and cosset him. Now, things had gone beyond any such point.

"Look," the warrior yelled, "look at this!"

He turned the Mage so that he could see the devastation that lay behind them. His voice could hardly be heard above the roar of battle, but Ramus-Bey responded nonetheless.

What the Mage could see caused him a deep distress, and a pain in his soul that surpassed anything that could come from his battered old body. The ground before them had been heavily scored by pulse fire, and was littered with the dead and dying. The Varnian ground force that had been pursuing them had now scattered. Some, those with the cannon capability, were attempting to return fire at the attack ships that cruised over them, casually dispensing such destruction. These craft were too swift and manoeuvrable for the ground warriors to effectively draw a bead, and so they became – literally – sitting targets.

Varn attack craft had joined the fray, seeking to defend their fellows on the ground. This bought the air battle closer to home and made it easier to assimilate.

"You better pray the Varn ships are good, because those were our own people trying to terminate us," Simeon yelled. "They all want us terminated, and you think this is not the time to take chances?"

The Mage's eyes blazed. "You fool, you still think it is an easy choice?"

Simeon shook his head. The Mage paused, and looked at the carnage around them. Warriors were dying, craft were being destroyed, all because of him. At least, that would be the explanation understood by the masses drawn into war. For this was just the beginning.

Ramus-Bey was heart-sick. This was not why he had studied for so many years. This was not why he had acquired such knowledge, and with it great power. This was not his responsibility, but it had been made his by the actions of others.

Now was the time to accept it. He turned to Simeon. "Very well. The time has come."

# CHAPTER EIGHTEEN

## Year Zero – Period Three

Simeon looked at the devastation that was being wrought around them: Ramus-Bey may consider that this was the right moment, but it was far from the right place. The Mage stood apart from the area of most carnage but in all truth, he may as well have been wearing a sign proclaiming his identity and role as the primary target.

"We need to get him into cover," Simeon yelled at Jenna, straining to make himself heard above the roar of battle. She assented after the most cursory of glances.

They took the Mage and pulled him low, eyes scanning the immediate area for anything that would offer them some kind of refuge. Ramus-Bey struggled against them.

"I will not hide any more," he proclaimed, suddenly puffed up by his own sense of importance. No man who could alter destiny should cower away.

"Can you put a protective charm around yourself while you work?" Simeon said.

"Well, no, not exactly, not if I have to concentrate," the Mage prevaricated, losing the edge of his arrogance. "It has been a while, and..."

"Then it will be a pity to be blasted to shreds before you get a chance to flex those magic muscles, won't it?" Simeon snapped, giving Bey no chance to argue as he pushed him into a trench carved by a previous blast of pulse fire.

The soil that lined the trench was still warm. Sweat spangled their foreheads as they crouched down, the depth of the blast area almost covering their height. The walls of the trench formed a sound barrier of sorts, cutting down the noise of the air attack craft and their fire. Despite the fact that they were now almost enclosed by dark walls of soil, the morning sky was made brighter by the implosion of pulse engines as battlecruisers were ripped asunder, the force of the blast making the daylight seem as night by comparison.

"Are you sure about this?" Jenna asked the Mage.

Simeon furrowed his brow. "What kind of a question is that? He's just said..."

Ramus-Bey stayed him with a gesture. "She's right to ask. I told you, I have no idea of what may happen, if anything. But it's something that I can't avoid. I have to try. If anything I've ever believed in actually meant something, then I have to..."

"Then we need to watch your back." Jenna spoke emphatically. "Sim, if he's going to try, then we need to keep him well protected."

"And we're here why, exactly?" The exasperated warrior questioned.

"Down here we can't see if the ground forces are making progress towards us," she continued, ignoring his peevish tone. "We need to keep scout out the ground above, so Ramus can get to work in peace."

The Mage allowed himself a smile. "An interesting definition of peace. Go, do what you must, leave me to prepare." Simeon and Jenna moved in opposite directions, leaving the old man hunkered down, breathing deeply with his eyes now closed, trying to shut out all stimuli as he prepared to cast.

Attack craft flew over the trench, holding fire. Were they waiting for them to emerge, or was it that they had no idea that they had taken refuge here? Simeon favoured the latter, as he knew the normal tactic when the enemy was located was just to blast the hell out of the area. The air wing of the military had never been known for their subtlety. As far as he was aware though, there was no bio-identification software that would enable the attack craft to single out Ramus, or himself and Jenna.

If anything, while the air forces battled each other and tried to penetrate the visual and bio-feedback murk that littered the battlefield, any real threat posed would come from the ground forces. The fact that they had not been as yet attacked was good. Even if their position had been identified, the land forces were still some way off.

Time to check. He risked getting his head blasted from his shoulders, but it was the only way to locate the opposing forces. He took a deep breath, feeling the bile bite the back of his throat. Cautiously – as though that would make any difference – he raised himself so that he could see over the lip of the trench.

The noise was overwhelming, almost physically battering him back into the trench. He turned through a full three-sixty degrees, appalled at the sight that greeted him.

The Varn land force knew where they were. They had almost entirely circled the trench. Fortunately, it had great length, so even in doing this they were still at long-distance blasting range, wherever there were groupings of them.

In numbers, they were much reduced from the force he had first seen earlier that morning. The air strike had devastated them, and he was able to count the groupings and those within them at a glance. Twenty small teams, dug in to as much cover as they could find. Each team was composed of four or five warriors. They were equipped with small and large cannon. Although they showed obvious intent towards closing in on the trench, they were pinned down by the constant passes of the

Bethel attack craft.

These small air attack vehicles could have easily wiped out the teams if not for the fact that they, too, were under attack. Varn attack craft kept hot on their tails, not allowing them to sweep the ground forces as they were forced to engage on two fronts.

It would seem that, temporarily, the primary target had been sidelined, if not forgotten, as the old enemies had easily fallen into old patterns of warfare. Sooner or later though, one side would triumph in the field.

Simeon pleaded to the Gods for a weapon. They answered this easily enough: the land around was littered with corpses, many of which still held the weapons they had so ill-used before their deaths.

Getting hold of one of these was, however, a problem for which he could not foresee even the Gods providing an answer.

Who needs the Gods when you have a Mage?


Ramus-Bey had calmed his fears. His frailties, both physical and otherwise, had been dismissed as superfluous. He had dug down deep within himself, and now felt that he had reached that place he had been but a few times before. That small island of calm that housed his true self, the man who had set out to attain knowledge, to attain control not over others, but over himself.

This was the man who could change things, who could stop the wasteful and disgusting battle that raged not just about them, but in the hearts and minds of those who had directed matters to this point.

He touched that within himself that had been lost for so long. He was not just heart, not just mind. He was the balance of these and in the exercise of that balance laid the knowledge of what was true. Not absolute truth, for that may not exist, but the truth of what was the right thing for him, when he used all of himself to make a decision.

He must stop this senseless waste by drawing on that power that he held within himself. He must bring it to the fore; harness, unleash and direct it so that the fighting would cease.

All doubts that he held about himself and his ability to do this must cease. It had been many anums, but he had not lost the skills.

Focusing his mind on his objective, and making a series of complex passes with his hands and fingers that externalised the tendrils of power that snaked from within his subconscious, he sought to bring his power into play.

The land around them shimmered and boiled. For a fraction of a moment, the rock became liquid. It passed beneath all those present in the area, just that touch too fast, but enough for them to register that it had been there. The colours, shapes and contours of the land blurred into an amorphous mass for an equivalent length of time. Again, not long enough to truly register, but enough to cause in all of those present a feeling of mild nausea.

Along the length of the trench, where Simeon, Jenna and Bey himself were these feelings were intensified. Both Simeon and Jenna threw up, unable to stop the pitch and yaw of their stomachs. An intense heat that made their clothes smoulder at the seams seized them.

When Simeon had gulped down hot, fetid air, gasping to stop the reflux, he raised his head again, daring another look over the lip of the trench.

He gasped again, but this time from a sense of profound shock. In front of him there was a large gap in the landscape. The rise and fall of a mountainous crop that had formed a barrier between the city of Ilvarn and the scrub area where they had pitched battle was gone. As simple as that. It was no longer there. In the blinking of an eye, millennia of rock had simply disappeared. In the distance, he could see the strange mix of old and new within the city, small air ships buzzing like flies around the constructs.

Between here and there lay nothing. Not in the sense that it was a void, but rather as though a giant hand had descended and scooped out the mass of rock like a child would scoop a handful of mud, leaving a deep pit and little else.

The ground forces were no longer paying the trench any attention. In awe, their attention had been taken by the strange sight that lay in the direction they had come. Overhead, the battleships and the smaller attack craft had stopped their dance of death. The larger craft were stilled, while the smaller craft now sped towards the giant pit, crossing time and again over it as they attempted to make sense of what they could see.

In the eerie silence that had descended over the plane, Simeon heard a small voice.

"Not exactly what I intended, but a reasonable start."

The warrior turned and saw that Ramus-Bey was standing, his head over the lip of the trench, surveying his work. Simeon started to run towards him, feeling as though he were moving in slow motion. He almost fell, and his momentum carried him into the Mage.

The pair of them stumbled, tumbling over each other onto the floor of the trench.

"A fine way to treat your Mage," Bey murmured. There

was, within his tone, a hint of the bombastic assurance that he had held when first Simeon had met him. Not something, the warrior felt, that would be of much good to them right now.

"You did that?" Simeon managed to croak out in a dry voice, his throat ravaged by the heat.

"I did," Ramus replied, drawing himself out from under the warrior and rising to his feet, dusting himself down. "And I'd remind you to have a little more decorum in how you treat the premier wizard of Bethel!"

"Who could have got his head shot off as he wasn't taking precautions, and Gods alone know it's big enough right now..."

"I have not been called upon to practice for many annums, as you well know, and under the circumstances..."

"It hasn't done anything yet," Simeon barked. "It's only going to be some bastard good if it gets us out of here! As it is, it damn near finished us off."

"You forget yourself," bristled the Mage.

"No more than you," retorted the warrior. "We've still got to get out of here!"

In the silence that had followed the Mage's charm, Jenna had been quick to recover. Thrown from her feet by the lack of equilibrium, she had rolled onto her knees and retched bile on to the hot earth. Deep within her, some instinct for preservation had told her to ignore the feelings that wanted her to roll over and cry from the pains that wracked and spasmed her body. A nasty voice in her mind wanted her to welcome the Varn and Bethel forces, to ask them to terminate her and put her out of her misery. It nagged, and she wanted to obey if only to shut it up and give her some peace.

But her instinct to live was greater than that. It pushed that small voice to the furthest reaches of her consciousness and made her haul herself to her feet.

Breathing deeply through her nose, she clutched at the wall of the trench, almost willing the world around her to stop spinning. She was facing away from the Mage, and she heard his words, though not their meaning. They came to her through a haze as though they were meaningless syllables. But enough for her to realise that she must take action.

Looking up above the trench, she beheld a sight much as Simeon was seeing, but with one difference. While the warrior could only see the astounding result of the Mage's actions, Jenna's instinct for preservation drew her attention to two things. First, that the ground force surrounding them at a distance was similarly in awe of the missing mountains; secondly, that there were a number of discarded weapons lying around the battlefield.

If she was quick, then perhaps she could take advantage of these two things.

Adrenaline and the desire to stay alive overriding all else, she hauled herself over the top of the ridge, Varnian clothing ripping on the jagged rock. She was glad. Her short Ensign's tunic was better suited to what she was about to do.

Keeping low, discarding the rest of the Varn clothing as she went, Jenna half-crawled, half-ran across the open ground that lay between her and her objective. A pulse cannon and blaster were within reach, if she ignored the corpses that surrounded them and the lack of cover.

What did it matter? If she had stayed in the trench, they were still trapped. As for the dead, they could no longer threaten her now that they were with the Gods.

She picked up two small cannon and three blasters, being careful to disentangle the webbing of the cannon from the corpses of the previous owners without attracting attention.

With the weapons gathered to her, she paused to look up. The ground forces were still drawn to the gap in the mountains, and the air forces were too concerned with recce'ing the area to spare a glance for one, lone figure.

Thanking fortune for favouring her thus far, she began to move back towards the trench. With every step she felt her heart pound, her stomach turn. Even with the weapons, because of the way in which she carried them, it would have taken her too much time to open fire should anyone spot her. She would be dead before she had a chance to squeeze the trigger.

She was aware of the trench behind her, and slid gracelessly down the wall to the floor, collapsing in a heap. Back in relative safety, she felt euphoric. She wanted to laugh out loud. In the heat of battle she had captured weapons. And while she – a mere holoship Ensign – had been doing this, the almighty Mage and his bodyguard had been arguing like women over the last prime cut in a meat market.

What, she wondered, would they do without her?

Simeon checked the small cannon, handed one to Jenna. He did the same with two of the three blasters. The third he checked, then offered to Ramus-Bey. The Mage shook his head.

"I cannot accept that."

"Take it," Simeon insisted. "Call it a precaution."

"Call it whatever you wish," Bey muttered as he grudgingly took the small arm. "I shall not use it. I will not."

"But someone might believe you would, which may make them think twice. Call it a deterrent."

"They called me a deterrent... look where it has got

Inan," Bey said bitterly.

"Time enough for that later," Simeon said gently. "The most important thing is that we get out of here with you in one piece. Question is, how?"

"And how soon?" Jenna added. "Ground and air forces are static while they try and work out what's going on and what they can do about it, but that won't last long."

"Should be simple enough. If he can do *that*," Simeon gestured vaguely in the direction of Ilvarn, "then he can charm us back to Belthan."

Bey grimaced. "Ideally, I could... but that result wasn't what I intended, exactly. So how much trust would you truly like to put in arriving back in one piece?"

Despite himself, Simeon grinned. Something of the old Ramus mixed with the new. Power and humility together. It was going to take a little getting used to.

"Fair point," he said. "I'm too young, she's too pretty, and you're too important to be killed. We need another plan. Though it's not much, I think I might just have one."

Orders had come through comm-receivers. *Stop gawping at the carnage caused by what was assumed to be magic, and concentrate on the objective.* Ramus-Bey must now be considered more of a threat. If magic had caused the mountain to move – and scans had revealed no tech traces – then the Mage was using his power. The consequences could be dire. Varn knew they could not counter with their own Mage for fear of retribution from other nation states. They had to prey on his poor physical condition to eliminate him.

The ground teams were clustered around the trench. Although at some distance, they were in range for their pulse cannon to effect damage.

While they peppered the area around the trench with pulse fire, Simeon and Jenna used their purloined weaponry to return some of that fire, hopefully deflecting the ground crews from measuring perfect aim.

Ramus-Bey sat on the floor of the trench, once more centering himself. He would not terminate these warriors, as they were only men and women who were fulfilling the duty laid down for them by their nation state, but he would remove them from the field of play.

A reasoned thought. Skeins of energy played out as passes of the hands and fingers, and...

The ground crews were gone. The firing ceased.

"Where..." Jenna began.

Bey grinned. "I wouldn't like to say exactly. Probably Ilvarn – maybe some swamp in the south if I got it too wrong. But safe enough."

"Nice sentiment, but we haven't got time for that," Simeon said, looking up. "It's only going to be a short while before the confusion clears and they realise what's happened. Then we'll have a full-scale air attack. We can't defend against that."

Bey assented. "I know."

He went into himself again. Jenna threw a questioning look over his head, directed to Simeon. The warrior shrugged. He had no idea how long it would take. They would just have to hope.

Above them the battlecruisers began to shift from their holding patterns, aloof from the action of the smaller attack craft. Each side had held their giant ships at a distance, unwilling to risk any more engagement until the battle lower down had been resolved. It was apparent though, that the loss of the ground forces had filtered through, and the battle cruisers were moving to engage and provide heavy-duty cover for the smaller craft, which began to disengage from their own offence/defence patterns, swooping in arcs that would bring them in for ground attack passes.

"You think he's going to get this right?" Jenna asked.

"What choice have we got?" Simeon shrugged. He looked up, beyond the rapidly – too rapidly – approaching small craft. The Varnian battlecruisers were gaining ground. "It's not like he could miss all of them surely?"


"Gods! No-one could survive that," whispered Commander Tilan Vash, officer-in-charge of the battlecruiser *Illyd*.

His helmsman had, under his watchful eye, piloted their ship at the head of the fleet, approaching the battle area in a flight pattern designed to cut off Bethelian battlecruiser paths to the air attack squadrons below them. There were a dozen cruisers left afloat, two more than in the Bethel fleet. That should be deterrent enough.

Like every other Varnian Commander, he had been a little stunned to see the Bethelian air attack craft turn and, instead of trying to deflect the Varn squadron from their path, join them in blasting the ground in and around the trench where their Intel told them that Ramus-Bey and his – well, kidnappers or rescuers, depending on which newscasts or military channels you believed – were holed up.

The squadrons pulled up, and the dust and smoke began to clear. What had once been a trench was now a blasted plain. Uneven, irregular rises and crops of rock and soil were now flattened, melted and blasted into a flat expanse of nothing. Whatever had been down there had been eradicated.

Helmsman Cavlar whistled. "They were all blasting, sir.

What's that about?"

Vash shook his head. A life-long warrior in the air fleet, he believed implicitly in following orders and to trust in his superiors. He couldn't for the life of him imagine how they would explain this, but he felt sure that there must be a reason somewhere behind it.

"Tyra, get Ministry One on the comm, see what they want us to do now that the enemy seems to have been eliminated," Vash murmured.

Comm Officer Tyra hit the comm-send sensor, preparing to deliver the message. She was stunned to silence when a strange hand gripped her wrist.

"I wouldn't, if I was you."

Vash and Cavlar spun round, reaching for their blasters.

"I really wouldn't do that, either." They were greeted by a second, female voice, and the sight of three battle-scarred individuals. Two of them – the woman, and the man who gripped Tyra's wrist – were holding blasters, with portable cannon strapped across their shoulders. The third individual – a wizened, tired looking old man – was staring distractedly around him.

"Quite pleased with this," he sniffed. "I never knew that a flight deck was so small. Could have done a whole lot worse, all in all."

The man laughed. "Don't be too pleased, this is only the start."

Vash could contain himself no longer. "Who – who are you?" he spluttered. "How in the name of the Gods did you get on my flight deck? And what in the name of the sacred places do you want?"

The tall man smiled, gently helped Tyra from her seat and directed her across the deck to where Vash and Cavlar were standing, and then sat down at her comm-station.

"I should have thought that the answers to all three questions were obvious, Commander. But the only one that really matters is the last. You, my new and trusted friend, are taking us home."

# CHAPTER NINETEEN

## Year Zero – Period Three

"You realise, of course, that once we break formation every ship in the fleet will realise that something is amiss?" Vash said with a self-satisfied smirk. "Your plan will never work."

Simeon sighed. "You saw those mountains vanish, right? You turned round to find us standing here when we weren't there a moment before, right?" He paused, waiting for Vash to cautiously assent. He continued: "Well, if that can happen, what's to stop us pulling this one off?"

Vash said nothing: he could see a flaw in the warrior's reasoning. Why did they need to commandeer a ship when they could do all of this? But he had one simple rule that had kept him alive to this point: never argue with a man who was armed, especially when you were not. It hadn't let him down yet, so he was going to keep trusting in it.

He indicated to Cavlar that he was to follow their instructions. With a further gesture, he also indicated that there were to be no attempts at deception. He recognised Jenna's Ensign uniform, and even though holoships were thought constructs, they worked on the same piloting principles. Any attempts to fool them, and they would soon be discovered.

Strangely, as the warrior directed Cavlar to turn the ship, Vash felt himself relax. There was nothing he could do, so he decided to sit back and see exactly how they planned to pull this off.

# Ilvarn - The Ministry

An emergency meeting was in session. The Chief Minister and his executive were seated around the conference table, a bank of holo-monitors suspended over the centre, offering them views from the air fleet, the ground forces, Intel satellites, and newsvid coverage from around the globe.

For the first time in over a day, the Chief Minister felt able to relax. The executive body, sensing this cautiously let a collective sigh escape.

"They are terminated. Bethel, too, played her part. Wherever we have to go from here, I think that every nation state can be in no doubt now that there is more to this situation than a simple division of blame. Gentlemen, I feel sure that war has, for the moment, been averted."

"Sir, while our relief at this cannot be too strongly conveyed, ought we to think about our own Mage? After all, the man had a part in the taking of Ramus-Bey, and has signally refused to assist us in the mopping-up operation. His loyalty to the nation state must surely be called into question?"

The Chief Minister fixed a look on the junior who had spoken. There were a myriad of reasons why he could not let Vixel be taken in and interrogated. Leaving aside the fact that he, himself, would be implicated in the twisted planning that had led them this far, there was also the problem of Vixel himself. He had remained aloof from this fight. Did he have the powers he professed? Could his judgement be trusted?

If the Mage had powers on a level with those shown by Bey, then he was dangerous. If he had been right about Bey, and this morning's display had just been the last flutterings of a senile talent, then what was Vixel truly capable of? More, his character must be considered. He had proven himself to be headstrong, egotistical, and erratic.

A danger to Inan? To Varn? More importantly, to the Chief Minister himself?

Finally, he answered the junior's question.

"Our Mage is an asset to the nation state of Varn. Until there is a man of equal power in the land, his status must remain unquestioned. His loyalty to the public and – more importantly – to other nation states is beyond question. Do I make myself clear?"

However, he was already pondering how practical it would be to effect an assassination of the Mage. Some dangers were best stamped on while still small.

Simeon had swiftly ascertained that the crew of a battlecruiser numbered one hundred and fifty, including the three flight deck crew before him. Unless called for, there were no routine tasks that would bring them to the deck. The trick would be to keep them at their posts and working as usual when they realised that the vessel had turned and headed for Bethel.

"All orders come from the flight deck, am I right?" questioned Jenna.

"Ah..." Vash's hesitation suggested he was forming a deception.

"Remember that, as a Kyan holoship Ensign, I served alongside Varn flight crew during the war," she added. He wasn't to know the truth, she reasoned.

Vash shrugged. "I can't see how you're going to do this, so what does it matter? Of course your assumption is correct."

"Then deliver new orders through the comm-system.

Varn is to strike back against Bethel oppression, and the current airborne fleet is to form the spearhead. As such, preparation will be made to turn and head for Belthan."

"Irregular, to say the least. From a purely academic point of view," Vash continued, his eye fixed on Simeon's weapon, "do you really expect the crew to accept this out of hand?"

Simeon smiled. "It's amazing what we'll swallow when it comes from a voice in authority, Commander. You will make it sound convincing, and they'll have no trouble following orders. Exceptional times make for exceptional orders, that kind of thing."

Vash shrugged. He found himself in an unsettled frame of mind. Resigned to the fact that he had little option other than comply or be killed, he was actually beginning to enjoy working out the reasoning used by the intruders, and to attempt to second guess their moves. For instance:

"I suppose you have given the matter of our power reserves some thought?" he said suddenly, stopping short of the comm-desk.

Jenna answered: "Battlecruisers have pulse engines that work on a recycle principle. The use of virtual perpetual generation allows them a propulsion capacity that will keep them afloat for a period without landing. Although swift motion eats the power faster, there's still enough on the average battlecruiser to circle Inan three times without needing to refuel. I'm guessing you weren't sent aloft this morning without a full emergency refit and check."

"Very good," Vash murmured. "I'm terribly, terribly impressed."

Jenna grinned at Simeon as Vash leaned into the comm-desk and delivered orders along the lines proscribed by the warrior. He was, it had to be said, extremely convincing. His voice was firm and commanding, his words chosen with care to demonstrate to his captors a complete lack of ambiguity.

"Will that do?" he asked, flicking off the internal comm-transmitter.

"You're being very co-operative," Simeon commented. "I wonder why?"

Vash shrugged. "I'm curious to see how you intend to carry this one off."

Simeon said no more to him, but turned instead to the Mage, who had remained silent.

"Well?" The warrior questioned.

"Yes," the Mage said at length, "it's time for me to take over, isn't it?"

# Belthan – The Ministry

A room similar to that in Ilvarn. A conference table and bank of holomonitors similar to that in Ilvarn.

There, the similarities end. The Chief Minister stares out of the window at the teeming streets below. The people are in uproar. Half of them demonstrate for war to be declared on the old enemy, the other half demonstrate for an end to that war, ignoring the fact that it has not yet officially begun.

"Chaos. The lack of order, the lack of discipline. Nothing is done, nothing is achieved. People running around without the slightest notion of why. Is this what this great nation state is about? Is this what we have become?"

The executive exchanged worried glances. None were able to judge the reaction that was required of them.

The Chief Minister turned to the assembled ministers.

"They are saying that I am behind this pre-emptive action. They are saying that, as the Chief Minister, I ordered this attack. Why are they saying this?"

Another exchange of nervous glances. A tall, blonde junior minister, nervously clearing his throat, took it upon himself to speak.

"Sir, your orders..."

"I gave no orders!" The Chief Minster turned and brought his fist down on the desk The crash sounded loudly in the otherwise hushed room, the holomonitors blinking and flashing their images in silence.

"But... but... I have the comm history here, sir," the junior stammered, brandishing a sheet. "I received an order from you, in my capacity as liaison with the air fleet arm of the military, to direct the air fleet to eliminate the Mage and the two people with him, on the grounds that he was likely to have been interrogated and mentally altered, making him a threat."

"I have never heard such complete shit in all..."

"Sir," another minister, with trembling hand, held up a print-out. "I was sent a reference and file copy of the message my colleague refers to... it was from your office, sir, from your personal comm."

"Give me that!" The Chief Minister snatched the printouts. He scanned them intently, then turned and looked out at the city below, his shoulders slumped. "I did not send this message. Do you believe that?" He turned and looked each of the men around the table squarely in the eye. Most averted their gaze. He laughed mirthlessly. "Of course you don't. Why should you? The evidence is against me."

He tailed off, looking down on the crowd. A heavy

silence fell on the room.

But for one man, it was difficult to hide his relief.


The problem faced by Ramus-Bey, Simeon and Jenna was this: they had succeeded in boarding and then commandeering a Varnian vessel. This had the capacity to get them back to Bethel in a very short period of time. The Varnian commander was being co-operative, and had delivered orders to his crew that would see the giant battlecruiser turn and set course for the rival nation state. These orders had even been delivered in a way that would not arouse suspicion. This part of the operation had run smoothly – far more so, in fact, than could have been hoped for at the outset.

There were, however, still problems to be surmounted. Firstly, although the crew of their vessel would follow orders, these were unique to the craft. Those Varn vessels around them would seek to intercept when communication could not be established. This was not to mention the battlecruisers of the opposing Bethel air fleet, who would feel no compunction in attacking an enemy craft that may suddenly turn and head for them.

If nothing else, being attacked by their own fleet would arouse the suspicions of the crew.

So it was imperative that something be done. A diversionary tactic to both carve a clear path, and to keep the crew of this vessel in the dark concerning their real intent.

"Put like that, how could I possibly refuse you?" Ramus smirked, glad to be given a chance to flex his skills once more. He had plans for when they reached Belthan, and any opportunity to clean the dust from his long-neglected practice would be more than welcome.

The first thing he did was to examine the holding patterns of the two air fleets. Both were still in the limbo that followed the devastation of the ground below, awaiting orders from their respective Ministries. Both fleets were poised for action, awaiting only orders or the provocation of attack. As soon as their ship left its place in the holding pattern, it would attract attention. A diversion would be necessary. Ramus-Bey was determined to stay true to his word. He would not cause the deaths of any warrior, on either side, if it were at all possible. Too many warriors had already tasted death because of him. He would not set them against each other.

But if... it was an amusing thought. He could not see how it could possibly harm any of the men and women populating the cruisers, and it would be a good test of his skills.

With a wry smile, he looked within himself and began to ritualise the powers he was drawing on with complex shapes proscribed in the air by his hands.

"Oh Gods alive, what is that?" Cavlar yelled, gesturing wildly at the port through which the rest of the Varn fleet was visible.

"That's someone's idea of a joke," Simeon murmured. But if it achieved their aim, he had no intention of any further comment.

It was a strange and unexpected sight. From nowhere, in the midst of the fleet holding pattern, three Ihere appeared, screeching and flapping their vast, leathery wings. The disruption they caused was immediate, as the battlecruisers nearest to the creatures took evasive action, invading the airspace of those cruisers and smaller attack craft near them, causing these in turn to tumble from their flight paths in evasive actions.

The Ihere was a mythical beast, part bird and part reptile,

with scaled wings, a feathered ruff, and three heads that snapped with razored bills at anything that came near. Unlike other creatures of their ilk, who survived still in small colonies on the edges of the wastelands of Hirvan, their eyes were not sharp: rather, they were dull with stupidity. Some said that the creature had never existed, other that the dullness of eye explained without further detail why they had long since been extinct.

There was, however, nothing extinct about their behaviour in the midst of the Varn air fleet. The small attack craft broke formation, heading in to attack, the larger vessels withdrew, their commanders realising that these creatures, despite their immense size, had a greater manoeuvrability than the battlecruisers.

None seemed to question that these creatures had appeared from nowhere, let alone that they should not, in fact, exist. The scrambled and confused welter of comm-messages that could be monitored told of only one thing, the immediate reaction to an immediate threat.

Threat it most certainly was. None of the firepower concentrated on the creatures seemed to have any effect. If anything, it seemed to make them increase in size and speed. Their darting heads and vast wingspans threatened to swat air attack craft like irritating insects, and to dent the fuselage of any battlecruiser slow to evade.

Such was the confusion caused that none of the commanders or pilots in the line of attack had so far realised that not a single casualty, not a single hit had been sustained.

"Got to give you that one," Commander Vash commented, shaking his head in disbelieving appreciation, "that's what I call a diversion!"

As the Varn fleet battled to keep shape and avoid devastation from this strange assault force, Vash directed

Helmsman Cavlar through the throng, avoiding both the Ihere and the battlecruiser as they sought clear airspace.

It was simple for the flight deck crew. As they progressed, so Ramus-Bey used his control of the thought forms to guide other craft from the flight path of their ship.

They attained clear airspace and increased speed. It was only then that Simeon and Jenna were able to see, and to admire, the breadth of Ramus-Bey's vision.

Some distance away, the Bethel air fleet stood off, their holding patterns preserved. They had presumably been viewing the attack on the Varn fleet with some bemusement. Such a tactic would not work on them. Besides which, it would be too simple for the Mage, and he wished to stretch himself. Not only was it vital that he sharpen his skills as quickly as possible, it was unlikely that the same kind of attack would have quite the same effect on a fleet that had already witnessed the like.

Pulling clear of the Varn fleet, the battlecruiser on which they travelled closed fast on the Bethel fleet. It was obvious that the commanders in the fleet could sense an easy target. To them, this was just a rogue vessel running scared.

The fleet broke formation, spreading across the sky. The flagship battlecruiser of the fleet – identifiable not from markings, but from the way it had formed the hub of the formation – moved forward to engage. It was the prerogative of the senior air commander to claim the first trophy.

Vash leaned across. "'He will fire at us you know. We have to fire first!"

Bey shook his head. "Not necessary."

His eyes closed, he began to hum tunelessly to himself. Simeon recognised this from countless nights on bodyguard duty. It was a habit, a quirk of age that he did this when his attention was fully focused. As it would have to be, the warrior realised, if he were to keep up the charm that now lay behind them, as well as solving the problem that lay before.

The two vessels closed on each other. With a gesture, Vash directed Cavlar to keep his nerve and continue on the current course even though the two vessels seemed to be on a collision course. Unless the Bethelian battlecruiser fired on them before impact.

The two ships came closer. Vash began to sweat. He could see his life ending in a ridiculous game of chicken.

Then it seemed as though his eyes could not be showing him what was really happening. The Bethelian ship seemed to turn up and in on itself, spiralling around, being stretched to an unnatural length and shape before heading back the way it had come.

As if this had been the cue for which they waited, the rest of the Bethel air fleet broke rank and flew at the Varn battlecruiser.

Each battlecruiser and small attack craft met with a similar fate. Each seemed to twist and turn on themselves, stretching unnaturally before finding themselves heading in the opposite direction.

"That's a nice little trick, but what about when they're behind us?" Vash queried.

"I think he'll have that one covered," Jenna commented.

Ramus-Bey smiled, but said nothing.

The Varn battlecruiser sped past the twisting and writhing shapes that constituted the Bethel air fleet. As the Varn ship headed towards the coast and out over the seas, the Bethel fleet gave chase. Yet, when they reached the point where sea met the land, they found themselves subject to the same phenomenon that had stopped them before. Coming out of the enforced turn, manoeuvring to try and evade whatever the barrier may be, they found themselves repeating the same phenomenon whichever way they flew. Splitting in different directions, the craft of the fleet found themselves distorting in the air in every direction, decreasing the area of untwisted space until they had turned themselves almost inside out, and had arrived at a point where stasis reigned, and they were frozen in the air.

"I – ah – I'm not sure I really want to know," a fascinated Vash asked, "but what exactly did you do to them?"

"Oh, I did nothing to the airships," Bey waved dismissively, "I just charmed the air so that their speed warped the spatial dimensions in proportion to their velocity. Inevitably, the more they tried, the more they just constricted their area of movement until they had nowhere to go. It was quite simple."

"I'll – ah – take your word for it," Vash murmured. He glanced from Simeon to Jenna, his eyes begging explanation. Simeon shrugged, some things were better left unexplained. Jenna merely smiled.

It had, the Commander reflected as he engaged the hyper-drive, been the most unusual mission he had ever flown.

He did not speak again for some time, until the coast of Bethel was in sight. During that time, the only problem they had encountered had been from the navigation and surveillance crew, who had expressed concern that they were the only Varn ship to escape the strangeness, and were now alone and approaching enemy shores. It had taken all of Vash's diplomacy – aided by the sight of Simeon and Jenna brandishing weapons – to reassure the crew that orders had changed due to the skirmishes back home, and that now they were on a reconnaissance mission.

It was, as he made all too clear, a poor excuse.

"You are right, of course," Ramus-Bey replied after some thought. He turned to Simeon. "With your consent?" And when the warrior assented, Bey continued to speak in normal tones, although his voice now carried to every man and woman on the battlecruiser by a simple series of passes.

"People of Varn, you have of course harboured doubts and concerns about this voyage. It is time to reveal truth. I am Ramus-Bey, Mage of Bethel. I have been travelling on your ship's flight-deck along with my two companions. Your Commander has acted with the utmost concern for your well-being, and has agreed to our demands in order to spare you. You are, indeed, lucky to have such a man at your head. He has pointed out to me that things can no longer be kept secret. He is correct, and I bow to his judgement.

"I have no argument with you or your nation state. Assuredly, agents of your government abducted me. But agents of my own attempted a similar thing. I am here because two people believed in integrity. They, like you, are humble serving warriors. I hope you will listen and understand, like them.

"We are entering what, to you, is enemy air space. In all honesty, I cannot say it is friendly as far as I am concerned either. I wish us to land in the heart of Belthan, and I am aware that we would be attacked and greatly outnumbered by Bethel craft simply because of our markings. If I declared my presence, I fear it would bring greater attack upon us.

"I hope you will trust me, I will trust you by telling of my actions. I will, as soon as I have finished speaking, cloak this ship so that no technology, or any magic short of Mage level, can reveal its presence. This is to ensure that I am not detected, and you are not exposed to any unnecessary risk. I wish you to land this ship in the grounds of the Bethel Institute, my home... where I am amongst friends. I thank you for your understanding, and wish to assure you that I shall cast charms in such a manner that you will not be at risk for your brave actions."

He stopped, nodded to himself, grunted, then said to Simeon: "Do you think I should have said something like 'end communication', just to let them know I was finished?"

The battlecruiser passed over the coast of Bethel without detection. It continued unheeded and until it came within view of the capital.

It was then that Ramus-Bey changed his mind.

"People of Varn" he said softly, his voice carrying to the minds of all the crew, "I have decided on another course. I intend to unmask this ship when we are over the centre of Belthan, but still keep a protective field around it for your safety. I wish for you to land this ship not in the Institute grounds, but in the central market square of the old city. For reasons of my own, I wish to announce my arrival to both people and government. I assure you, however, that I shall take every precaution to ensure your continued safety."

He ceased, nodding to himself once more.

Simeon was puzzled. "Why the change?"

Ramus-Bey smiled gently. "Because of you, dear boy." When he noted Simeon's puzzled expression, he explained: "Your actions have shown me something. That we have the power to take the fates into our own hands and make them something other than what we are given if we remain passive. True, not often do we have the power to make a great difference, but nonetheless... you did, and I can.

"I wanted to cut myself off from the mass of people. I wanted nothing to do with them as I had my own interests to pursue. Yet, in doing that, I was too blind to see that I allowed myself to be used by the Ministry. I am not some absurd weapon with which they can threaten the planet, yet I allowed myself to be presented as such. I, and my fellow Mages were treated like sacks of grain, sold and bartered at market. That is not what we should be about. The people should not fear us. Vixel may have a darkness in him that mars his being, but at least he was smart enough to see this before I did. Well, it's time to change that."

Simeon had many questions he wanted to ask, but there was too little time, already the battlecruiser was passing over the outer fringe of Belthan.

The Mage cancelled the cloaking charm, and replaced it with a protective field. The ship slowed to manoeuvre its bulk over the market square central to the old sector of the capital, and gently put down. Before the hum of the pulse propulsion had died away, the ship was surrounded by warrior security.

"Time to make a stand," Ramus said decisively. "Are you with me?"

Simeon and Jenna exchanged glances, then assented. Neither had the slightest notion of what, exactly, he intended to do, but both knew they could trust him.

The crew of the battlecruiser lined up to watch the Mage as an exit ramp was lowered. Flanked by Simeon and Jenna, Ramus-Bey began to descend.

Warriors began to move forward in ranks, weapons

raised for attack. Their orders had been given, regardless of the man who stepped down.

Bey raised a hand, gestured simply.

The warriors were immobilised, finding themselves heavy-limbed to the point of being unable to stand. They sat, feeling gravity increased to a point where they could not lift their weapons. Weaker than new born babes, they could only stare as Ramus-Bey uttered his first words back on home soil.

"Men and women of Belthan, you are the first to know that your Ministry has, as of now, been relieved of a responsibility that they are unfit to administer. This is now a truly free nation state."

# CHAPTER TWENTY

## Year Zero - Period Three

News of the Mage's arrival travelled swiftly. Before he had even reached the Ministry building, newsvid crews and holocams were hovering around the area, trying to capture every last moment and relay it to the waiting planet. The whole of Inan watched with their breath stilled, wondering what developments were to take place, and how this would affect the status of a world on the brink of war.

Two men, on separate continents, had reason to watch and wonder with a little more trepidation than any other.

Vixel had retreated to the depths of the Institute in Ilvarn, and had sealed himself in with a charm that would brook no admittance. He knew that his Chief Minister awaited him. Fear would haunt their dealings from this time on, and there could never be the trust or mutual interest that had led to their plotting. Perhaps that was as well; look where it had got them. The Chief Minister was forever paranoid, and Vixel was an outcast in his own small realm. Wherever he went from here, wizards and adepts would not welcome him. But then again, did this matter? As he watched the newscasts, he realised before any others that this was a world about to change forever.

A view he would have been amused to find that he shared with Daliel. The squat, scarred Intel chief sat alone in a darkened room, lit only by the glow of a bank of holomonitors, deep in the bowels of the Military building. The events he watched unfurl were only a short distance from where he sat. It would have taken only moments to leave his chamber and watch it in solid reality. That, however, would have been a little too much to take.

The dream was over. His planning, his cunning, his skills at manipulation and subterfuge, built over many years, all of this was now as dust.

He had little doubt that the warrior he saw walking with the Mage knew at least a little of the plot in which he had been an unwitting puppet. He had picked Simeon 7 because he had believed him to be a fool. He had seriously misjudged the boy's character. What he had thought of as stupidity had been naiveté. Another time, another place and he would have liked him at his side. As it was, he stood as an enemy that would be implacable. He had grown in stature as a warrior, and shown tenacity in the face of adversity that would make him a foe to be reckoned with.

Daliel sighed. Even if Simeon and Jenna had not guessed the extent of the plot, even if Ramus-Bey had not woken from his age-induced stupor, even if he had thus far managed to conceal the workings of his scheme... all of it would count for nothing.

The junior minister would crack. Daliel had instilled fear in the young man. He had marked him down, put him in his place. From the very beginning he had manoeuvred the situation so that he could play on the weaknesses and vanities of the politician. He had made him believe that he had the upper hand, revealing his own dominance when the time was right. He had used the boy's fear of him to keep him in line, to manipulate him, and through him, the situation.

But that fear would now go against him. Who was the greater foe? It was no contest. Faced with the Mage, the boy would crack and reveal all.

An irony that his greatest asset – the ability to instil fear – could also be his biggest downfall. Ah well, it had been a good run, and he had almost succeeded. Better to try and fail than to stay in the ranks and be a good warrior, sent to your death for fools who knew nothing of pain, suffering and humiliation.

Although he had little time left to him now, he would not hurry. With a sorrowful sigh, Daliel rose and walked across the room. Behind a wall hanging, there was a safe. The walls of the Military building were of old stone, and this safe had been artfully concealed. Only Daliel knew of its presence. The mason who had installed it had met with an unfortunate accident at a busy junction, less than a period after he had finished the work. Such a shame.

The Intel chief opened the safe and extracted the contents. Money, papers with a new identity, and a tech disk. This was the true treasure. He had information on a programme writer in the Ministry building who was one of the brightest rising stars in tech. It was the kind of information that such a woman would not wish to be made public. Daliel had arranged to loose this information, for a price, of course. There was always a price.

It had been her greatest work. A virus that responded to a name or an image. It could be fed into the Intel network, and through this into the public networks. It was undetectable until it came across a certain name or image. Thus triggered, it would erase any such information. In an age of tech, there was little enough paper information. Even that which did exist would have to be transferred by means of tech. Who could lose? Maybe, eventually, someone would catch on and send a fragile piece of paper by air fleet. But that was only a maybe.

The name was his. The image was his. Once he inserted

this disk, transferred the virus to the mainframe, it would spread.

He would disappear

Daliel inserted the disk. A few keystrokes and the programme entered into the system with no trace of its origin. A beautiful piece of work, and a fine memorial to a great talent.

He was done here. He looked around at the chamber. This was the hub of his small, dark empire. In some ways he wouldn't be sorry to leave it. The idea of fine weather appealed. Praal always welcomed traders, and he would enjoy pitting his wits against their best talents on an open market.

An air ship was waiting for Intel personnel. He could take it to Kyas then switch to a public flight. The last physical trace would end there.

Yes, it all worked itself out nicely. Not, perhaps, as he had planned, but... Daliel pocketed the papers and the money. He was still alive, and likely to remain so. He left the chamber, holomonitors flickering silently, without looking back.

While the news teams waited outside, Ramus-Bey walked unimpeded through the Ministry building until he reached the chamber where the Chief Minster and the Executive stood, expectant. There had been no attempt to impede his progress. After his display at the landing of the battlecruiser, it seemed to be a pointless exercise.

As they made their almost-stately progression, it crossed Simeon's mind that this was as close to a display of absolute power as he had ever seen. Acquiescence as the only path. Indeed, since their descent from the battlecruiser, Ramus had been given no reason to use any magic.

There was danger there. It brought home to Simeon exactly what he had been protecting, exactly what the nation states had been using as political currency.

The genuflection of the Chief Minister and the Executive as they entered the chamber did nothing to dispel this feeling.

"Ramus... I...I'm glad to see that..."

The Mage dismissed the stammering politician with a gesture. "No you're not, you ordered your own people to fire on me. You, Varn, everyone, all the same. All intoxicated with your own power and scared of anything that is greater. Perhaps you might have succeeded. Catch me unawares and I am frail in physique. But from your attitude, I can see that you realise that any attempt to terminate me would be at best fruitless."

"There have been misunderstandings..."

"That is what you call them?" said Bey.

"Miscommunications, untruths, blackened reports to mislead," the Chief Minister continued, undaunted. "We were acting in what we believed to be the best interests of our nation state, of yours."

"Patriotism, eh? The last refuge of the scoundrel. Last refuge of the moron, more likely. You act in my best interests if that is the case, for I am of this nation state. Yet I cannot see how termination benefits me."

"The greater good..."

"Which of course, you decide. You and this cabal," Bay sneered, indicating the Executive. "You few who decide what is best for all. To the extent of bringing me into your plans and precipitating a situation that would not, otherwise, have existed. Was that the greater good?"

"We can only do what we think is best."

"You, sir, do not think at all!" Bey roared. "At least," he continued in a softer tone, "of anything other than yourselves."

"So this is what you want, is it?" the Chief Minister said flatly. "The chance to claim the power that we represented through you. That is what you seem to be saying, that you know better."

Ramus-Bey drew a deep breath, shook his head. "You are partly correct. I do seek to claim something. But it is that which you took from me forcibly."

Simeon and Jenna were amused by the furrowed brows and puzzled expressions that greeted this speech. It would seem that no-one in the Executive could quite comprehend the Mage. From the way he was looking at them, Simeon could see that some of the testy old man he had first known was about to bubble to the surface.

"Oh, for the sakes of all the Gods, just let me broadcast to Inan. I have something to say, and I'm going to say it anyway, one way or another. The ordinary people will understand. Even if they don't, they should at least be given a chance."

It was a source of some amazement to Simeon how fast the media and the government could move when they felt themselves under threat. Bureaucrats and Executives who, under normal circumstances, would take almost an entire period to respond to even the most simple of requests had shown an instant response to the demand of Ramus-Bey.

Power. Its use was something that Simeon could feel like a drug rush. And this at one remove. How was the Mage reacting? As he watched Bey, a figure of calm in the midst of sudden, confused activity, he found himself for the first time in a long time unable to read the man.

Before nightfall in Belthan, everything was in place for the broadcast. To accommodate the crowds who had gathered, and also the large number of newsvid teams from around Inan, the broadcast was to be held in the square which housed the Ministry and military buildings.

The chill night air had the edge taken from it by arc lighting that powered down from all four corners of the square. The crowds were held back by warrior security, yet there was no sense that they would surge forward and become a threat. They were subdued. Like everyone. *Like me*, Simeon thought as he surveyed them. We're all waiting for our fate to be determined. It was, by others, every day of our lives: but this would be the first time to be fully aware of it.

Ramus-Bey was calm. He had said nothing to Simeon or Jenna regarding the content of what he wished to say. His demeanour gave no clue. Not even when he was informed that newsvid crews had been admitted to every Ministry building in every nation state of Inan. Holomonitors suspended in the square to give a large-screen, real-image view of every capital showed Mages seated next to Chief Ministers. Those of Kyas and Turith seemed anxious, even though they tried not to show it. The Chief Minister and Mage of Praal were as impassive as ever. It seemed to Simeon that, even if the world were to be on the brink of destruction, this race would shrug, let their Mage resolve matters with a gesture, then continue. Or else they would accept his decision to let matters be, and for the Gods to determine their fate. Finally, the image from Varn showed the Chief Minister sitting apart from Vixel. Both men were turned from each other, and the Mage looked as though he would rather be anywhere else. However, either through curiosity or concern, it was imperative he be there to hear what Ramus-Bey had to say.

Finally, the moment came for the Mage to speak. Bey, seeming a little stiff, sat behind a make-shift desk, the Chief Minister – looking less than happy – at his side. He was cued-in, and Simeon gripped Jenna's hand tightly as he felt a hush descend over the whole of Inan.

Ramus-Bey began by detailing what had happened to him. He was thorough and precise, describing the initial attacks, his abduction, and his eventual rescue and return to Bethel. He was punctilious in his description. Where there were matters of assumption, he emphasised this. When he had completed this description, he relaxed. He had wanted to be precise, and now the moment had come when he had gone beyond a mere report.

"People of Bethel and Varn, take note of what has occurred. These nation state governments, who purport to have the authority and skill to rule Inan, cannot even engineer the termination of one frail old man and his bodyguard. If they had any competency, I would not be here now. They are so concerned with double-dealing each other, both within their own executive and without, that they cannot see what is happening in front of them. Furthermore, they conspire in their idiocy without considering what may happen if they push to the point where magic comes into play. Now they are terrified! Now, when it is of their own doing!

"Mark this well. They hold up the Mage as a symbol of ultimate power, then attempt to manipulate this symbol with no thought of the power which they expect other nation states to fear. Frankly, if you can follow that logic and make sense of it, then I would like you to explain it to me, for I fear I am at a loss.

"But yet there is some good that may come from this farce. Like, I am sure, my fellow Mages, I have been too long away from the world and its ways. The search for knowledge has caused all of us to separate ourselves from the mainstreams of Inan. We have forgotten the aims and desires of those who choose another path. We have, perhaps, forgotten part of what it is to be a whole person.

"In doing this, we have lost sight of the motivations and desires of our fellows. It is this that has led to such a situation as the one in which we find ourselves. We, as Mages, allowed ourselves to be used as trophies. We cause great fear. We can also bring great security. On us has been bestowed a mantle that we did not ask for, and which we are, I suspect, unwilling on the whole to accept. As a result, we have turned our backs on this, we have abdicated our responsibilities and let others speak and act for us.

"This cannot continue. What has happened to me proves, I feel, that we cannot tolerate this situation

"We have two choices. First, we can separate ourselves from the executive body of the nation state to which we belong. Together, acting independently of all government, we can form a body which will oversee the running of Inan. We can use the knowledge and wisdom which we, allegedly, possess, to maintain this world of ours as we see fit. If we choose to exercise our power, then there is little alternative to this."

He paused. Simeon could almost feel a physical wave of confusion sweep across Inan. What the Mage was suggesting was nothing less than the handing over of all power to a cabal of ancients, rendering all governments and military redundant overnight. But, as he looked at the old man, he felt that there was something else.

"Of course, that is not the only way. Who can decide that they have the right to rule over another man? Surely, if the pursuit of knowledge and enlightenment teaches us nothing else, then it teaches us that the more that we know, the more we have to know. The simpler the decision, the harder it can truly be to arrive at a true and just conclusion. The hardest thing of all in this life that we have – this life that we, as students of the great truths, have prolonged in order to study those very truths – is to decide what is right for us as individuals. How, then, can we decide what is right for others?

"Our alternative path is to have nothing to do with nation states or governments. To treat our Institutes as independent and autonomous. We must withdraw from the world in a political sense, and not allow ourselves to be used, or to be drawn into the schemes of those base enough to seek to control others. Each must learn to be the ruler of his own life.

"I would urge my fellow Mages to follow this path. It is my preference. There may be those who would point out that a Mage without alliance has the capability to destroy at will. To this, I would point out two things. First, the very nature of our studies should negate this fear. Secondly... well, as at least one of us knows, there are always checks and balances. There are no islands: every action sparks a reaction, and in this way we are able to track the progress of our fellows... whether they wish this or not."

Simeon watched the holomonitors. Vixel shifted uncomfortably, a movement that would not have gone unnoticed by his peers. Simeon allowed himself a smile: all systems of government had mechanisms for accountability. This was how Vixel was made answerable to his Chief Minister. Similarly, Ramus-Bey was tacitly proposing that this be followed through magically.

The Varn Mage was not the only one to be so affected. Within the crowd, Simeon could feel a wave of mixed emotion spread. Fear for the future, hope that it would be a better world, anticipation for a time to come.

It would be like that across the planet. Inan was changing. Change was always feared, a step into the dark and the unknown.

As abruptly as he had started, Ramus-Bey finished. He stood up and walked away from the newscast. As he approached Simeon and Jenna, he looked back over his shoulder at the crowd behind him. They were subdued, but unsettled. The Chief Minister was looking over his shoulder, unsure of what to do. An attitude echoed by the members of the executive and the warriors – both foot-soldiers and high ranking officials – who were gathered for the broadcast.

The Mage turned to Simeon and Jenna. "Time, I think, for us to be gone."

"That's it?" Jenna queried.

Bey grinned and nodded. "There isn't anything else to say to them. It isn't really my problem any more. Not unless I'm asked for help. I rather think that it may be some time before I'm bothered in that way."

The Mage walked past them and into the Ministry building. With a last, lingering look at the crowd, their mood echoed by the images on the holomonitors from around the planet, Simeon and Jenna followed him.

Inside the old building, now empty, their footsteps resounded around the corridors. Bey led them towards a rear entrance.

"And we're going where, exactly?" Simeon asked.

"Back way, avoid the crowds, the sort of thing you'd be doing for me," Bey murmured. "Before I leave, I wanted to talk privately with you."

"Where are you going?" asked Jenna.

The Mage smiled. "Not far. Just back to the Institute. I have friends I wish to see. Friends I have not treated perhaps as I should in the past. But there's time to make amends for that. There is much to rebuild, and not just the physical damage caused by those who abducted me. There is a trust, a calm, a way of living and learning that we need to re-establish, perhaps make better than before."

"That's good to hear," Simeon said before falling into an awkward silence.

"That's all you have to say about it?" Bey quizzed with a sardonic tone, his eyebrow raised.

"What else is there? You no longer have any need of my services."

"You think not?"

Simeon shrugged. "There's no-one to attack you now, at least, no-one obvious. Besides which, you don't need me. Back when this started, you were unaware that you had physical failings that others would seek to exploit; that you could be attacked in that way. I think you know now how wrong that was. The same is true of your magic: you thought your body strong and your magic weak. Now that you know that the reverse is true, that awareness allows you to be prepared"

Bey shook his head. "And that's the only reason I'd want you to join me? You don't think you'd have something to offer, something that I think would be good for us at the Institute? I've taken note of the way in which you've handled those small pieces of magic you know. You've got a certain talent, you know... but apart from that, does it not occur to you that I would be pleased to have you around just to call you friend?"

Simeon said nothing for a moment. Then, with a glance to the woman at his side, he said: "I would be honoured, and I would be glad to call you friend, too... but there are other things..."

Ramus-Bey grinned. There was a twinkle in his eye that betrayed him. He may be old, but he was not that out of touch.

"And who's to say that the lovely Ensign Jenna would not be welcomed? True, we have been male academies up to now, but times are changing everywhere else."

"I think perhaps they should have changed a lot sooner," Jenna countered with a chuckle, "though perhaps you wouldn't have been as devoted to your studies."

"Perhaps, but will you not consider it?"

Simeon shook his head, after some consideration. "I would be glad to call on you, but it can't be my home. And not just because of Jenna, although that is a consideration. I... I have spent my life being a warrior, and because of the lack of opportunity I believed that I was a poor warrior. I now know that this is not the case. These are going to be uncertain times, and there will be need of men and women who know how to fight."

"You think I have precipitated another war?" Bey seemed genuinely saddened. "Is that really what you think of my decision?"

Simeon put his hand on the old man's shoulder. "No. There won't be a war, but there will be fighting. There has to be, as people learn how to make choices. There will be injustice, and there will be people needed to balance this. The peace that we thought was peace was nothing but a fraud. This time we can have a true peace, but it will be a painful birth. It's going to be an – ah – interesting time for people like Jenna and me. I just hope that we can make the right choices along the way."

The Mage embraced them both. "I have faith in your sense of justice, of truth." He stepped back. "I'd also put money on you in a fight. Any time."

Without another word, but with a smile that told them all, Ramus-Bey turned and walked away from them, his footsteps echoing through the stone corridors of the empty building. They could hear him even after he had turned around a corner at the end of the corridor, and had passed from view as well as from their lives.

At least for the moment.

Simeon sighed, and embraced Jenna. "Well, are you ready for this?"

"No," she said into his shoulder. "Are you?"

He laughed. "No. I don't think so. Don't think I ever really was, ever really will be. But it hasn't stopped either of us so far, right? So we might as well see what the Gods have in store for us."

They turned and walked back towards the front of the building, where the people of Belthan – and the whole of Bethel, and of Inan – awaited the future.

Whatever that may be.

# THE END

**Andy Boot** has written twelve novels in the post-apocalypse series *Deathlands*, and two in the longest-running crime series currently in print, *The Executioner*. Previous to this he wrote four non-fiction books covering true crime, the paranormal, and horror films. Before that he was a journalist. After this, he'd like to be rich.

coming
January
2007...

Now read the first chapter from the second book
in the exciting *Dreams of Inan* series...

DREAMS OF INAN

# STEALING LIFE

## Antony Johnston

COMING JANUARY 2007

ISBN 13: 978-1-905437-12-2
ISBN 10: 1-905437-12-9

£6.99 (UK)/ $7.99 (US)

# CHAPTER ONE

He'd been told the apartment would be empty while he robbed it. But it wasn't.

In fact, he'd been told it would be empty by the young woman sitting on the edge of the bed. She had long, dark hair, a slim boyish figure and dark brown eyes on pale skin. Her figure was a little too straight, her mouth a little too large, but these features seemed to suit her. In the right light, the woman was certainly pretty.

The woman smiled at him. "Hello, Nicco. Right on time."

But Nicco wasn't looking at her. He was looking at the fat man sleeping next to her.

Nicco reached through the circular hole he'd made in the glass and opened the window. He swung his legs over the windowsill and tip-toed toward the woman across a deep pile carpet. "Keep your voice down," he whispered. "What in the fifty-nine hells are you doing here? What's *he* doing here?"

"Relax, lover." She wore almost nothing, a silk slip that barely covered her, and as she spoke she crossed her legs and looked up at Nicco. "I drugged him. He'll be out for about four hours. I wanted to see you. I never see you at work."

Her name was Tabathianna, but everyone called her 'Tabby'. She and Nicco were what he called 'part-time' lovers, which meant they slept together occasionally, but he didn't return her calls. And she was also a whore.

"I could have just walked through the front door if I'd known," said Nicco. "You were supposed to take him out! What if he wakes up?"

Tabby gripped Nicco's collar, pulled him down and

kissed him. "I told you, he's drugged. I put enough black grain in his beer to keep him out for hours. He just didn't want to go out. Not even for a romantic walk on the harbour."

Nicco looked at the sleeping man and thought of Azbatha's Northern harbourfront, a ghost town of empty warehouses and docking platforms punctuated by rusting cranes and shipping cartons. The only major business still operating there was an old shipbuilding firm that had diversified into airships just months before the bottom fell out of the surface cargo industry. All the other shipbuilders had gone under, and with no ships there was no inbound cargo, and with no inbound cargo there was no work for the docks. The city council was desperately trying to reinvigorate the area with 'business incentives' and backhanders, hoping that surface trade would pick back up in these unfamiliar times of peace. But the smart money had already moved to airships. Azbatha International, the city's central airship station, saw hundreds of vessels packed with cargo come and go every day.

By this time of night the harbour's regular inhabitants would rob a man like Tabby's client blind, deaf and dead. Nicco wondered about her idea of romance, and thought that the man had probably gotten off lightly.

Nicco gently removed Tabby's hands from his collar, stood up and looked around the apartment. He was here now, he may as well steal whatever he could. He certainly needed the money, and the whole thing would have been a waste of time if he left empty-handed. Besides, leaving empty-handed would upset Tabby, and he didn't want that. Whatever the state of their sexual relationship, Nicco had known her since they were both children.

He opened the bedroom door and walked into the lounge. Tabby followed him, pulling the door closed again behind her, and together they looked around at the sumptuous decor.

"Was I right?" Asked Tabby. "It's all worth something, isn't it?"

She was right. Nicco could see the man had spent a lot of money to make this place look legitimate. But for a thief, everything had a catch. Two original paintings by the famed Varnian painter Arno Ven Ladall hung on the walls, one above the fireplace and one adjacent to the window. They were worth thousands... but would be very difficult to fence. Nicco was no expert, but the design on the hearth rug looked like a hand-woven depiction of the Three Praalian Mountain Kings myth, worth almost as much as one of the paintings... but Praalian rugs were thick and heavy. Nicco had brought a backpack, not a truck. Next to the holovid unit was an art deco statuette in the central Varnian style, a high-foreheaded caricature carved from the region's famous white, heavy stone... but the stone was also famous for its brittle nature, prone to cracking if merely lifted incorrectly. It would take at least two men to remove it safely, and there was only one of Nicco.

His mind turned to smaller things, looking for jewellery, valuable books, cash. But if there was anything like that in the apartment, it wasn't in this room. He glanced in the kitchen, but as he'd suspected, there was as much chance of this man lighting an oven as Nicco marrying a policewoman.

"It's not looking good," he said. "It's all worth a lot, but I can't take any of it. This isn't a home for him, it's a place he visits. It's got about as much soul as my mother's corpse."

Tabby tutted. "You shouldn't say things like that. It's bad luck to speak ill of the dead."

Nicco ignored the admonition. He'd spoken ill of his mother often enough when she was alive. He didn't see what difference it would make now that she rested at the bottom of the Nissal Straits.

He moved through to the bathroom. The bath had gold taps which could fetch a tidy sum, but with the man still inside the apartment Nicco wasn't about to wrench them off and flood the place. Drugged or not, some things just made too much noise for a thief's comfort. He settled for the bath plug and soap dishes, also made of gold.

He heard Tabby calling in from the lounge. "What about this?"

Nicco walked back to see her pointing at an enchanted orb, floating three feet above the coffee table. It was a couple of inches in diameter and pulsed with a soft, blue-green iridescent light. The enchantment was beautiful, subtle. Probably not from Turith itself. Varn, perhaps? Or Praal, like the rug? One of those weird places where everyone used magic, no doubt.

"This must be worth something," said Tabby, "And you can easily carry it out. You could probably fit it in your pocket."

Nicco hesitated. "I'm not sure... I only know one wizard who's a fence, and frankly, I don't trust him that much."

Tabby looked at him with disapproval. "It could be worth a fortune!"

"Magic just gives me the creeps. You can't touch it, half the time you can't see it... How can you trust something like that?"

Tabby giggled, teasing him. "Big Nicco Salarum, frightened by a little magic. Come on, it's not going to bite you, is it? It's just a bit of glass."

Nicco supposed she was right. He sighed and reached for the orb.

It shrieked.

Nicco let go, but the loud, high-pitched whine didn't stop. It must have been some kind of alarm, probably powered by the same enchantment that kept the orb floating above the table. Regardless, it was the final straw for Nicco. With a silent vow never to take job suggestions from Tabby ever again, he moved to the bedroom door. Then he realised it was slowly opening.

Naked as the day he was born, Tabby's client opened the door and blinked at Nicco.

It had been Tabby's idea. She'd been with the mark before, a wealthy industrialist from Jalakum, in the centre of the Turithian archipelago. A wealthy *married* industrialist, more to the point, and so he came to Azbatha, famed city of vice, the Pit-On-Stilts, the most dangerous and overcrowded city in Turith, to satisfy his lust. Which was often enough that he'd bought an apartment in Riverside, the wealthiest neighbourhood in Azbatha, to use while he and his libido were in town. This apartment. He'd bought it under the guise of needing a place to stay while doing business in Northern Turith, and certainly no-one would argue that in Azbatha, an apartment was probably more secure than a hotel. In fact, he really did use it for legitimate business sometimes, so the apartment was filled with expensive goods. From the art hanging on the walls to the gold bath taps, from the Praalian hearth rug to the enchanted floating orb in the lounge, when Tabby had seen the apartment she figured a good thief could turn most of its contents into a tidy sum of money.

And Nicco Salarum, as Tabby well knew, was a very good thief.

She'd told Nicco about the businessman's apartment four periods ago. The businessman had come to town and called on Madame Zentra, asking for a young woman with dark hair. Madame had sent Tabby, one of the brothel's more experienced girls. The businessman had picked her up on a crowded street corner in a hired groundcar and taken her back to his apartment. It was forty-five stories up, but when Nicco went to case it he saw that the building's exterior was easily scalable with a combination of monofilament wire and omnimag grips, his preferred method of solo climbing.

(Nicco knew some burglars who used enchanted tools to get them up Azbatha's trademark skyscrapers, such as floating boots, sticky gloves or even light-bending cloaks that rendered the wearer invisible. But Nicco was a traditionalist at heart. He preferred technology to magic. Even in Azbatha the paths of thieves and wizards crossed often enough for Nicco to know he wouldn't trust any of them as far as he could kick them down the stairs. What happened when your floating boots suddenly stopped working at the fourteenth floor? Even assuming you survived, wizards didn't exactly hand out receipts.)

That evening, Nicco also saw what Tabby hadn't told him—that it really was about the most expensive place you could find in Azbatha, complete with high-tech security and a permanent guard patrol. Getting in via an apartment window would be easy, but doing it without tripping an alarm was an altogether different challenge. Social engineering to disable alarms, like the old 'unexpected electrician call-out' ruse, worked well enough... on lazy, gullible and downright stupid people. But any Azbathan security firm comprised of stupid people would be bankrupt within days.

So Nicco decided to pass. Good thief or not, he didn't think the profit margin was sufficiently high to risk being target practice for a bunch of bored and trigger-happy ex-cons playing at cops.

But the reason Tabby hadn't told him about the security was because she hadn't seen it. It transpired that the businessman had an arrangement, no doubt an expensive one, with the in-house security firm to preserve his dignity and minimise the risk of wagging tongues. When he was in town and 'entertaining', the security patrols ignored him and anything going on in his apartment. Cameras were switched off, patrols innocently missed out his corridor, and guards made themselves scarce when they saw him walking up the steps to the lobby. The apartment was extremely secure but only when it was vacant.

Nicco found all this out the next time the businessman visited Azbatha, six weeks later. Six weeks is a long time in theft, and Nicco had all but forgotten about the man by then. But that night he was casing a warehouse on the other side of town, clambering around in the eaves doing his due diligence, when a dark blue groundcar pulled up at the roadside and waited. Nicco froze. It wasn't a part of town known for streetwalkers or kerb crawlers, and for a moment he thought perhaps he'd missed a security camera, that he was about to be chased down by an over-eager guard.

Then Nicco heard the clatter of high heels. He craned his neck out and saw a tall, dark-haired woman in a long coat and evening dress walk toward the car. Nicco didn't recognise the woman—some high-class escort from the other side of town, by the look of her—but he did recognise the businessman's face as he opened his car door and invited her in. Nicco wasn't an overly spiritual man, but he could take a hint from the cosmos. He followed them, this time focusing on any changes in the security pattern when the businessman was at home. That night, he observed all the deliberate lapses. But he still wanted more certainty of the arrangements before he'd consider the job a good one, so he shrugged it off and moved on.

The next time he came to Azbatha, the businessman called Madame Zentra again. Tabby, by now convinced the businessman was an easy mark for someone like Nicco, was ready to connive her way into the job if she'd had to. But that hadn't been necessary. The businessman had asked for her by name. Apparently, the high-class escort had been a little too high-class for this client's particular peccadilloes.

A plan was hatched. The businessman always paid for a full night, so Tabby would get the sex over with, then insist he took her out on the town. A holokino show, a quick drink, a walk along the sea front perhaps. She'd come up with something. And as she explained her brilliant and foolproof idea to Nicco over several jars of beer in the bar next to Madame Zentra's place, tossing back her hair and giggling about how much money he could fence it all for, Nicco had decided that by the watery saints, she really would think of something and it really was a brilliant and foolproof idea.

When he woke the next afternoon it was with a clearer and more sober view of Tabby's plan. But he also knew she was trying to help his current and somewhat dire situation. Nicco was in a sizeable amount of debt to Wallus Bazhanka, famed mob boss of Azbatha, after losing a trailer full of high-performance skycars. The loss was unavoidable—the only alternative that didn't involve being arrested was to silence the guard who saw him, a guard who shouldn't have been on duty in any case. But Nicco had never even seriously injured anyone in the course of his work, much less killed someone. It was a badge he wore with pride, and he wasn't about to start now.

So Nicco dumped the trailer in the ocean and made a getaway. To him it was the only viable option, but Bazhanka didn't see it that way. To Bazhanka it was the careless and unnecessary loss of one hundred and fifty thousand golden fish, Azbatha's currency. And he expected Nicco to compensate him. Nicco gave Bazhanka sixty thousand straight away, everything he had saved except for ten thousand to keep him afloat. But it wasn't enough to get the mob boss off his back. Now he wanted the balance, ninety thousand golden fish, and the payment deadline was running out. Bazhanka offered Nicco the chance to pay it off in kind by working for him, but Nicco refused. Owing Bazhanka was bad enough, and the thought of being on his payroll made Nicco sick. He'd find the money some other way. Nicco had already amassed fifteen thousand in loot, all of it fenced and converted into money as quickly as possible, but if he was going to meet the deadline he couldn't afford to turn anything down.

So he decided to go ahead and rob the businessman. Maybe Tabby's plan would work, after all.

Nicco would never know. Because here he was, having scaled forty-five stories of apartment exterior in the sub-zero temperatures of a Turithian winter to get through the poxy bedroom window, and not only had Tabby not taken the businessman out, but now he'd recovered from the black grain she slipped him.

Nicco weighed his options. He could clobber the businessman and make a hasty exit, but that would leave Tabby in potential danger. Nicco couldn't abandon her, not if the businessman worked out the scam. He hesitated, but it was too late. Nicco had given the businessman enough time to work out what a black-clad man with a backpack was doing in his apartment. He punched Nicco in the guts.

Nicco lost his breath in a single gust. His knees buckled. The bodyweight that had shaken off Tabby's black grain so quickly also gave the businessman's blow a hefty power.

Tabby's voice rose a couple of octaves as she shouted, "Hit him! Hit him!"

Nicco could barely hear her over the shrieking orb. Was she talking to him? The businessman loomed over him, and Tabby was still screaming. "I got up for a drink of water I found him in here he was trying to rob you and he had a gun and I couldn't scream or he'd kill me!" She backed into a corner as she screamed, circling round toward the holovid box.

Nicco scrambled backward on his hands and heels as the businessman advanced on him. *Clever girl*, he thought. *Obvious, but very plausible*. He hoped the businessman would overlook the complete absence of a gun in Nicco's hands.

Now that Tabby was above suspicion, he turned to the situation at hand. Nicco kicked upward, driving his foot into the businessman's groin with enough force to turn him a darker shade of pink. He also made an "O" shape with his mouth, but no sound came out. Or perhaps

Nicco just couldn't hear him over the screeching from the enchanted orb. He could hear Tabby, though—the girl could scream—and suddenly, she stopped.

Then he saw her calmly walk up behind the businessman and smack him over the head with the Varnan statuette.

It smashed into a hundred pieces, littering the floor with fine white powder. The businessman stood stunned and motionless for a moment. Then he collapsed on top of Nicco, knocking the wind out of him again.

Tabby helped Nicco out from under the businessman's unconscious body, then ran into the bedroom. Nicco paused a moment to grab the orb and throw it down on the floor. Like the statuette, it smashed, and the piercing alarm finally stopped. Nicco sighed, caught his breath and followed Tabby into the bedroom. He expected her to be dressing, ready to make a quick getaway. Which she was, but not in the manner Nicco expected. Tabby stood by the window, still in her slip, ready to climb out.

"What in the fifty-nine hells are you doing?" Nicco said.

"Well, we'd better escape, hadn't we?"

"We're forty-five stories up, and it's minus eight out there! No, get some clothes on and leave through the front door. The guards will just think he's finished with you." Tabby paused, considering his suggestion, so Nicco pulled her towards him and kissed her. "*Trust* me."

That did the trick. As Nicco moved to the window Tabby pulled her clothes out from an untidy pile on the floor, starting with a sequined top. "All right," she said, "But what about you? You could come with me."

Nicco shook his head. "Too suspicious. And there's no way I could pass for your pimp in this get-up." He stepped onto the windowsill. "I'll see you soon, all right? Just get out of here and back to Madame Zentra's as quickly as you can." Then he leapt out of the window.

Nicco was confident Tabby would be all right. Even if the businessman did suspect her, he was hardly likely to call the police. Besides, half of the Azbathan force was on Madame Zentra's client list.

Nicco caught the monofilament he'd left hanging from the window frame and slid down it at full speed. Sparks flew from his steel-palmed gloves. As he passed the twelfth floor he hit the switch on his semigrav belt to slow his descent, then hitched his belt clip to the wire and casually rappelled his way toward the ground. At the sixth floor he stopped completely, hidden from view behind one of the city's enormous, ubiquitous and downright gaudy holovid billboards. Those billboards pumped out enough light to fill a stadium, keeping Nicco safe from the prying eyes of police skycars.

He pulled the omnimag grips from his belt and hit the seals. A low hum, then a quiet slurping sound and a soft green light signaled the grips were in place and coupled to the molecular frequencies of the building's surface material. Hanging by one arm, he cut the monofilament—let it hang there, it couldn't be traced back to him—then used the grips to move across the wall, ignoring the crowded street below.

With four million people crammed into one hundred square kilometres and nowhere to build but up, the streets of Azbatha were always crowded whatever the time of day or night. No floating housing projects or thought-form supported malls here. Azbathans were nothing if not arcano-Luddites, and with the serious business of rebuilding society in a time of peace foremost on the agenda, any city councillor stupid enough to suggest paying wizards to maintain flying cities would be lynched before he got the words out. Luckily for Nicco, and the city's myriad other thieves, this peculiar brand of pragmatism meant Azbathan architecture was born more of necessity than aesthetics. It did nothing to invite admiration, and the added street-level dangers of pickpockets, muggers and beggars kept the collective Azbathan gaze aimed firmly at street level. The surest way to tell a tourist wasn't by their clothing or accent, but by the angle of their neck.

Nicco moved round to the rear of the apartment building, where the only illumination was the dim light of Inan's moons. He dropped to the ground behind a refuse cannister, just to be safe. He replaced the omnimag grips on his belt and put the belt in his backpack. Then he opened his jacket, reached inside and squeezed a small, fabric-covered nodule attached to the lining. Colour spilled across the coat from the collar downwards, turning black to red. Three seconds later, the jacket was bright crimson.

It wasn't exactly a disguise, but Nicco's tanned skin— darker than the normal Turithian pale hue—already marked him out in most cops' eyes as trouble waiting for the right moment. Anything he could do to break up his all-black ensemble and make himself look less a potential criminal would make his journey easier.

And it was only a short journey. Eight blocks East, catch a skywhale ferry across the Nissal River, then ten blocks South to his equipment lock-up. Normally he might have taken a more circuitous route to avoid being seen or followed, but it was very unlikely that the businessman would even raise the alarm, much less involve the police. Nicco relaxed, hauled his backpack onto one shoulder, shoved his hands in his pockets and stepped out to join the incessant wave of foot traffic on the main street.

He was so relaxed that he didn't notice the large groundtruck start following him six blocks from the ferry port. He didn't even notice when the truck stopped and ejected four identically tall, thin and pale-skinned men two blocks later.

He noticed their footsteps when they ran up behind him, but by then it was too late.

# Abaddon
# Books